The Elson Readers—Book Five
A Teacher's Guide

Catherine Andrews

B.A. English Education, National Board Certified, Teacher of English, International Baccalaureate/Bartow High School

Mary Jane Newcomer

B.A. English Education, Teacher of English, Frostproof Middle-Senior High School, Frostproof, Florida

Lake Wales, Florida

Publisher's Note

Recognizing the need to return to more traditional principles in education, Lost Classics Book Company is republishing forgotten late 19th and early 20th century literature and textbooks to aid parents in the education of their children.

This guide is designed to accompany *The Elson Readers—Book Five,* which was reprinted from the 1920 copyright edition. This guide contains all the original questions and exercises from the reader along with suggested answers. It also includes new "Extended Activities" that reinforce and enhance the original study sections.

We have included the same glossary and pronunciation guide of more than 1380 terms at the end of the book that is included in the reader, and which has been updated with pronunciation notation currently in use.

The Elson Readers—Book Five, which this volume is meant to accompany, has been assigned a reading level of 1060L. More information concerning this reading level assessment may be attained by visiting www.lexile.com.

ISBN 978-1-890623-29-6

Designed to Accompany
The Elson Readers—Book Five
ISBN 978-1-890623-19-7
Part of
The Elson Readers
Nine Volumes: *Primer* through *Book Eight*
ISBN 978-1-890623-23-4

On the Cover:
Ali Baba Counted Forty of Them from *The World's Fairy Tale Book,* pub. by G. Harrap & Co. Ltd., London (book illustration) by Monro Scott Orr (b. 1874)
Private Collection/Bridgeman Art Library

Table of Contents

Part II: Stories of Adventure

Part III: Great American Authors

Appendix

The Elson Readers—Book Five

A Teacher's Guide

How to Use This Book

This *Teacher's Guide* was developed to provide teachers with a guideline for appropriate, grade-level, student responses to the questions found in the "Notes and Questions" sections of the reader. Some extension activities have been added to those discussion questions in this manual and may be used at the teacher's discretion to reinforce comprehension and appreciation of the work in question. Vocabulary worksheets have also been added at the end of each major section in the *Teacher's Guide* to encourage students to broaden their use of language.

Teachers may wish to have students begin with "Part One" and read the book in order, or they may pick and choose the works that fit their classroom goals. The parts are not sequential; however, skills introduced in one part may be reinforced in later parts allowing students to practice and master the various literary skills as outlined in the objectives found at the beginning of each major section in the *Teacher's Guide*.

These questions and activities were designed to give the students a greater understanding of the world around them and a deeper appreciation for the contributions of those who have helped to build that world. In addition, students will receive instruction in the qualities so essential to their development as future productive citizens in the world they will inherit.

Instructional Aids—Additional aids have been provided for instructing and evaluating students' progress in the "Appendix."

A Note about This Guide

Teachers and students alike may notice a difference in punctuation, capitalization, and spelling between the prose and poetry sections in the reader. Rules concerning these matters have changed since the original reader's publication, and we have decided that in the prose sections it would be in the best interest of the student to update these items so they will learn these rules as practiced today. However, the stories remain completely unabridged. We have exercised constraint, and typical changes consist of, for example: commas used in place of semicolons when appropriate, lowercase treatment of words not personified, or hyphenated spelling of words being contracted to modern spellings. We have, however, followed the traditional editorial practice of not changing these items in works of poetry, leaving these matters to the prerogative of the poet.

Language is always changing, and when the student notices these changes it is often a good place to start a discussion on topics such as: personification, comma usage, "up" or "down" style of capitalization, etc.

We have used *The Chicago Manual of Style,* 14th Edition, published by the University of Chicago, as our primary reference for these changes.

The reader was originally published just after World War One and many discussion questions refer to this great event. These questions can often be used to start discussions on that war and conflicts that occured after it. See the "Appendix" for a brief description of World War One.

Finally, we have provided references to Internet sites that may be useful for some of the exercises. These sites are the property of their creators, not Lost Classics Book Company, and we take no responsibility for their content. Considering the very changeable nature of the Internet, these sites may or may not exist by the time of printing and should only be considered a starting point for research.

Part I: Nature—Humor—Home and Country

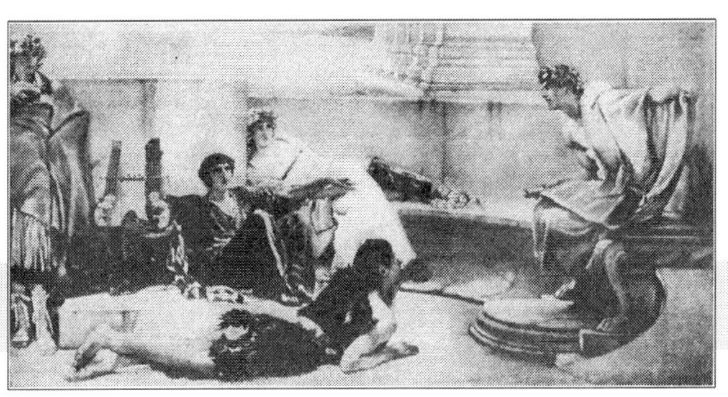

In This Section—

Objectives—

By completing "Part I," the following objectives will be met:

1. The student will use effective reading strategies to construct meaning and identify the purpose of a text including:
   a. using illustrations
   b. defining unfamiliar words
   c. retelling and summarizing
2. The student will determine the main idea or essential message and identify relevant supporting details and facts of a text.
3. The student will read and organize facts from the text and other sources to make a report, outline, and perform an authentic task.
4. The student will prepare for writing by focusing on the topic and organizing supporting details in a logical sequence.
5. The student will draft and revise writing in cursive.
6. The student will produce final documents that have been edited for correct spelling, punctuation, and grammar.
7. The student will write for a variety of audiences and purposes.
8. The student will write in a variety of genres including narrative and expository writing.
9. The student will use reference materials (dictionaries, encyclopedias, maps, charts, photos, and electronic reference) to gather information.
10. The student will write a business letter.
11. The student will use speaking strategies effectively such as eye contact, gestures, and visuals to engage the audience.
12. The student will identify the development of plot and how conflicts are resolved in a story.
13. The student will identify and understand similarities and differences among the characters, settings, and events presented in various texts.
14. The student will identify the author's purpose and point of view.
15. The student will identify and use literary terminology such as rhyme scheme, personification, simile, end rhyme, and alliteration.
16. The student will respond critically to fiction, nonfiction, poetry, and drama.
17. The student will recognize cause-and-effect relationships in literary texts.
18. The student will respond to a text by explaining how the motives of the characters or events compare with those in his or her own life.
19. The student will understand the qualities necessary for people to become good citizens and apply those qualities to his/her personal life.
20. The student will understand the qualities necessary to develop good character.

Turk, The Faithful Dog, p. 21

1. **How does this story prove the intelligence of Turk?**
   Turk understood what his owner instructed him to do.
2. **How does it prove his fidelity?**
   "Rather than lose the guinea, he allowed himself to be half killed." Turk remained faithful to his owner at the risk of losing his own life.
3. **Here are two qualities that every man should desire to possess. Do you think many men, set upon by robbers, would act as bravely and as faithfully as Turk? Give reasons for your answer.**
   Answers will vary. The two qualities are bravery and faithfulness.
4. **What do you know of the author?**
   Refer to the biography on page 29:
   Samuel White Baker (1821-1893) was an English engineer and author. At the age of twenty-four he went to Ceylon, where he soon became known as an explorer and hunter of big game. With his wife he later explored the region of the Nile River. He is the author of *True Tales for My Grandsons*, from which "Turk, the Faithful Dog" is taken.
5. **Class readings: The conversation between Mr. Prideaux and the butcher, page 26, line 9, to page 27, line 26 (2 pupils).**
6. **Outline for testing silent reading. Tell the story in your own words, using these topics: (a) Turk's adventure; (b) how the mystery was explained.**
   (a) To prove Turk's intelligence to his friends, Mr. Prideaux sent him with a guinea to a friend's house. It was a stormy night, and Turk was gone a long time. Long past midnight Turk returned "shivering with wet and cold." When Mr. Prideaux gave him a bath, he discovered Turk had wounds "of a serious nature." Mr. Prideaux was mystified at how Turk received his wounds.
   (b) The next day while walking past a butcher's shop, Turk was attacked by another mastiff. The butcher ran out surprised that Turk had retaliated when attacked. He explained to Mr. Prideaux that the night before, Turk did not fight back.

Mr. Prideaux then realized that rather than lose the guinea, Turk allowed himself to be beat by the other dog.

7. **You will enjoy reading "Cap, the Red Cross Dog" (in *Stories for Children,* Faulkner).**
8. **Find in the glossary the meaning of: alert, mission, dejected, besmeared, brindled, docile, relaxed, crestfallen.**
9. **Pronounce: hearthrug, anecdote, guinea, toward, extraordinary, calm.**

Extended Activities:

1. For a reading check, have students answer true or false to the following statements:

T. a. Turk, the faithful dog, was a mastiff.

F. b. After dinner, Mr. Prideaux and his guests discussed extinct animals.

T. c. According to Mr. Prideaux, Turk's intelligence was very remarkable.

F. d. To prove Turk's faithfulness, Mr. Prideaux sent Turk to the butcher's shop to fetch a package.

T. e. Turk returned later that evening having been in a fight with another dog.

2. Have students complete a web on fidelity (faithfulness). A web is a graphic organizer that helps students to visualize how a variety of ideas connect to a topic. Webs can be simple or complex. Webs provide the learner with opportunities to recall prior knowledge and identify patterns of information.

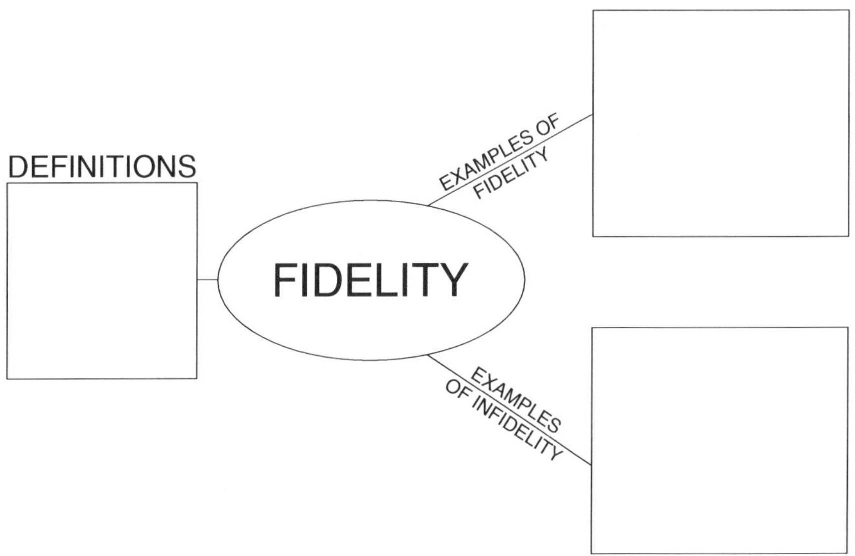

NAME______________________________CLASS__________DATE______

TURK, THE FAITHFUL DOG, P. 21

1. For a reading check, answer true or false to the following statements. Circle one.

True False a. Turk, the faithful dog, was a mastiff.
True False b. After dinner, Mr. Prideaux and his guests discussed extinct animals.
True False c. According to Mr. Prideaux, Turk's intelligence was very remarkable.
True False d. To prove Turk's faithfulness, Mr. Prideaux sent Turk to the butcher's shop to fetch a package.
True False e. Turk returned later that evening having been in a fight with another dog.

2. Complete a web on fidelity (faithfulness).

DEFINITIONS

FIDELITY

EXAMPLES OF FIDELITY

EXAMPLES OF INFIDELITY

Our Uninvited Guest, p. 30

1. **Why was Jimmy not popular with the farmer's wife?**
   She had just milked a cow, and he came to her standing on his hind legs scaring her. He then drank half the milk from the pail.
2. **Why do you think the children liked the bear?**
   "Like them, he was full of fun and mischief and he would play as long as anyone cared to play with him."
3. **Do you think they would have enjoyed the party more, or less, if there had been no "uninvited guest"?**
   Answers will vary.
4. **Class readings: The description of the supper, page 31, line 7 to page 32, line 26.**
5. **Outline for testing silent reading. Tell the story of the "Uninvited Guest," using these topics: (a) the bear and how he was liked; (b) the bear's actions at the children's party; (c) the boxing match.**
   a. Jimmy was a bear who was liked by all the children. He was full of mischief and fun. For example, he climbed into Mr. W—'s bed, and he scared the farmer's wife.
   b. At the children's party, Jimmy was awakened by all the noise. All the children ran to the window to see him. When one child opened the window slightly, Jimmy slipped through into the room. He went straight towards the food and ate most of it.
   c. After Jimmy was full, he wanted to play. All the children romped around with him. Jimmy raised his paws as if to box a girl. She accepted the challenge and did well for awhile. Jimmy then hit her hard, and she didn't want to play anymore. Jimmy was let back outside.
6. **You will find interesting stories in *Bear Stories Retold from St. Nicholas*, Carter, and in *The Biography of a Grizzly*, Seton.**
7. **Find in the glossary the meaning of: unanimously, unwittingly, sleight-of-mouth, tawny, muzzle, intruder.**
8. **Pronounce: blancmange, haunches.**

Extended Activities:

For a reading check, have students answer true or false to the following statements:

F. 1. Jimmy was liked best by the farmer's wife.
F. 2. The children had a party to celebrate Jimmy's birthday.
T. 3. Jimmy slipped into the room through a window.
T. 4. Jimmy boxed with a girl at the party.
T. 5. Jimmy was let outside when he hit a girl with his paw.

NAME______________________________**CLASS**__________**DATE**______

OUR UNINVITED GUEST, p. 30

For a reading check, answer true or false to the following statements. Circle one.

True False 1. Jimmy was liked best by the farmer's wife.

True False 2. The children had a party to celebrate Jimmy's birthday.

True False 3. Jimmy slipped into the room through a window.

True False 4. Jimmy boxed with a girl at the party.

True False 5. Jimmy was let outside when he hit a girl with his paw.

Hunting the American Buffalo, p. 34

1. **What makes this story "exciting," or "thrilling"?**
   Roosevelt and his companion trying to track the bison, not knowing if they would find them or be seen by them, makes this story exciting.
2. **How does the writer let you know his feelings?**
   He explains that he grew anxious. He describes the bison as being magnificent creatures which shows his admiration and respect for these animals.
3. **What proof of Roosevelt's good sportsmanship is found in the second paragraph on page 34?**
   He did not like that his companion would have shot animals unnecessarily, and that he would kill the cows and calves.
4. **Class reading: From page 35, line 3, to page 36, line 13.**
5. **Outline for testing silent reading. Tell the story briefly, using these topics: (a) the discovery; (b) the pursuit; (c) the first view; (d) the end of the story.**
   a. Roosevelt and his friend were hunting bison. They traveled around looking for them, as well as moose and sheep. While traveling through a valley, Roosevelt's companion found hoof marks of a small band of bison.
   b. They followed the trail to a little lake, through some woods, and to a meadow. They then came to some open glades.
   c. Nearing the edge of the glades, they saw three bison: a cow, a calf, and a yearling. They waited for the bull to appear. After some time, he finally appeared at the edge of the glades.
   d. Roosevelt aimed low behind the bull's shoulder and shot him. The other bison ran, disappearing in the forest. Roosevelt and his companion retrieved the bull.
6. **Find in the glossary the meaning of: daybeds, glade, skirted, yearling, trophy.**
7. **Pronounce: bison, boundary, frequented, knoll, melancholy, remnant, incline, strewn.**

The Birds and I, p. 38

1. **Why does the author say that the springtime belongs to "the birds and me"?**
   They both wallow in it—the author says "We know when the mayflowers and the buttercups bloom. We know when the first frogs peep. We watch the awakening of the woods. We are wet by the warm April showers. We go where we will and we are companions."
2. **When may we say the birds are our partners and when our servants?**
   We can say the birds are our partners when we let the birds be free, but they are our servants when our hearts are set on killing or catching them.
3. **What different ways of dealing with birds are spoken of? Which way does the writer prefer?**
   One way to deal with birds is to shoot them and another is to leave them alone. The author prefers to leave the birds alone and let them be free.
4. **How can you encourage the birds to live near you?**
   You can encourage birds to live near you by feeding the cats and keeping those away who would harm the birds. You can plant trees and bushes and let some grow into tangles where birds might build their nests.
5. **What do you gain if you persuade them to do this? Find an answer to this question in the poems that follow.**
   We gain joy and happiness.
6. **What birds come to trees near your home?**
   Answers will vary.
7. **How are birds helpful to mankind?**
   They help mankind enjoy and appreciate nature.
8. **You will find interesting stories and pictures of birds in *The Burgess Bird Book for Children*, Burgess.**
9. **Find in the glossary the meaning of: acquainted, explore, wary.**
10. **Pronounce: partners, again.**

Extended Activity:

1. Have students complete the following research presentation:

Your assignment is to choose a topic dealing with ornithology. Ornithology is the study of birds. Research your topic and write a five paragraph paper. The paper must include at least one illustration. Possible topics are: a particular bird species, bird families (i.e. woodpeckers, eagles), bird orders (i.e. birds of prey, song birds), bird calls, Audubon Society, endangered birds, bird nests, bird flight, and bird classification.

The research paper should be written in blue or black ink and in cursive. Be sure you plan your writing before you compose the final paper. The following map may be helpful in planning your writing and verifying there is enough information.

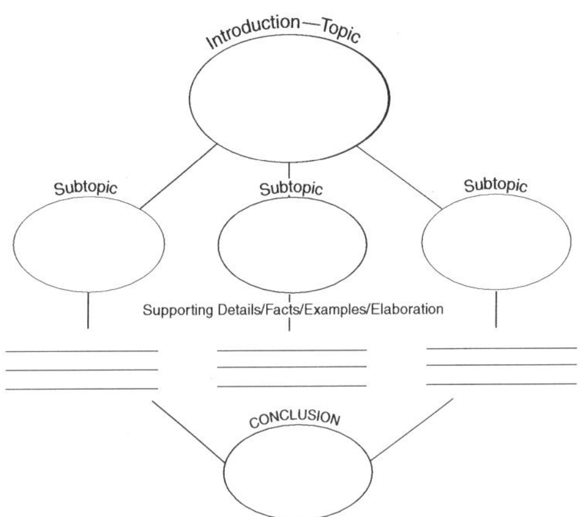

The presentation should be a minimum of two minutes. It must include at least one visual. This may be props, posters, pictures, video, overhead slides, computer and/or television. Arrangements should be made ahead of time with the teacher for use of materials. Each student will be graded on proper treatment of the topic as well as proper elements of public speaking.

PRESENTATION EVALUATION

	Poor		Satisfactory		Excellent
Eye Contact	◇	◇	◇	◇	◇
Emphasis	◇	◇	◇	◇	◇
Rate	◇	◇	◇	◇	◇
Volume	◇	◇	◇	◇	◇
Length	◇	◇	◇	◇	◇
Visual	◇	◇	◇	◇	◇
Organization	◇	◇	◇	◇	◇

2. Have students select a poem about birds from the reader to illustrate or students can write their own poem about birds. Using the poem have students make a zig-zag book.

Directions:

a. For the cover use pieces of cardboard covered with construction paper.

b. The front of the book must have a picture that illustrates the theme of the poem, the poem's title and author. If the student wrote the poem, have them write their name.

c. On the inside they must make one continuous page of artwork that illustrates the poem.

d. They may type the poem on the computer or hand write it using black ink. All lettering must be solid and easily read.

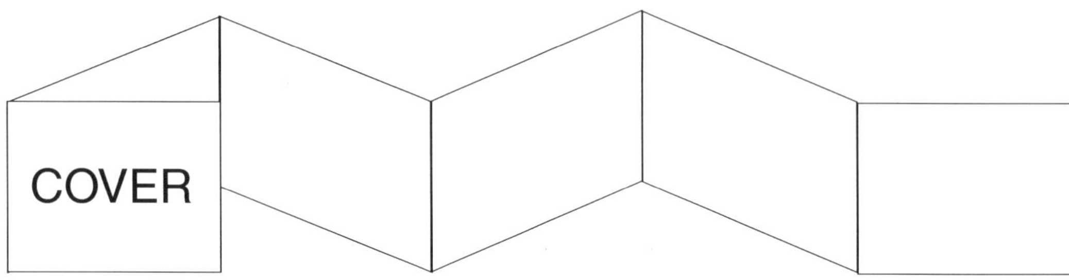

NAME______________________________ **CLASS**__________ **DATE**______

THE BIRDS AND I, P. 38

1. Choose a topic dealing with ornithology. Ornithology is the study of birds. Research your topic and write a five paragraph paper. The paper must include at least one illustration.

   The research paper should be written in blue or black ink and in cursive. Be sure you plan your writing before you compose the final paper. The following map may be helpful in planning your writing and verifying there is enough information.

   The presentation should be a minimum of two minutes. It must include at least one visual. This may be props, posters, pictures, video, overhead slides, computer and/or television. Arrangements should be made ahead of time with the teacher for use of materials. You will be graded on proper treatment of the topic as well as proper elements of public speaking.

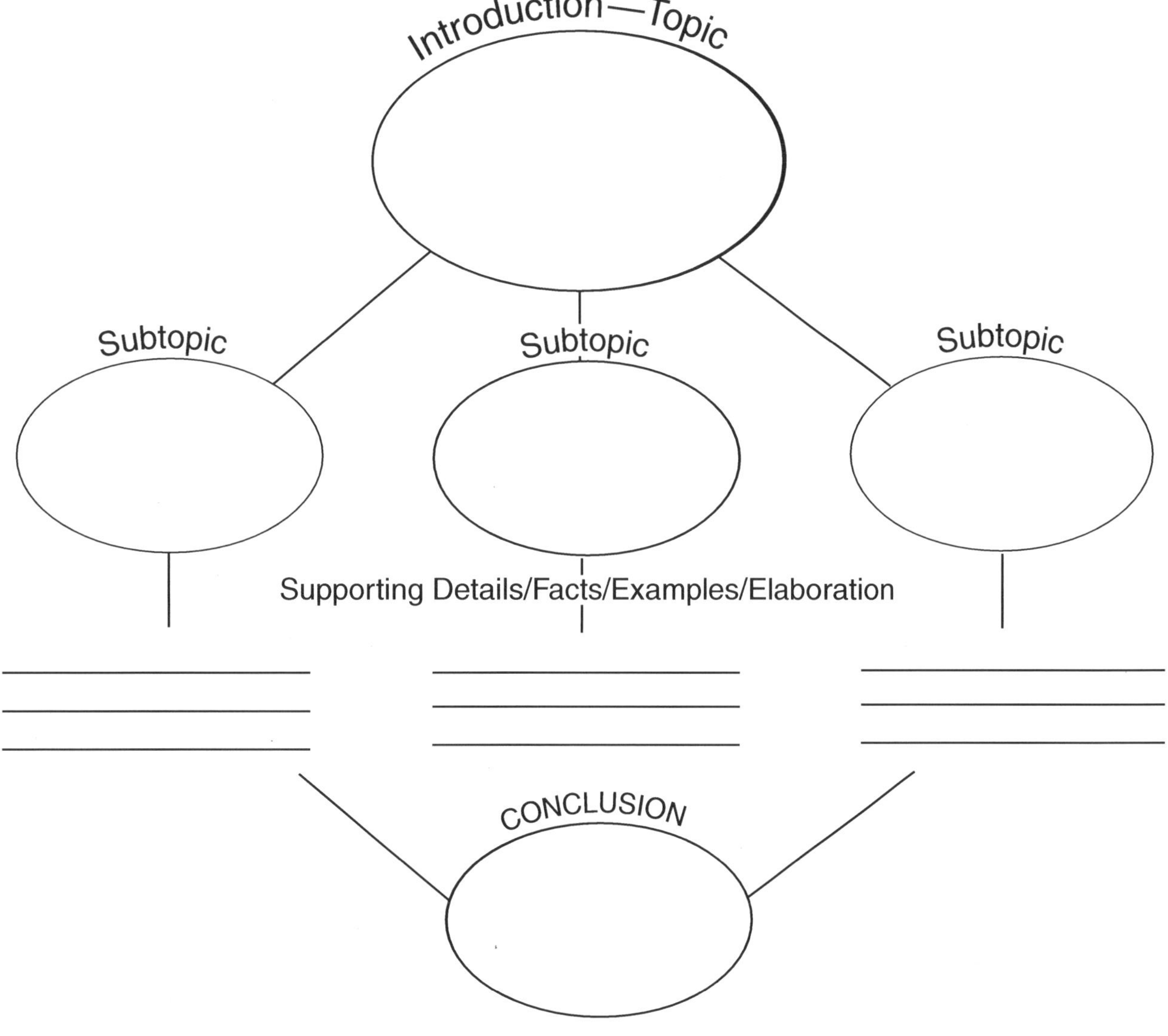

2. Select a poem about birds from the reader to illustrate or you may write your own poem about birds. Using the poem, make a zig-zag book.

Directions:

a. For the cover use pieces of cardboard covered with construction paper.

b. The front of the book must have a picture that illustrates the theme of the poem, the poem's title and author. If you wrote the poem, write your name.

c. On the inside you must make one continuous page of artwork that illustrates the poem.

d. You may type the poem on the computer or hand write it using black ink. All lettering must be solid and easily read.

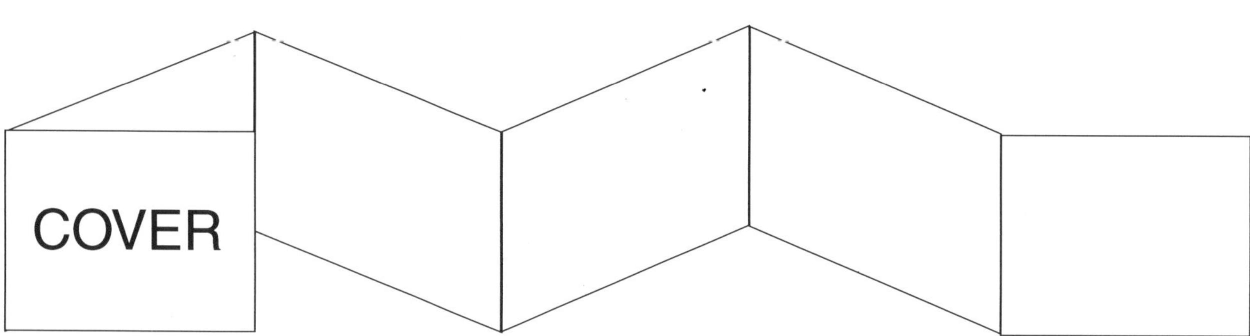

The Brown Thrush, p. 40

1. **Who is supposed to be speaking in the first two lines?**
   A child is speaking in the first two lines.
2. **Who asks the question in the third line?**
   The author asks the question in the third line.
3. **Who answers the question?**
   The thrush answers the question.
4. **Find the answer to the question in the first stanza.**
   The question is "what does he say?" He says:
   "Oh, the world's running over with joy!
   Don't you hear? Don't you see?
   Hush! Look! In my tree
   I'm as happy as can be…"
5. **Why is the little bird so happy?**
   He is happy because he is free.
6. **What will make him unhappy?**
   He will be unhappy if someone meddles with the eggs in the nest or harms him.
7. **How can you help to make the world "run over with joy"?**
   You can help make the world "run over with joy" by being good and letting the birds remain free.
8. **You will enjoy hearing "Songs of Our Native Birds" and "How Birds Sing," Victor records by Kellogg.**

Sing On, Blithe Bird, p. 41

1. **To what does the poet compare the eyes of the birds?**
   The poet compares the eyes of the birds to glittering beads.
2. **Find the lines that tell why the bird is not afraid of the poet.**
   "I passed them by, and blessed them all; I felt that it was good
   To leave unmoved the creatures small whose home was in the wood."
3. **How do you think the birds know their friends?**
   The birds know their friends are people who do not harm them.
4. **What happiness does the poet get because of his kindness to the birds?**
   The poet is happy when the birds sing.
5. **Read the lines that another poet who loved birds has written about his love for them:**
   He prayeth well who loveth well
   Both man and bird and beast
   He prayeth best who loveth best
   All things both great and small;
   For the dear God Who loveth us,
   He made and loveth all.

6. **You will find helpful suggestions in the illustrated Farmers' Bulletins, *Bird Houses and How to Build Them*, and *How to Attract Birds*, sent free by the Department of Agriculture, Washington, D.C.**
   ***Visit the Department of Agriculture website to locate the latest bird bulletins.**
7. **In the "Forward Look," on pages 19 and 20, you were told that the poets and wise story writers of nature help us to see the beauty that lies in the great outdoor world. Mention instances of help that you have received from the stories and poems you have read in this group.**
   Answers will vary.
8. **Find in the glossary the meaning of: peer, glittering, trims, spray, blithe, measures.**

The Violet and the Bee, p. 43

1. **What did the Violet ask the Bee?**
   She asked, "Who are you?"
2. **What surprised the violet?**
   The violet was surprised by the size of the bee.
3. **What is the violet's "eye glasses of dew"?**
   Violet's "eye glasses of dew" are the dew drops on her.
4. **Find in the glossary the meaning of: quoth, publican, tax.**

Four-Leaf Clovers, p. 44

1. **To whom is the four-leaf clover supposed to bring good luck?**
   The four leaf clover will bring luck to those who have hope and faith, to those who love and are strong and to those who work and wait.
2. **Which do you think will give greater happiness, to earn something by hard work or to gain it by chance? Why do you think so?**
   The greater happiness will come to those who work hard because they will appreciate life more than those who don't work hard.
3. **What does the poem say we must have?**
   We must have hope and faith.
4. **What does the poem say we must do?**
   We must love and be strong.
5. **If we have all these things and do all these things, shall we need to hunt for the four-leaf clover to bring us good fortune? Why?**
   No, if we have all these things and do all these things, we won't need to find the four leaf clover for luck; we will have made our own good luck.
6. **Commit the poem to memory.**

Jack in the Pulpit, p. 45

1. **What time of year is described in this poem?**
The time of year described in this poem is springtime.
2. **Who make up the congregation when Jack in the Pulpit preaches?**
The congregation is made up of anemones, buttercups, clovers, daisies, dandelions, and geraniums.
3. **How does the poet make the flowers seem like people?**
The flowers seem like people because the author gives them human qualities (personification). For example, the violets smile, the clovers wear bonnets, the daisies clasp their fingers as if in prayer, and the dandelions are proud of their hats.
4. **How many of the flowers described in this poem are familiar to you?**
Answers will vary.
5. **Which flower is most beautifully described? Find the lines that give the description.**
Answers will depend on the student's preference.
6. **Why are we not told about the sermon?**
We aren't told about the sermon because the speaker did not hear it; she was busy looking at all the people. Refer to lines 19-22:
"We heard not the preacher
Expound or discuss;
But we looked at the people
And they looked at us."
7. **What was the congregation doing during the sermon?**
The congregation was looking around during the sermon.
8. **What did they see? What did they hear?**
They saw:
"…all their dresses
Their colors and shapes,
The trim of their bonnets,
The cut of their capes."
They heard: "…the wind-organ
The bee, and the bird"
9. **Find in the glossary the meaning of: drooping, beaming, gauze, assembled, text, worship, expound.**
10. **Pronounce: anemones, guileless, languidly.**

SEPTEMBER, P. 48

1. **What is meant by the harvest of the sedges?**
   Sedges are tall grass-like plants with heads of seeds. When the seeds fall off it is like a harvest.
2. **How are the "asters in the brook" made?**
   Asters are flowers that look similar to daisies. Their color ranges from white to pink. The flowers beside the brook are reflected in the water.
3. **Which lines in the last stanza tell us what September brings?**
   September brings "summer's best of weather, and autumn's best of cheer."
4. **What things mentioned in this poem have you seen?**
   Answers will vary.
5. **Read again what is said on pages 19 and 20 about the poet as a magician. What beauty of nature does the poet show you in the following lines?**

   And asters by the brookside
   Make asters in the brook

   The poet is describing the beauty of the asters' reflections in the brook.
6. **Find in the glossary the meaning of: sedges, flaunt, flutter.**
7. **Pronounce: gentian, dusky.**

OCTOBER'S BRIGHT BLUE WEATHER, P. 50

1. **What comparison is made in the first stanza between June and October?**
   The sun, skies, clouds, and flowers of June are compared to one hour of October's bright blue weather.
2. **Why is the bumblebee described as "loud"?**
   The bumblebee is loud because he is hurrying to the flowers that are dying fast.
3. **Compare the description of the goldenrod in "September."**
   In "September" the goldenrod is yellow and in this poem it is "dying fast."
4. **Compare the description of the apples in this poem with the description of the apples in "September."**
   In "October's Bright Blue Weather" the apples are lying on the ground, but in "September" they are still on the tree weighing down the branches.
5. **Find the line that tells why the "gentians roll their fringes tight."**
   The "gentians roll their fringes tight,
   To save them for the morning"
6. **What is the color of the woodbine leaves?**
   The woodbine leaves are redder than the apples.
7. **What are the "wayside things" usually called?**
   The "wayside things" are weeds and wild flowers that grow alongside the road.
8. **What do good comrades like to do in October?**
   In October good comrades "seek sweet country haunts."
9. **Why are we sorry to have October go?**
   We are sorry to see October go because we will miss the "bright blue weather."
10. **Find in the glossary the meaning of: fragrant, twining, aftermath, haunts.**
11. **Pronounce: rival, vagrant, freighting.**

NOVEMBER, P. 52

1. **What signs of autumn are mentioned in the first stanza?**
   "The leaves are fading and falling
   The winds are rough and wild
   The birds have ceased their calling."
2. **What signs of the coming winter are mentioned in the second stanza?**
   The day grows darker and colder.
3. **Where have the birds gone?**
   In the winter time birds normally migrate southward.
4. **What is meant by the word "here" in line 4 above?**
   ("Line 4" is referring to the sixth stanza, line 4) "Here" means winter.
5. **Why are the brooks "dry and dumb" in November?**
   The brooks are "dry and dumb" because in winter the water freezes over.
6. **Is this true in all parts of the country?**
   No, this is not true to all parts of the country. In southern states, it does not snow.
7. **What are we told about the spring in "October's Bright Blue Weather"?**
   The "springs run low" in October.
8. **What will happen when the winter is over?**
   "And when the winter is over,
   The boughs will get new leaves,
   The quail come back to the clover,
   And the swallow back to the eaves.

   The robin will wear on his bosom
   A vest that is bright and new,
   And the loveliest wayside blossom
   Will shine with the sun and dew."
9. **Where does the swallow build his nest?**
   The swallow builds his nest in the eaves.
10. **What wonder of nature, about which you read on pages 19 and 20, does the second stanza tell you?**
    The second stanza tell us about the magic of nature. It seems the roses have died, but the "roots will keep alive in the snow."

11. How can the snow help keep the roots alive?
The snow keeps a protective covering over the roots. Snow is like a blanket.

12. In what stanza is this thought repeated?
This thought is repeated in the last stanza.

13. Find in the glossary the meaning of: fading, quail, eaves.

Extended Activities:

1. Stanzas are the divisions of lines in a poem. They are much like paragraphs in an essay. Have students identify the number of stanzas in "November." There are seven stanzas. Students may go back through the text and identify the number of stanzas in the other poetry selections.

2. Alliteration is a figure of speech that refers to the repetition of beginning sounds such as "merry mermaids make music." Have students identify alliteration in the poem "November." Can they find alliteration in the other poetry selections?

Stanza 1: fading, falling
Stanza 2: doth, darker and roots, red, roses
Stanza 3: quail, clover
Stanza 4: none
Stanza 5: dry, dumb
Stanza 6: winds, wild
Stanza 7: roots, roses

NAME______________________________**CLASS**__________**DATE**______

NOVEMBER, p. 52

Alliteration is a figure of speech that refers to the repetition of beginning sounds such as "merry mermaids make music." Identify alliteration in the poem "November." Can you find alliteration in the other poetry selections?

Stanza 1:____

Stanza 2:____

Stanza 3:____

Stanza 4:____

Stanza 5:____

Stanza 6:____

Stanza 7:____

TODAY, p. 54

1. **Find the lines that explain why the day is called a "new day."**
   "Out of Eternity
   This new day is born;
   Into Eternity,
   At night will return."—second stanza.
2. **Find the lines which remind us that the day will pass quickly.**
   "Behold it aforetime
   No eye ever did;
   So soon it forever
   From all eyes is hid."—third stanza.
3. **The poet tell us in the first stanza to "think"; what does he want us to think about?**
   He wants us to think about how we will spend our day. He asks "wilt thou let it slip useless away?"
4. **Find the same lines in another stanza. Why did the poet repeat these words?**
   It is in the last stanza also. The poet repeats these words because they are important.
5. **Read the short story that follows, and tell whether Titus and the poet have the same idea of a "useless" day.**
   The Roman emperor, Titus, won the love of all his people by his kindness and generosity to those who were in trouble. One night at supper, remembering that he had not helped anyone that day, he exclaimed, "My friends, I have lost a day!"
   Yes, the poet thinks that something must be done for the day to not be wasted. Titus, who helped people, thought a day was wasted if he did not help someone.

Extended Activity:

Have students keep a journal of their activities for one week. At the end of the week have them answer the following questions:

1. What did you learn this week?
2. What is one good thing that happened?
3. What is one thing you would have done differently? Why?
4. Did you make good use of your days? Why or why not?

NAME______________________________CLASS__________DATE______

TODAY, P. 54

Keep a journal of your activities for one week. At the end of the week answer the following questions:

1. What did you learn this week?

____

____

____

____

2. What is one good thing that happened?

____

____

____

____

3. What is one thing you would have done differently? Why?

____

____

____

____

4. Did you make good use of your days? Why or why not?

____

____

____

____

The Night Has a Thousand Eyes, p. 55

1. **What are the eyes of the night?**
   The eyes of the night are stars.
2. **What is the eye of the day?**
   The eye of day is the sun.
3. **How many eyes does the poet say the mind has?**
   The mind has a thousand eyes.
4. **How many eyes does he say the heart has?**
   The heart has one eye.
5. **In which line are we told what the eye of the heart is?**
   The line is: "The eye of the heart is love."
6. **On page 20 you read that the poet is a magician whose words open for us the fairyland of nature. What have the words of this poet done for you?**
   Answers will vary.
7. **Memorize the poem.**

Adventures of Baron Munchausen, p. 59

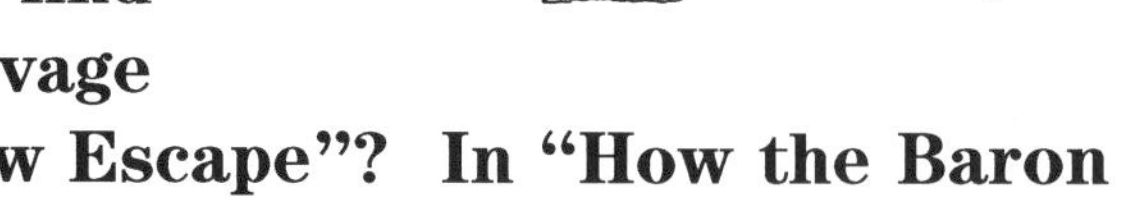

1. **What extravagant statements do you find in the story "The Savage Boar"? In "A Narrow Escape"? In "How the Baron Saved Gibralter"?**

   "The Savage Boar"—The boar's tusk went through the tree and he weighed five tons.

   "A Narrow Escape"—The lion was 40 feet in length. The Baron was surrounded by a lion, a crocodile and poisonous snakes all at one time.

   "How the Baron Saved Gibralter"—It is hard to believe that the cannon traveled as far as the Baron said it did.

2. **Which of the incidents mentioned do you think is the most ridiculous?**

   Answers will vary.

3. **What do you think of the proof given by the author to prove the truthfulness of the last story?**

   Answers will vary.

4. **Which of the sources of humor mentioned on page 58 does this story illustrate?**

   "Monstrous exaggeration" is the source of humor mentioned.

5. **Find in the glossary the meaning of: boar, encounter, tusks, riveted, gigantic, abyss, severed, whereupon, exaggerations, ramparts, touchhole, recoil, repelling, dismounted, hold.**

6. **Pronounce: Munchausen, projected, harrowing, Monsieur.**

The Blind Men and the Elephant, p. 63

1. **How could blind men "see" the elephant?**
   They could "see" the elephant by feeling it.
2. **To what did each compare the elephant?**
   The elephant was compared to a wall, a spear, a snake, a tree, a fan, and a rope.
3. **Explain the comparison each made.**

1. broad and sturdy side	wall
2. round, smooth, sharp	spear
3. squirming trunk	snake
4. knee	tree
5. ear	fan
6. swinging tail	rope

4. **Why is comparison a common way of describing objects?**
   Comparisons help us better understand things.
5. **Point out instances of its use by other authors in this book.**
   Students should be encouraged to look for comparisons as they read. Possible answers are listed below:
   The Grapevine Swing .... Peck.......... lightheart/wildrose
   A Visit from St. Nicolas.. Moore .... reindeer/eagles
   A Visit from St. Nicolas.. Moore .... cheeks/rose
   A Visit from St. Nicolas.. Moore .... nose/cherry
   A Visit from St. Nicolas.. Moore .... mouth/bow
   A Visit from St. Nicolas.. Moore .... beard/snow
   A Visit from St. Nicolas.. Moore .... smoke/wreath
   A Visit from St. Nicolas.. Moore .... belly/jelly
   The Name of Old Glory.. Riley.......... flag/sail in the blast
   Somebody's Mother .... unknown... boys/flock of sheep
   Casabianca .... Hemans .... flames/banners in the sky
6. **Why were these blind men all "in the wrong"?**
   They were in the wrong because they each describe only one aspect of the elephant.
7. **How far was each "in the right"?**
   They each described one aspect about the elephant correctly. Refer to the chart in question three.

8. **What makes this poem humorous?**
   Answers will vary.
9. **What may we learn from this story?**
   We learn that sometimes we need to know more than just a part of something to understand it completely.
10. **Find in the glossary the meaning of: learning, observation, approached, wonder, resembles, marvel, grope, disputed, stiff.**
11. **Pronounce: sturdy, wondrous, scope.**

Darius Green and His Flying-Machine, p. 65

1. **What did Darius Green believe that men would soon be able to do?**
   Darius Green believed that men would soon be able to fly. "The air is also man's dominion and that with paddle or fin or pinion, we soon or late shall navigate."
2. **What did Darius determine to use as material for his machine?**
   Darius used "wax and hammer and buckles and screws,
   And all such things as geniuses use;
   Two bats for patterns, curious fellows!
   A charcoal-pot and a pair of bellows;
   An old hoop-skirt or two, as well as
   Some wire and several old umbrellas;
   A carriage-cover, for tail and wings;
   A piece of harness; straps and strings;"
3. **Why did he not tell his brothers what he was trying to do?**
   He did not tell his brothers what he was trying to do because Darius thought they would not understand: "But I ain't goin' to show my hand to mummies that never can understand…"
4. **When did he plan to try his machine?**
   He was planning to try his machine on the Fourth of July.
5. **Find the lines that tell what he imagined he would do.**
   Darius imagined that he will "…astonish the nation, and all creation, by flying over the celebration."
6. **Find the lines that tell what he really did.**
   Darius tries to fly, but falls immediately to the ground: "Away he goes! Jimminy! What a jump! Flop - flop - an' plump to the ground with a thump!"
7. **What did he say was the unpleasant part of flying?**
   The unpleasant part of flying was the landing: "He said; 'but the' ain't sich a thunderin' sight O'fun in 't when ye come to light."
8. **Mention some inventions that people once thought**

were as impossible as the boys thought this flying machine was.

Answers may vary. Some inventions that people once thought were as impossible as the flying machine were the submarine, helicopter, telephone, and light bulb.

9. **Mention some inventors at whom people once laughed but who are now honored.**

   Answers will vary. Some inventors at whom people once laughed were Galileo, Thomas Edison, and Alexander Graham Bell.

10. **In what way does the author make his story humorous?**

    Answers will vary, but some ways the author makes this story humorous is the funny things Darius uses to build his machine and the suspense created by the brothers trying to spy on him. He also uses the dialect—use of local language—to add humor.

11. **Notice Darius's language on pages 67 and 68. The writer shows by such words that Darius was not a well-educated boy. Are persons often judged by the way they talk?**

    Answers will vary.

12. **In Wildman's *Famous Leaders of Industry*, you will find interesting facts about Orville and Wilber Wright. You will enjoy reading *The Boys' Airplane Book*, Collins.**

13. **Report any current news on airplane development, airplane mail routes, etc., that you can find.**

14. **Find in the glossary the meaning of: soaring, lank, gimlet, yore, pinion, tinkered, mummies, quirk, crevice, weasel, cunning, ancient, helm, ruefully.**

15. **Pronounce: Darius, aspiring, genius, awry, grimace, droll, Daedalus, Icarus, almanacs, phoebe, calked, breeches, accoutered, pagans, jaunty, stanched.**

Extended Activities:

1. Dialect is a way of speaking that is characteristic of a certain place or group of people. Writers often have their characters speak in dialect to make them more realistic and intriguing. To write dialect, writers have to spell the words the way they sound. Have students read page 67, lines 5-30 aloud. Then have students rewrite the dialogue using correct English grammar.

Suggested answer:

"Birds can fly,
And why can't I?
Must we give in,"
Says he with a grin,
"The bluebird and phoebe
Are they smarter than us?"
Just fold our hands and see the swallow
And the blackbird and the catbird, can they beat us?
Does the little, chattering, sassy wren,
No bigger than my thumb, know more than men?
    Just show me that!
    Or prove the bat
Has more brains than are in my hat,
And I'll back down, but not until then!"

2. The poem "Darius Green and His Flying Machine" is an example of a narrative poem. Narrative poems tell a story. They contain all the elements of a regular story. Have students read the account of Daedalus and Icarus below and translate it into a narrative poem adding any details and descriptions they imagine.

In Greek mythology Daedalus was an accomplished craftsman. One day he upset King Minos, who was ruler of Crete where Daedalus lived. King Minos imprisoned Daedalus and his son Icarus. Daedulus being the skilled inventor, made wings of wax so they could escape by flying. It worked; however, Icarus flew too near the sun, which melted his wings and he fell and drowned in the sea.

NAME______________________________**CLASS**__________**DATE**_______

DARIUS GREEN AND HIS FLYING-MACHINE, P. 65

1. **Dialect is a way of speaking that is characteristic of a certain place or group of people. Writers often have their characters speak in dialect to make them more realistic and intriguing. To write dialect, writers have to spell the words the way they sound. Read page 67, lines 5-30 aloud. Then rewrite the dialogue using correct English grammar.**

2. The poem "Darius Green and His Flying Machine" is an example of a narrative poem. Narrative poems tell a story. They contain all the elements of a regular story. Read the account of Daedalus and Icarus below and translate it into a narrative poem adding any details and descriptions you imagine.

In Greek mythology Daedalus was an accomplished craftsman. One day he upset King Minos, who was ruler of Crete where Daedalus lived. King Minos imprisoned Daedalus and his son Icarus. Daedulus being the skilled inventor, made wings of wax so they could escape by flying. It worked; however, Icarus flew too near the sun, which melted his wings and he fell and drowned in the sea.

Birthday Greetings, p. 76

1. **What is usually meant by "drink your health"?**
   "Drink your health" according to the glossary usually means to "wish you good health when beginning to drink, usually at a meal."
2. **What play on the meaning of these words gives a humorous turn to them?**
   Lewis Carroll is intending "drink your health" literally and not figuratively - as "drink your health" usually means.
3. **What remedy does the author suggest the doctor will prescribe for Gertrude?**
   He suggests that next year Gertrude will drink the author's health.
4. **What does the author call this humor?**
   He calls it nonsense.
5. **The author was a serious man, yet he believed in the value of wholesome fun. Of what great poet did you read, on page 57, who also believed in the value of a hearty laugh?**
   John Milton also believed in the value of a hearty laugh.

Extended Activities:

1. What other phrases are used figuratively that would be humorous if taken literally?

   Raining cats and dogs
   Bull in a china shop
   Eat crow
   Out of the frying pan and into the fire
   Take a bull by the horn
   Don't cry over spilled milk
   Two heads are better than one
   Get up on the wrong side of the bed

2. If students enjoyed reading this story by Lewis Carrol, have them read "Jabberwocky" and "The Walrus and the Carpenter," also by Lewis Carrol, and see if students can identify any other kind of nonsense in these poems.

NAME______________________________CLASS__________DATE______

BIRTHDAY GREETINGS, p. 76

1. What other phrases are used figuratively that would be humorous if taken literally?

2. Read "Jabberwocky" and "The Walrus and the Carpenter," also by Lewis Carrol, and see if you can identify any other kind of nonsense in these poems.

THE WIND AND THE MOON, P. 77

1. **Why did the wind want to blow out the moon?**
   The wind wanted to blow out the moon because the moon stares, and the wind said, "I hate to be watched."
2. **What natural changes in the shape of the moon take place each month?**
   The moon goes through a 28-day cycle. The moon phases are:

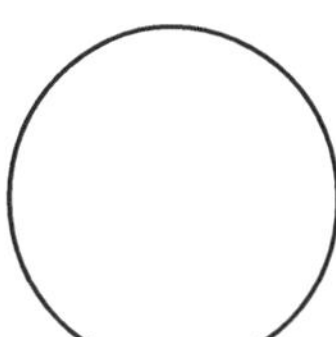

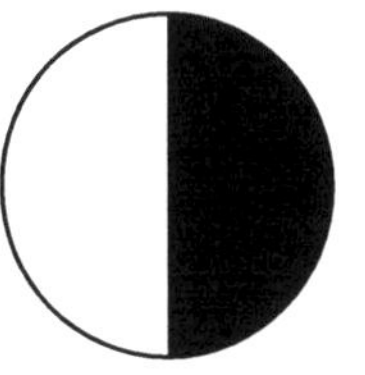

3. **What really caused it to disappear?**
   When the moon is at the New Moon stage, we cannot see it. The changes in the moon occur because of the rotation of the earth and the reflection of the sun on the moon.
4. **What did the wind do when he thought he had succeeded?**
   "He took to his revels" and "He leaped and hallooed with whistle and roar."
5. **Find the lines that tell how the wind felt when he saw the moon grow broader and bigger.**
   The wind said, "What a marvel of power am I!"
6. **Find the lines which tell that the moon did not know that the wind was blowing.**
   "Motionless, miles above the air, She had never heard the Great Wind blare."
7. **What qualities does this story give to the wind?**
   The wind possesses the qualities of perserverence and determination.
8. **Do you know any person who has these qualities?**
   Answers will vary.
9. **The poet aims in this poem to amuse us; by what means does he do this?**
   The poet amuses us by telling us a light-hearted story explaining how the moon changes.
10. **Find in the glossary the meaning of: muttering, sledge, wedge, grim, matchless, blare.**
11. **Pronounce: revels, hallooed, radiant.**

Home, Sweet Home, p. 87

1. **What words in the first stanza are repeated in the refrain, or chorus?**
   The poet repeats these lines in each stanza:
   "Home, Home, sweet, sweet Home!
   There's no place like Home! there's no place like Home!"
2. **What is it that the poet says "hallows," or blesses, us when we are in our homes?**
   "A charm from the sky" hallows us in our homes. The glossary defines a charm as "something with magic power."
3. **With what word in the second stanza is "cottage" contrasted?**
   "My lowly thatched cottage" is contrasted with an exile, one away from home.
4. **What does the second stanza tell us that the poet had at home and missed afterwards?**
   The poet had "The birds, singing gaily, that came at my call
   Give me them—and a peace of mind dearer than all!"
5. **What is it that really makes home beautiful?**
   Answers may vary but may mention that a beautiful home is built with love and filled with family and friends who care for us.
6. **What great service do our mothers perform?**
   Mothers soothe our cares and charm us with their love.
7. **What does page 84 tell you of the value the love of home is to a nation?**
   Since our nation is a collection of homes, our love of home affects our love of nation. As we work to build our homes and communities, we, in turn, build our nation.
8. **Explain the expression "splendor dazzles in vain," line 7, page 87.**
   The glossary defines the "splendor that dazzles in vain" as "a bright show of glory does not tempt." The excitement and lure of distant lands may draw citizens away, but those splendors can never replace the value of one's home and country.
9. **Find in the glossary the meaning of: humble, hallow, charm, fond, soothe, beguile, roam.**
10. **Pronounce: exile, solace.**

Extended Activities:

1. Have students read a copy of the old traditional cowboy song "Home on the Range." Have students compare and contrast these two poems about home. What qualities do both homes share? How does life in each home differ?

> Oh, give me a home where the buffalo roam,
> Where the deer and the antelope play,
> Where seldom is heard a discouraging word,
> And the skies are not cloudy all day.
>
> Where the air is so pure, and the zephyrs so free,
> The breezes so balmy and light,
> That I would not exchange my home on the range,
> For all of the cities so bright.
>
> How often at night when the heavens are bright
> With the light from the glittering stars,
> Have I stood here amazed and asked as I gazed
> If their glory exceeds that of ours.
>
> Oh, I love these wild flowers in this dark land of ours,
> The curlew I love to hear scream,
> And I love the wild rocks and the antelope flocks
> That gaze on the mountaintops green.
>
> Oh, give me a land where the bright diamond sand
> Flows leisurely down the stream;
> Where the graceful white swan goes gliding along
> Like a maid in a heavenly dream.

2. Have students create a four-stanza poem describing their homes. Possible stanza topics may include: favorite location, activities, people, and memories.

NAME______________________________ **CLASS**__________ **DATE**______

HOME, SWEET HOME, P. 87

1. **Read below the old traditional cowboy song "Home on the Range." Compare and contrast these two poems about home. What qualities do both homes share? How does life in each home differ?**

Oh, give me a home where the buffalo roam,
Where the deer and the antelope play,
Where seldom is heard a discouraging word,
And the skies are not cloudy all day.

Where the air is so pure, and the zephyrs so free,
The breezes so balmy and light,
That I would not exchange my home on the range,
For all of the cities so bright.

How often at night when the heavens are bright
With the light from the glittering stars,
Have I stood here amazed and asked as I gazed
If their glory exceeds that of ours.

Oh, I love these wild flowers in this dark land of ours,
The curlew I love to hear scream,
And I love the wild rocks and the antelope flocks
That gaze on the mountaintops green.

Oh, give me a land where the bright diamond sand
Flows leisurely down the stream;
Where the graceful white swan goes gliding along
Like a maid in a heavenly dream.

Same:____

____

____

____

____

Different:_____________________________________

____

____

____

____

2. **Create a four-stanza poem describing your home. Possible stanza topics may include: favorite location, activities, people, and memories.**

The Grapevine Swing, p. 89

1. **Why does the poet call the old plantation "The fairest spot of all creation"?**
   The poet describes the old plantation as the fairest spot of all creation, located "Down by the deep bayou…Under the arching blue." It brings back so many happy childhood memories.
2. **What does he mean by "the long, slim loop"?**
   "The long, slim loop" was the grapevine swing hanging from the "moss-green trees."
3. **For what "days gone by" does the poet sigh?**
   The poet longs for days gone by when he was "Swinging in the grapevine swing."
4. **What picture do lines 6, 7, and 8, page 89, give you?**
   These lines describe a barefoot boy in an old, torn, straw hat, jumping happily onto his grapevine swing.
5. **What tells you that the swing was near the bayou?**
   The poet says the grapevine swing hung down by the deep bayou and would swing "out o'er the water lilies bonny and bright."
6. **What is compared to the wild rose?**
   The boy's heart was "as light as a wild rose tossed by the breeze."
7. **Why do you think the poet would "barter it all for one day's romp"?**
   The poet says he is tired, heartsick, and turning gray from the stresses of life. He'd trade it all for one carefree day back on his grapevine swing.
8. **Find in the glossary the meaning of: creation, bonny, reckless, fretted, wend, pomp, fame.**
9. **Pronounce: bayou, arching, laughing.**

Extended Activities:

1. Sensory details are vivid images that appeal to one or more of the five senses: sight, touch, smell, sound, or taste. Peck's poem uses many sensory details of sight and sound to describe his happy boyhood memories. Have students complete the chart with as many of these details as they can.

Suggested Answers:

Sight	Sound
arching blue	wind over cotton and corn
to the loop I'd spring	laughing where birds sing
brown bare feet	I shouted and laughed
hat-brim torn	mocking bird joined in
water lilies bonny and bright	
fevered mart	
moss-green trees	
romp in a swing	
wild rose tossed by the breeze	

2. Have students write a poem about a special place in their early childhood that begins with Samuel Peck's first words: "When I was…" Be sure to include sensory details.

NAME______________________________CLASS__________DATE______

THE GRAPEVINE SWING, P. 89

1. **Sensory details are vivid images that appeal to one or more of the five senses: sight, touch, smell, sound, or taste. Peck's poem uses many sensory details of sight and sound to describe his happy boyhood memories. Complete the chart with as many of these details as you can.**

Sight	Sound

2. **Write a poem about a special place in your early childhood that begins with Samuel Peck's first words: "When I was…" Be sure to include sensory details.**

When I was… ____

____

____

____

____

____

____

Lullaby of an Infant Chief, p. 91

1. **What things mentioned in the first stanza show that the baby has great possessions?**
   The baby's father was a knight, his mother was a lovely, bright lady, and the woods and glens belonged to him.
2. **How would the warders protect the baby?**
   They would guard his rest with their bows and blades to fight any enemies who came near.
3. **What words could be used instead of "blades"?**
   Have students use a thesaurus to locate possible answers. Swords, bayonets, tomahawks, machetes, etc., may be options.
4. **What will this baby have to do when he becomes a man?**
   When he becomes a man, he will have to pick up the hard work of manhood; "For strife comes with manhood."
5. **What will the trumpet and drum mean to him then?**
   The trumpet and drum may be calling him to war to fight for his people.
6. **How can you tell that this baby lived a long time ago?**
   The poet uses old English terms and spelling such as thee, babie, and thy. His father was a knight, his mother, a lady, and bugles brought warnings. We would not use those terms in modern English.
7. **Find in the glossary the meaning of: sire, knight, lady, glens, towers.**

Extended Activity:

Words at the ends of two or more lines of poetry that rhyme are said to have end rhyme. Rhymes can then be organized in patterns called rhyme schemes: lines that rhyme are assigned the same letters of the alphabet beginning with A. Have students identify the rhyme scheme of this poem. It is as follows: AABB CCDD EEFF. Have students identify the rhyme scheme of other poems in "Part I."

NAME______________________________CLASS__________DATE______

LULLABY OF AN INFANT CHIEF, P. 91

Words at the ends of two or more lines of poetry that rhyme are said to have end rhyme. Rhymes can then be organized in patterns called rhyme schemes: lines that rhyme are assigned the same letters of the alphabet beginning with A.

Identify the rhyme scheme of this poem.

____

Identify the rhyme scheme of other poems in "Part I."

Poem 1)______________________
TITLE

____
RHYME SCHEME

Poem 2)______________________
TITLE

____
RHYME SCHEME

Poem 3)______________________
TITLE

____
RHYME SCHEME

Poem 4)______________________
TITLE

____
RHYME SCHEME

Poem 5)______________________
TITLE

____
RHYME SCHEME

The First Thanksgiving Day, p. 92

1. **When did the events related in this story take place?**
   These events took place in 1621, after the Pilgrims had gathered their crops and prepared for the cold winter ahead.
2. **Who was the governor of Plymouth at this time?**
   William Bradford was the governor of Plymouth.
3. **What proclamation did he make?**
   "Ye shall gather with one accord, and hold, in the month of November, thanksgiving unto the Lord."
4. **What did the governor say that God had done for the colony?**
   "He hath granted us peace and plenty, and the quiet we've sought so long; He hath thwarted the wily savage, and kept him from wrack and wrong."
5. **Who did he say should be invited to the feast?**
   They were to invite the Sachem—the Indian chief.
6. **What meat did the Pilgrims have at their first Thanksgiving dinner?**
   The Pilgrims ate fish, deer, bear, and "wild game from the greatest to least."
7. **What fruits did they have for the feast?**
   Their fruits were plums, grapes, oranges, peaches, and pine.
8. **What fruit is meant by "pine" in line 12, page 93?**
   The pine could refer to the fruit of the pine tree—pine nuts.
9. **What did the colonists do "with glad accord" before they sat down to their feast?**
   The colonists listened "to Elder Brewster as he fervently thanked the Lord."
10. **Find the lines that tell what Massasoit said when he ate of the feast.**
    "He muttered, 'The good Great Spirit loves His white children best.'"
11. **Why is it a good thing for America to have a day set apart each year for us to give thanks for our blessings?**
    Answers will vary, but could include references to the wealth of our great country, our freedoms, and our families.
12. **Find in the glossary the meaning of: store, sheaves,**

clearings, wrack, dames, mayhap, befall, slaughtered, appointed, summoned, fervently, sate, braves, brawny.

13. **Pronounce: therefore, franchise, wily, sachem, pumpkin, matrons, corselet, Massasoit, granaried.**

Extended Activities:

Have students choose one of the following characters from the first Thanksgiving Day: Governor Bradford, a hunter searching for wild game, a young girl or woman preparing the food, Miles Standish, Massosoit. Have them brainstorm, completing the web before they begin writing. Big circle: character; smaller circles: When I first heard about a Thanksgiving Day, I…; On the big Thanksgiving Day, I…; As I look back on that day, I'll never forget… After the web is complete, have students write a story (or poem if they prefer) using descriptive, sensory details to describe the sights, sounds, smells, and tastes of the day. Students should plan, write, and edit their work. Then they should write a final draft.

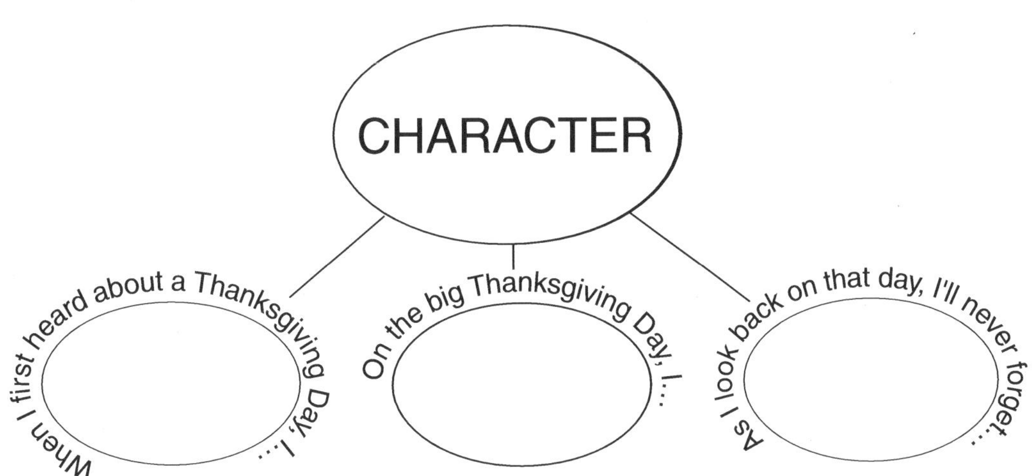

NAME________________________________ **CLASS**__________ **DATE**______

THE FIRST THANKSGIVING DAY, P. 92

Choose one of the following characters from the first Thanksgiving Day: Governor Bradford, a hunter searching for wild game, a young girl or woman preparing the food, Miles Standish, Massosoit. Brainstorm, completing the web before you begin writing. After the web is complete, write a story (or poem if you prefer) using descriptive, sensory details to describe the sights, sounds, smells, and tastes of the day. You should plan, write, and edit your work. Then you should write a final draft.

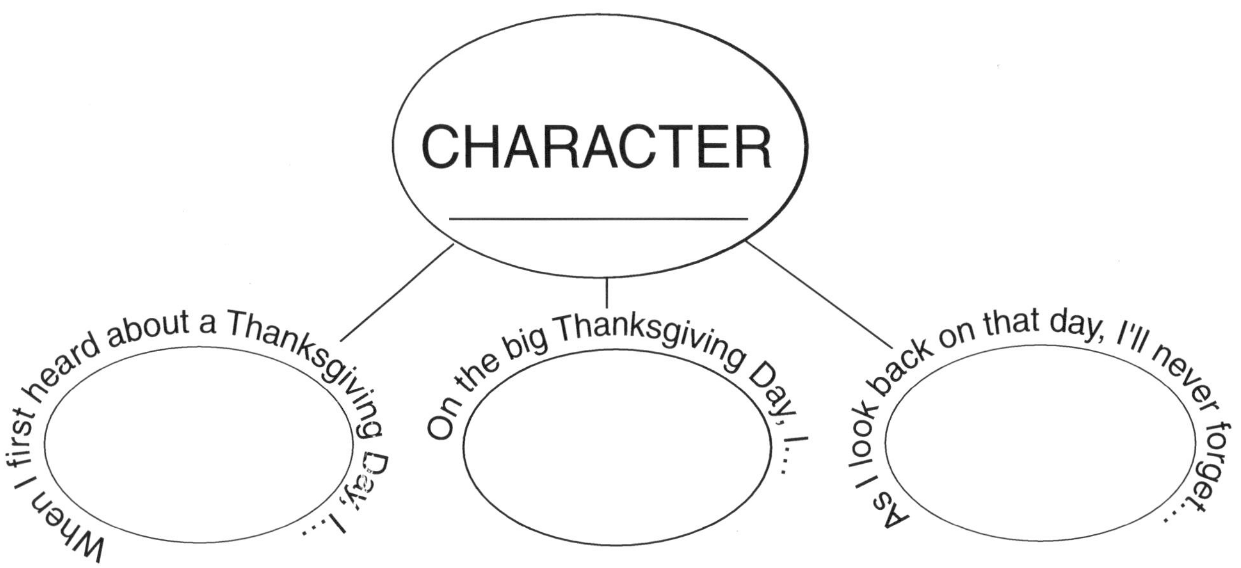

Examples, elaboration, details

______________ ______________ ______________

______________ ______________ ______________

______________ ______________ ______________

______________ ______________ ______________

A Visit From St. Nicholas, p. 95

1. **What picture do the first eight lines of this poem give you?**
The poet describes the house on Christmas Eve: decorations hung, a family in bed, and a quiet calm throughout the house.
2. **Does this picture seem real to you?**
Answers will vary based on students' personal Christmas experiences.
3. **Of what were the children dreaming?**
The children saw "visions of sugarplums" dance through their heads. Sugarplums were a small ball or disk-shaped candy.
4. **What word do you use instead of sugarplums?**
Responses will vary.
5. **What picture do you find in lines 7-10, page 96?**
The poet describes St. Nick's arrival in a "miniature sleigh and eight tiny reindeer."
6. **What is the next picture? Find the lines that make it.**
The poet describes St. Nick's reindeer. "More rapid than eagles his coursers they came, And he whistled and shouted and called them by name: 'Now Dasher! now Dancer! now, Prancer and Vixen! On, Comet! on, Cupid! on, Donder and Blitzen! To the top of the porch, to the top of the wall, Now dash away, dash away, dash away all!'"
7. **To what is the swiftness of the reindeer compared?**
The reindeer are swifter than eagles.
8. **What words show how lightly the reindeer flew through the air?**
They flew through the air like "dry leaves that before the wild hurricane fly, When they meet with an obstacle, mount to the sky."
9. **Find the lines that picture St. Nicholas after he came down the chimney.**
Lines 25, page 96, to line four, page, 97, picture St. Nicholas. The picture begins with: "He was dressed all in fur…" and ends with "He was chubby and plump—a right jolly old elf;"
10. **Which of all the pictures in the entire poem can you see most distinctly?**
Answers will vary.

11. Which do you like best?

Answers will vary.

12. What did you read in a "Forward Look," pages 83-86, about the value of home festivals? What does a love of these festivals do for us? What should we lose if we did not celebrate them?

"A Forward Look" says "festivals bind men more closely together, make them one, join them to their native land." Sharing these festivals causes people "to work together to make the community a better place in which to live." Without them, we would lose our sense of community and love for our country.

13. Find in the glossary the meaning of: clatter, coursers, hurricane, obstacle, twinkling, tarnished, encircled, elf.

14. Pronounce: miniature, tiny, chimney, droll.

Extended Activities:

1. A collage is a piece of art consisting of a variety of materials (pictures, paper, cloth, wood, and/or words) that center on a single topic. Have students create a collage of their favorite holiday celebrations.

2. Have students sketch a portrait of the following characters in the poem: the children, Mamma in her kerchief, Papa in his cap, St. Nicholas. Then have students draw thought balloons that show what each character is thinking based on the poem.

NAME______________________________CLASS__________DATE______

A VISIT FROM ST. NICHOLAS, P. 95

1. **Create a collage of your favorite holiday celebrations.**

2. **Sketch a portrait of the following characters in the poem: the children, Mamma in her kerchief, Papa in his cap, St. Nicholas. Then draw thought balloons that show what each character is thinking based on the poem.**

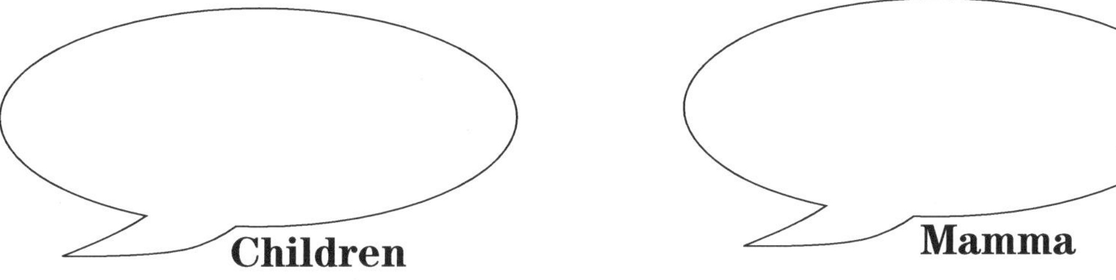

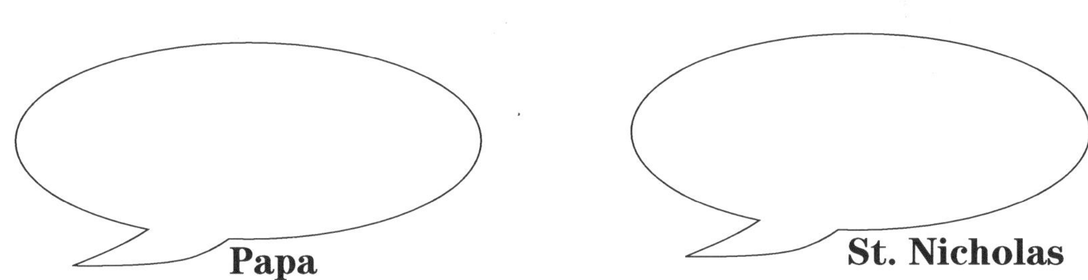

THE LAND OF LIBERTY, P. 98

1. **What parts of our country are noted for pine forests?**
   Pine trees can be found throughout North America including Eastern Pines, Southeastern Pines and Western Pines. Have students research types of pines found in their area of the country.
2. **What things about America call forth the love of the poet?**
   The poet identifies many things that he loves: pine-clad hills, gushing rills, sunshine, storms, rugged rocks, rivers, fields, vales, dells, dales, forests, valleys, flowers, his country's name.
3. **Does he have all parts of America in mind, or some part that he knows well?**
   The poet describes America from north to south, from east to west.
4. **What name does he give America?**
   The poet calls America, "The Land of Liberty."
   Why does this "echo deathless fame"?
   The poet believes America's fame will never die.
5. **Name one of the "mighty streams that seaward glide."**
   Answers will vary but may include any of America's great rivers: Mississippi, Missouri, Arkansas, Colorado, Hudson, Potomac.
6. **What does the poet say makes the forests beautiful?**
   The forests are beautiful "For there the wild bird's merry tone I hear from morn till night; And there are lovelier flowers, I ween, Than e'er in Eastern lands were seen, In varied colors bright."
7. **This poem is similar in many ways to the national hymn, "America." Compare it with the words of the hymn in as many ways as you can.**

"America"	"The Land of Liberty"
My country 'tis of thee	The Land of Liberty
Sweet land of liberty	I love my country's pine-clad hills
From every mountainside	Her rough and rugged rocks
I love thy rocks and rills	gushing rills
Thy woods and templed hills	rugged rocks
	I love her forests

8. **Commit to memory the last three lines of the poem.**
9. **Why is our country called "The Land of Liberty"?**
   America is "The Land of Liberty" because of the freedoms we enjoy: freedom of religion and freedom of speech along with political and economic freedom. We can move freely throughout our great land, enjoying its vast beauty and many contrasts as mentioned by the poet.
10. **Find in the glossary the meaning of: gushing, rills, rugged, rear, vales, dells, lone, ween.**
11. **Pronounce: hoary, fantastic, haunts, echo.**

Extended Activity:

Nouns and adjectives are two parts of speech that name and describe things around us. Nouns name a specific person, place, thing or idea. Adjectives describe those nouns. The poet identifies many nouns that make up our great country and uses vivid adjectives to help us visualize those places. Identify the nouns in the poem with the adjectives that describe them.

NOUNS	ADJECTIVES
hills	pine-clad
rills	thousand bright gushing
rocks	rough rugged
heads	hoary
forms	wild fantastic
rivers	deep wide
streams	mighty
fields	smiling
vales	pleasant
dells	shady
dales	flow'ry
rest	peaceful
forests	dark lone
bird	wild
tone	merry
flowers	lovelier
lands	Eastern
colors	varied bright
forests and valleys	fair
air	morning
fame	deathless

NAME________________________________CLASS__________DATE______

THE LAND OF LIBERTY, P. 98

7. This poem is similar in many ways to the national hymn, "America." Compare it with the words of the hymn in as many ways as you can.

"America"	"The Land of Liberty"

Nouns and adjectives are two parts of speech that name and describe things around us. Nouns name a specific person, place, thing or idea. Adjectives describe those nouns. The poet identifies many nouns that make up our great country and uses vivid adjectives to help us visualize those places. Identify the nouns in the poem with the adjectives that describe them.

NOUNS	ADJECTIVES

The Flag of Our Country, p. 100

1. **Each paragraph in this selection has a separate message. Does the first paragraph fit America only, or could an Englishman say the same thing about his national flag, and a Frenchman of his?**

   Anyone could express the same thing about his country's flag.

   What then is the thing that *any* flag represents to the citizen of the country to which he belongs?

   A flag represents home and country to its people and symbolizes the love they share for their country.

2. **What facts peculiar to America does the third paragraph give you?**

   The paragraph describes the stars and stripes of our American flag and what each stands for.

3. **How many stripes has the flag?**

   The flag has thirteen stripes that represent the "original union of the thirteen states to maintain the Declaration of Independence."

4. **How many stars were in the first American flag?**

   The original flag had thirteen stars to "proclaim that union of states constituting our national constellation, which receives a new star with every new state."

   How many are there now?

   There are now 50 stars on the flag—one for each state.

5. **What is meant by "union past and present"?**

   The stars and stripes are a symbol of our union with the founding fathers and early settlers who helped to build and make our country great.

6. **"White is for purity"—in what way does this express the ideals of the founders of our country?**

   The founders of our country visualized a land of equality, fairness, and peace for its people where we could be free from weakness, harsh lives, and disunity—a land of purity in our deeds and words.

7. **How does it express the motives that led the United States to enter World War One?**

   The United States entered World War One to defend the right to maintain our purity—freedom, justice, and peace.

8. **If we had desired to gain new territory by fighting in this war, would the flag have been honored?**

The flag would not have been honored. America was not interested in gaining new territory, but in defending freedom .

9. **How does the quality of justice appear in the course of America in the war?**

America fought to make the world a safer place, a place of justice for all.

10. **What injustice did our soldiers and sailors fight against?**

Our soldiers fought against the injustice of great nations who sought new territories, trade, and commerce without regard for the people in those territories.

11. **Find in the glossary the meaning of: rippling, reverence, bunting, proclaim, original, maintain, constituting, valor, cherished.**

12. **Pronounce: symbolizes, sublimely, alternate, constellation.**

Extended Activity:

The American flag went through several stages of design before it finally became the flag we have today. Have students research the history and development of our flag. Create a replica of the flag in each stage. Possible stages include: Continental Colors, First Official U.S. Flag, Star-Spangled Banner, Betsy Ross Flag, Great Star Flag, Flag of 1818, Old Glory, Civil War Flag, 37 Star Flag, 45 Star Flag, 48 Star Flag, and the 50 Star Flag.

The following websites are helpful resources:

http://www.anyflag.com/history/greatsta.htm

http://www.law.ou.edu/fedflag.html

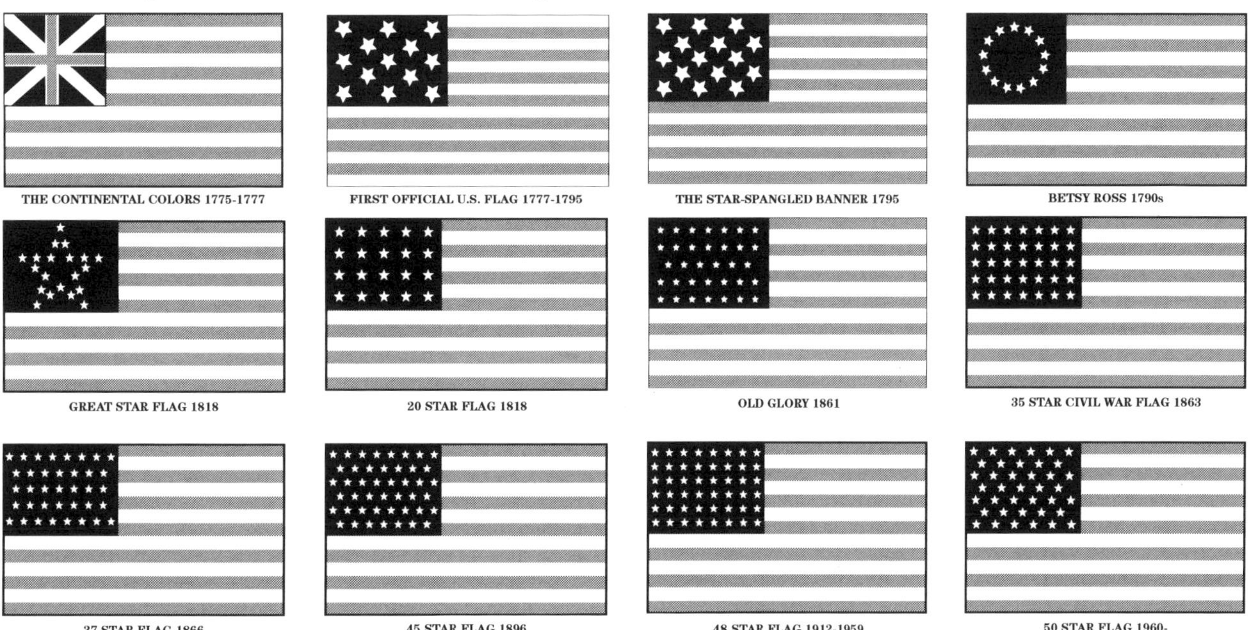

NAME________________________________CLASS__________DATE______

THE FLAG OF OUR COUNTRY, P. 100

The American flag went through several stages of design before it finally became the flag we have today. Research the history and development of our flag. Create a replica of the flag in each stage. Possible stages include: Continental Colors, First Official U.S. Flag, Star-Spangled Banner, Betsy Ross Flag, Great Star Flag, Flag of 1818, Old Glory, Civil War Flag, 37 Star Flag, 45 Star Flag, 48 Star Flag, and the 50 Star Flag.

THE NAME OF OLD GLORY, P. 101

1. **It is said that the name "Old Glory" was given the flag by Captain William Driver, of the brig *Charles Doggett*, in 1831. Why is this a good name for the American flag?**
"Old Glory" represents the glory of our great country as seen in the selections in this section entitled "Our Country and Its Flag."
2. **The first stanza describes the beauty of the flag. What words or lines tell you about the *appearance* of "Old Glory"?**
"Your stripes stroked in ripples of white and red, With your stars at their glittering best overhead—By day or by night."
Which words or lines tell you about the *personality* (pride, freedom, joy) of the flag?
"Who gave you, Old Glory, the name that you bear With such pride everywhere As you cast yourself free to the rapturous air And leap out full-length, as we're wanting you to?"
3. **What is meant by "long, *blended* ranks of the gray and the blue"?**
"Long blended ranks of the gray and blue" refer to the soldiers in uniform, regardless of rank or station, over whom Old Glory fluttered.
4. **What response does the flag seem to make?**
"The old banner lifted, and faltering then, In vague lisps and whispers fell silent again."
5. **The second stanza gives the effect produced by the flag upon the poet. Where is he?**
The poet is at war "seeing you fly and the boys marching by."
How does he feel?
"There's a shout in the throat and a blur in the eye And an aching to live for you always—or die, If, dying, we still keep you waving on high."
6. **In the last stanza, compare what is said about the parts of the flag and their meaning with what Mr. Sumner told you in the preceding selection.**
The last stanza describes the flag with its "driven snow-white and the living blood-red" stripes and stars as a symbol of unity. Mr. Sumner also describes the flag with its colors and the unity they represent.

7. **Find in the glossary the meaning of: faltering, thrilled, blast, driven, symbol.**
8. **Pronounce: rapturous, christening, audible.**

Extended Activity:

After researching the designs of the American Flag (see extended activity in "The Flag of Our Country") identify the flag design that was flying when the poet wrote this poem. (This was probably the Flag of 1818.)

NAME______________________________CLASS__________DATE______

THE NAME OF OLD GLORY, P. 101

Identify the flag design that was flying when the poet wrote this poem.

The Star-Spangled Banner, p. 104

1. **What lines in the poem are explained by the historic note on page 105? (see below)**

Biographical and Historical Note. Francis Scott Key (1780-1843), a native of Maryland, was a lawyer and poet. His patriotic poem, "The Star-Spangled Banner," which has become the national anthem, made him famous.

The incidents referred to in this poem occurred during the War of 1812. In August, 1814, a strong force of British entered Washington and burned the Capitol, the White House, and many other public buildings. On September 13, the British admiral moved his fleet into position to attack Fort McHenry, near Baltimore. The bombardment of the fort lasted all night, but the fort was so bravely defended that the flag was still floating over it when morning came.

Just before the bombardment began, Francis Scott Key was sent to the admiral's frigate to arrange for an exchange of prisoners, and was told to wait until the bombardment was over. All night he watched the fort, and by the first rays of morning light he saw the Stars and Stripes still waving. Then, in his joy and pride, he wrote the stirring words of the song which is now known and loved by all Americans—"The Star-Spangled Banner."

"O say, can you see, by the dawn's early light, What so proudly we hailed at the twilight's last gleaming? Whose broad stripes and bright stars, through the perilous fight, O'er the ramparts we watched were so gallantly streaming; And the rocket's red glare, the bombs bursting in air, Gave proof through the night that our flag was till there."

2. **The poem expresses the love and reverence felt by the patriots when the flag is endangered by the attacks of armed men in war. What is said on page 84 about the danger to our country in a time of peace?**

"But now that peace has come, it is not so easy to forget self in a loyalty to our country and its flag. It is easy to be on guard when we know that an armed enemy is close by; it is not easy when the enemy is hidden, and the guns are silent."

From what people?

"These hidden enemies of our country do not fight in armies; they are the bad citizens who are scattered about; often you do not realize who they are."

Can you do anything to prevent this danger?

We can show our love for home and country by our "service, willingness to help others. The man or woman who thinks only of his own good time or his own fortune is a bad citizen."

3. **Where was the reflection of the flag seen?**

"In full glory reflected now shines in the stream."

4. **What is the meaning of "thus" in line 1, page 105?**

"O thus be it ever, when freemen shall stand Between their loved homes and war's desolation" that "the Star-Spangled

Banner in triumph shall wave O'er the land of the free and the home of the brave." The poet is saying that he hopes the flag will always fly, whether in times of peace or times of war.

5. **What land is the "heav'n-rescued land"?**
The "heav'n-rescued land" refers to the United States.

6. **What does the poet mean when he speaks of the "Power that hath made and preserved us a nation," line 4, page 105?**
The poet acknowledges God as the "Power that hath made us and preserved us a nation."

7. **Find the words that must be our country's motto.**
"And this be our motto, 'In God is our trust.'"

8. **Do you think this national song cheered the American soldiers in the last two World Wars?**
Answers will vary but will likely agree that the song did cheer the soldiers.

9. **Explain why you think the picture on page 98 (right) aptly illustrates "Our Country and Its Flag."**

Answers will vary.

10. **Find in the glossary the meaning of: dawn, gleaming, host, discloses, beam, triumph.**

11. **Pronounce: haughty, vauntingly, pollution, hireling, desolation.**

Extended Activity:

Have the students research the War of 1812, the war in which the flag flew that inspired this poem. Students can display their research by creating a class time line or a mural that depicts scenes from their topics. Possible research topics may include but are not limited to: Lake Erie Victory, British Blockade, Shelling of the Chesapeake, Dolley Madison saving the portrait of Washington, Uncle Sam, the burning of the nation's capital, Fort McHenry, the *Essex* voyage.

The Boyhood of Lincoln, p. 106

1. **What were the hardships suffered by the young Lincoln in the Indiana wilderness?**
His hardships included: poor housing, sickness, death, hunger, and cold.
2. **What do you learn about Lincoln's reading?**
He had only three books which he knew almost by heart.
About his school life?
He was often the head of his class and "spelled down" the other students.
3. **What was the first book Lincoln owned, and how did he get it?**
His first book was *The Life of Washington*. He had borrowed it, and one day rain blew through the cracks between the walls and soaked it "almost into pulp." So he told the man from whom he had borrowed the book. The man made him pay for the book by making him pull up cornstalks by the roots to feed the cattle for three days.
4. **What do you suppose Lincoln learned from the life of Washington?**
Answers will vary but may include references to Washington's bravery, honesty, and great leadership.
5. **How did Lincoln fix in his memory things that he wished to remember?**
Everything he wished to remember, "he would copy it on a shingle, because writing paper was scarce, and either learn it by heart or hide the shingle away until he could get some paper to copy it on."
6. **What characteristics of the boy help to explain why he afterwards became such a great man?**
Abraham Lincoln's hard work, ability to endure hardship and his honesty helped him to become a great man.
7. **You will enjoy reading *The True Story of Lincoln*, from which this selection is taken.**
8. **Find in the glossary the meaning of: forlorn, shanty, princely, wilderness, epidemic, shiftless, ash-cakes, slab, guidance, ciphering, clapboard, pulp.**
9. **Pronounce: Aesop, bade.**

Extended Activity:

Have students research further details of Lincoln's early life. A good encyclopedia or the Internet are excellent resources. Have students create a three-dimensional model of Lincoln's early cabin or school classroom, paying close attention to the details found in their research. Materials may include Lincoln Logs, straws, craft sticks, or other natural materials.

Washington with General Braddock, p. 110

1. **Tell what you can of the contest for territory in America between the French and the English.**

   Answers will vary. A possible student research resource is *A History of the United States and Its People* (Lost Classics Book Company) which includes a chapter on the English and French wars in America. In brief, the two countries battled for American territory for many years. The colonists were frequently caught in the middle of these clashes experiencing untold atrocities from both sides. The event as told in "Washington with General Braddock" occurred in 1754.

2. **Who was General Braddock and for what was he sent to America?**

   General Braddock, who commanded the British and colonial troops, came to America to drive out the French.

3. **Compare Washington and General Braddock in as many ways as you can.**

   Washington and Braddock were both generals, both were respected leaders, both were brave. However, their styles of leadership differed widely. Washington understood the dangers of war in the woods while Braddock was more concerned with the order and beauty of his troops. He refused to heed Washington's experienced advice.

4. **Why did Washington do all he could to help General Braddock in spite of the fact that he knew Braddock was not acting wisely?**

   Washington was a man of honor fighting for his country, so he chose to help Braddock in spite of Braddock's poor strategies.

5. **How did Washington gain glory from the engagement?**

   He came out of the clash a hero. He "protected the rear of the retreating army, carried off the dying general, and, cool and collected in the midst of all the terrible things that were happening, saved the British army from slaughter, buried poor General Braddock in the Virginia woods, and finally brought back to the settlements what was left of that splendid army of the king. He was the only man in all that time of disaster who came out of the fight with glory and renown."

6. **What are you told on page 84 about the value to us of studying the lives of great Americans?**

   "Through these stories we learn what the flag really means and what it has cost, and we love our country as we love our mother."

   What do you owe to Washington and Lincoln?

   We owe them our respect for their leadership, bravery, and love of country that made America great.

7. **Find in the glossary the meaning of: advisers, situation, caution, ford, array, gallantly, huddled, collected, disaster, renown.**

8. **Pronounce: Duquesne, Monongahela, mortally wounded.**

Extended Activity:

1. Have students research the design and layout of early American forts such as the one at Fort Duquesne. Students can then create a model of the fort as it may have appeared when General Braddock led his troops to conquer the French troops there.

2. Washington was an outstanding role model of patriotism, service, honor, and citizenship as he fought for the freedoms we enjoy. All of those characteristics are still essential today in order to keep America strong. In the web below, choose one of the following themes: patriotism, freedom, citizenship, honor. Write your theme in the hub of the wheel. On the spokes around the wheel, list what that theme means to you.

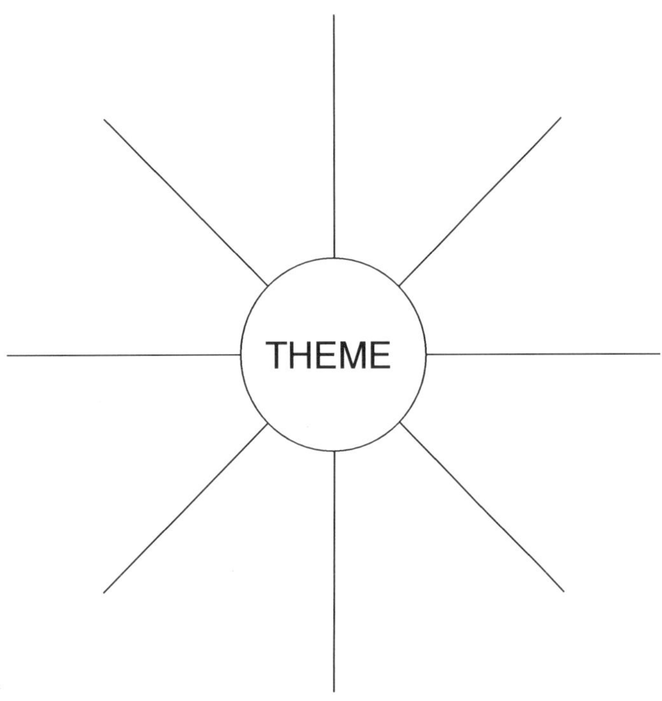

NAME________________________________**CLASS**__________**DATE**______

WASHINGTON WITH GENERAL BRADDOCK, P. 110

1. Research the design and layout of early American forts such as the one at Fort Duquesne. Then create a model of the fort as it may have appeared when General Braddock led his troops to conquer the French troops there.
2. Washington was an outstanding role model of patriotism, service, honor, and citizenship as he fought for the freedoms we enjoy. All of those characteristics are still essential today in order to keep America strong. In the web below, choose one of the following themes: patriotism, freedom, citizenship, honor. Write your theme in the hub of the wheel. On the spokes around the wheel, list what that theme means to you.

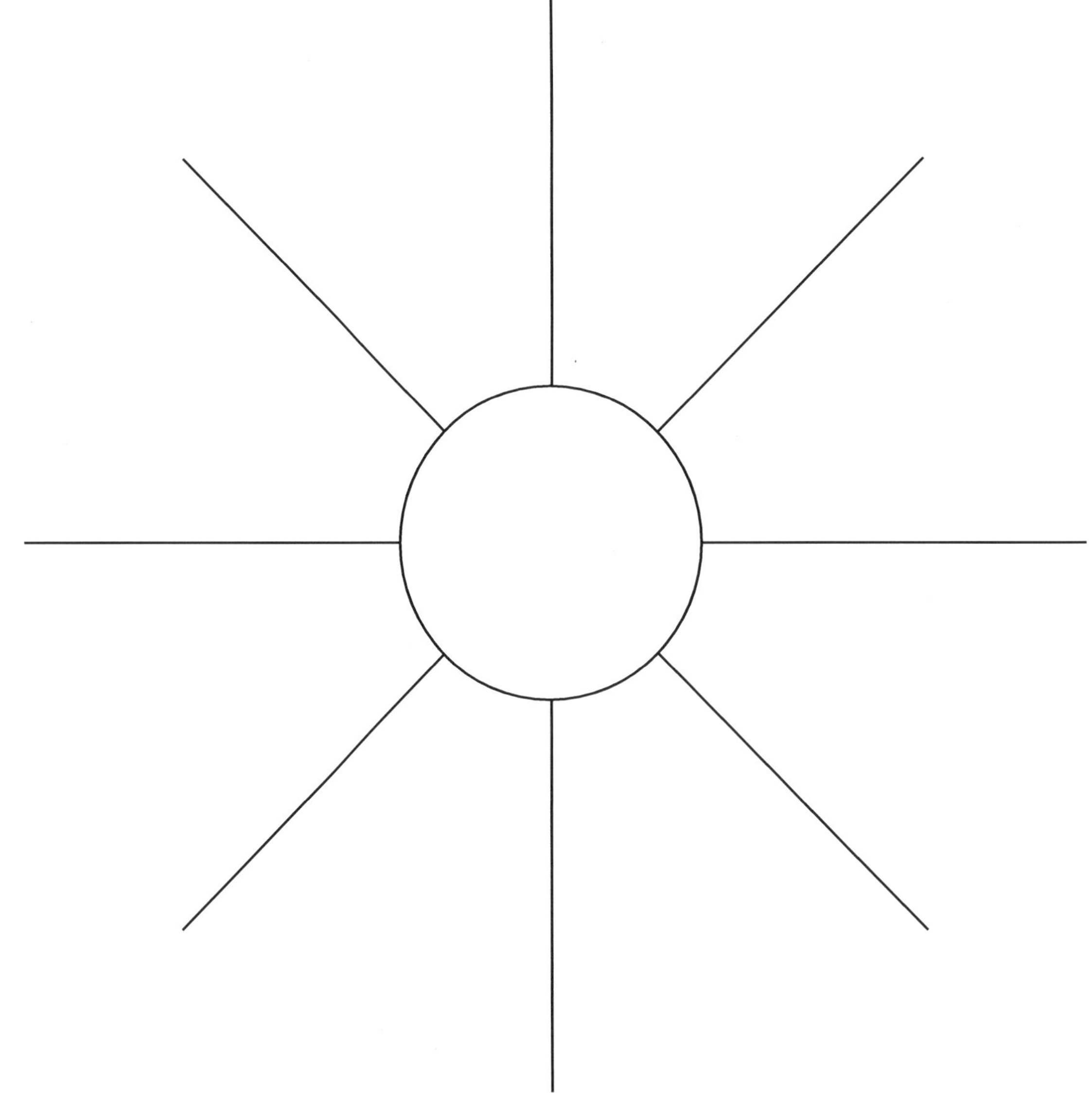

Somebody's Mother, p. 113

1. **Here is a story about a boy who saw a chance to do a service and did it; how was he different from his companions?**
   His companions ran past her without offering to help. The boy, on the other hand, "paused beside her and whispered low, 'I'll help you across if you wish to go.'"
2. **What were they interested in?**
   They were thinking about freedom from school and playing in the snow.
3. **Wasn't he also eager to do what they did?**
   Yes, he was "the gayest laddie of all the group."
4. **Why did he stop and help the old woman?**
   He told his friends, "She's somebody's mother, boys, you know, For all she's aged and poor and slow; and I hope some fellow will lend a hand to help my mother, you understand, if ever she's poor and old and gray, When her own dear boy is far away."
5. **How did the woman feel toward the boy?**
   That night in her prayers she prayed, "God be kind to the noble boy who is somebody's son and pride and joy."
6. **How do you think his own mother would have felt if she had seen him?**
   She would have been proud of his behavior.
7. **Why is this incident a splendid example of service?**
   The young boy put others' wishes above his own.
   How was this boy doing his part as a good citizen?
   In "A Forward Look" we read that a good citizen is willing to help others. If we consider only our own plans, we are unworthy citizens.

Extended Activity:

Have students complete the following assignment:

Think of a time you or someone you know was a star and helped someone who needed assistance. Complete the star by answering the following questions. Who did the good deed? When or where did the good deed take place? What was the good deed? How did the person helped respond? How did the person doing the deed feel when it was over?

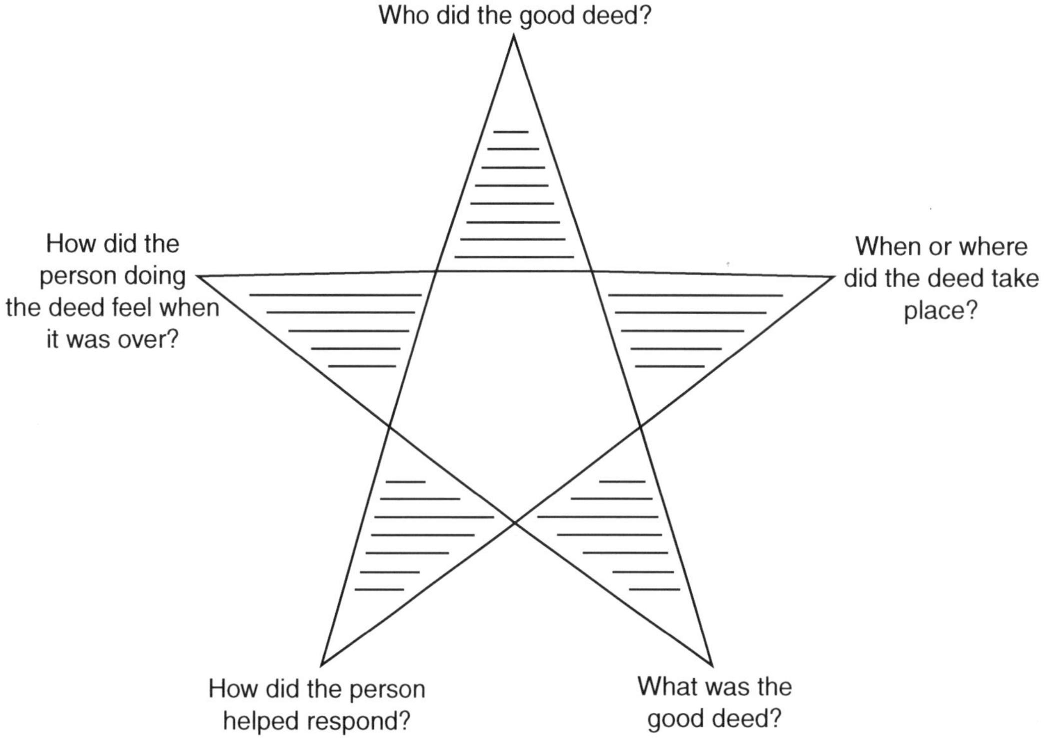

Name______________________________**Class**__________**Date**______

Somebody's Mother, p. 113

Think of a time you or someone you know was a star and helped someone who needed assistance. Complete the star by answering the following questions. Who did the good deed? When or where did the good deed take place? What was the good deed? How did the person helped respond? How did the person doing the deed feel when it was over?

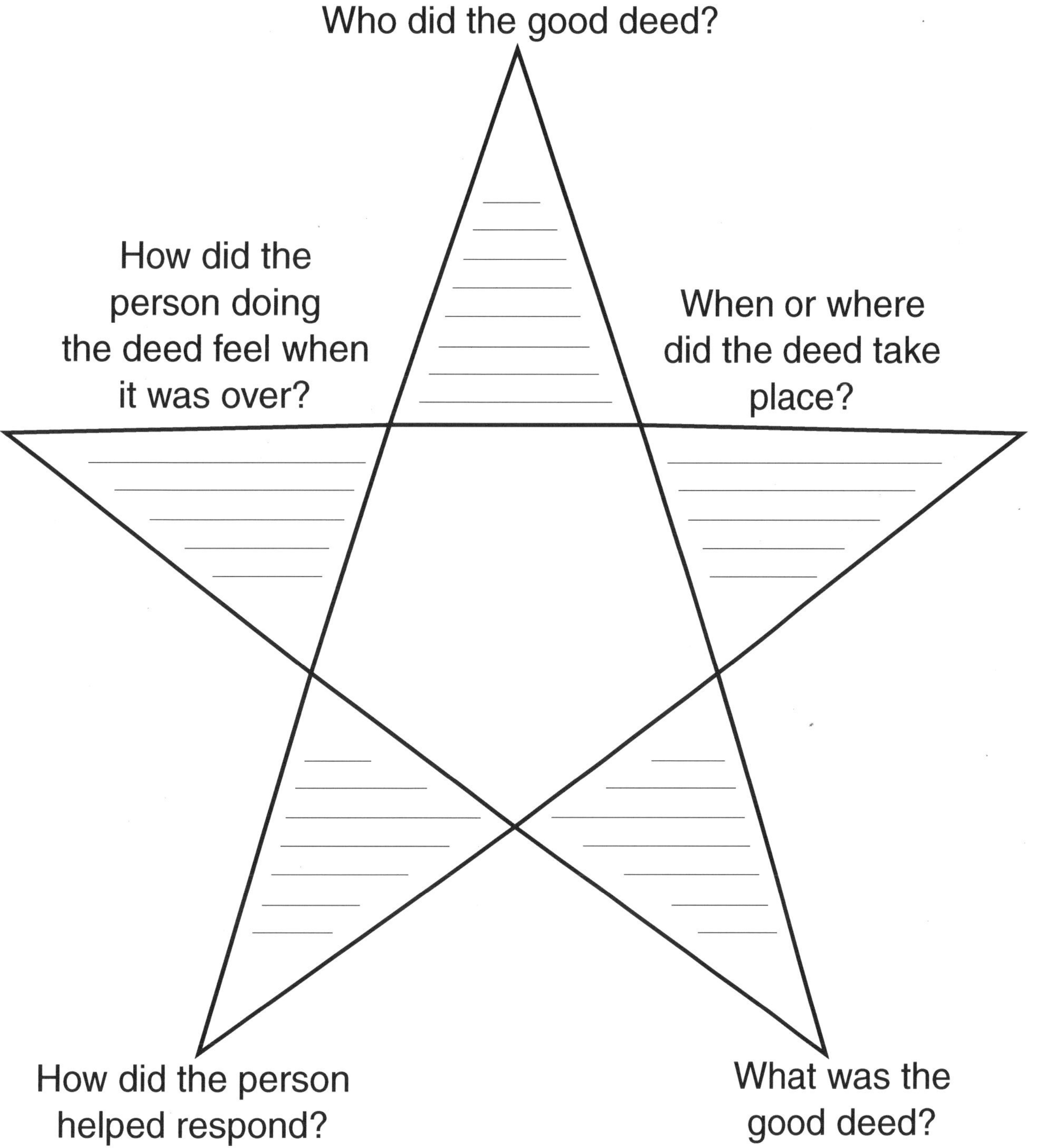

The Leak in the Dike, p. 115

1. **What purpose do the dikes of Holland serve?**
   The dikes form a barrier to keep the high tide from flooding the low lands.
2. **There were no Boy Scouts in those days, but here is a story of a boy who would have been a good member of the Scouts. Why?**
   Part of the Boy Scout oath includes the promise "To do my duty to God and my country…to help other people at all times." This boy fulfilled that promise by saving his country and helping his people.
3. **What service did Peter's mother call him to render?**
   "Come, Peter, come! I want you to go, while there is light to see, to the hut of the blind old man who lives across the dike, for me; and take these cakes I made for him."
4. **Had he done such things before?**
   The poet does not indicate whether or not the boy has run such errands before, but he was a brave boy, unafraid to tackle any task.
5. **How did the blind man think of Peter?**
   "Yet somehow he caught the brightness which his voice and presence lent; and he felt the sunshine come and go as Peter came and went."
6. **How did Peter find the danger?**
   Peter was gathering flowers when he heard the "low, clear, trickling sound."
7. **What would many boys have done?**
   Many boys would have run away in fear to get help.
8. **How did he stop the leak in the dike?**
   "He forces back the weight of the sea with the strength of his single arm."
9. **What would have happened if he had grown afraid or tired?**
   The leak would have grown to a raging torrent.
10. **Peter saw a duty to be performed and was brave enough to do it, though it was not easy, and might have cost him his life. What were the results of his quick wit and courage?**
    He saved the land and its people.

11. **How was Peter doing his part as a good citizen?**
    He saw a need and did his part to fulfill the need, even though he put his life in danger.
12. **Find in the glossary the meaning of: prattle, presence, anxious, trickling, stoutest, save, astir, yester, stricken.**
13. **Pronounce: chafe, sluices, loosed.**

Extended Activity:

Have students complete the following chart:

An effective way to understand a piece of literature is to ask questions about the work as you read. Answering the questions who, what, when, where, why, and how will aid you as you read. Complete the chart on "The Leak in the Dike."

Who is the main character?	
What is he asked to do?	
Where is the event taking place?	
When does the event occur? (time of day)	
Why was he considered a hero?	
How did those around him respond?	

Name______________________________ Class__________ Date______

The Leak in the Dike, p. 115

An effective way to understand a piece of literature is to ask questions about the work as you read. Answering the questions who, what, when, where, why, and how will aid you as you read. Complete the chart on "The Leak in the Dike."

Who is the main character?	
What is he asked to do?	
Where is the event taking place?	
When does the event occur? (time of day)	
Why was he considered a hero?	
How did those around him respond?	

CASABIANCA, P. 120

1. **How did it happen that the boy was alone on the "burning deck"?**
   His father had sent him there to complete a task, and he would not leave his post without his father's permission, even though everyone else had fled.
2. **Find two lines in the third stanza that tell how the boy showed his faithfulness and his "heroic blood."**
   "The flames rolled on—he would not go without his father's word."
3. **Why is his father called the "chieftain"?**
   His father was the captain of the ship.
4. **What did the boy ask his father?**
   "My father! Must I stay?"
5. **Why did he remain in such great danger when he might have saved himself?**
   He believed that obedience was more important than safety.
6. **What was it that "wrapped the ship in splendor wild"?**
   The "wreathing fires" "wrapped the ship in splendor wild."
7. **What made the "burst of thunder sound"?**
   In the biographical notes it tells us the "powder magazine exploded" which caused the "burst of thunder."
8. **What things are mentioned as fragments which "strewed the sea"?**
   The fragments were the "mast, and helm, and pennon fair, that well had borne their part; but the noblest thing which perished there was that young, faithful heart."
9. **Why is it good for us to read such a poem as this?**
   Answers will vary but may reflect the concepts referred to in "A Forward Look." We learn to become good citizens by reading about others who show love for home and family, loyalty to country and service to others.
10. **What service did Casabianca do for all of us?**
    He was an example of a true citizen who put obedience and duty ahead of his own interests.
11. **Find in the glossary the meaning of: chieftain, unconscious, booming, despair, fragments, pennon.**
12. **Pronounce: heroic, shroud, helm.**

Extended Activity:

Writers of good literature choose words carefully to create mental pictures or imagery that capture the minds of their readers. In "Casabianca" the poet uses several different expressions to create the image of a ship in flames. Have students list all the references they can find that create that imagery.

Answers include: burning deck; flame shone round him o'er the dead; flames rolled on; fast the flames rolled on; Upon his brow he felt their breath; while o'er him fast…the wreathing fires made way; they wrapped the ship in splendor wild; they caught the flag…and streamed above the gallant child like banners in the sky.

NAME______________________________**CLASS**__________**DATE**______

CASABIANCA, p. 120

Writers of good literature choose words carefully to create mental pictures or imagery that capture the minds of their readers. In "Casabianca" the poet uses several different expressions to create the image of a ship in flames. List all the references you can find that create that imagery.

Tubal Cain, p. 123

1. **What did Tubal Cain first make on his forge?**
   He "fashioned the sword and spear."
2. **Why did he think that his work was good?**
   His weapons were sharp and strong and would enable men to become kings and lords.
3. **What did men say about him?**
   They sang, "Hurrah for Tubal Cain, Who hath given us strength anew! Hurrah for the Smith! hurrah for the fire! And hurrah for the metal true."
4. **How did Tubal Cain feel when he saw what men were doing with the products of his forge?**
   When he saw that men used their swords to kill other men, he said, "Alas, that ever I made, Or that skill of mine should plan, The spear and the sword for men whose joy Is to slay their fellow-man!"
5. **What did he do then?**
   "And for many a day old Tubal Cain sat brooding o'er his woe; and his hand forbore to smite the ore, and his furnace smoldered low."
6. **What made his face "cheerful" at last?**
   He decided to make plowshares instead of weapons.
7. **Is it better to make instruments of war or tools for industry?**
   Answers will vary but may reflect that both have their place.
8. **Why was Tubal Cain happy when he made plows?**
   Instead of killing each other, men joined hands in friendship and worked together to build their land.
9. **Was he working for money, or for service?**
   He performed a service to humanity.
10. **Explain the last four lines.**
    While the plow is a useful tool, the sword may still be needed against oppression and tyranny.
11. **Find in the glossary the meaning of: fashioned, handiwork, wrought, anew, lust, brooding, forbore, plowshare.**
12. **Pronounce: hurrah, wield, carnage, smoldered, stanch.**

Extended Activity:

The poet created this poem based on a brief reference to Tubal Cain in the Bible in Genesis 4:22. In a Bible look up the following references and compare and contrast them to the poet's description of Tubal Cain's actions:

Isaiah 2:4
Joel 3:10
Matthew 5:9

NAME______________________________**CLASS**__________**DATE**______

TUBAL CAIN, P. 123

The poet created this poem based on a brief reference to Tubal Cain in the Bible in Genesis 4:22. In a Bible look up the following references and compare and contrast them to the poet's description of Tubal Cain's actions:

Isaiah 2:4

Joel 3:10

Matthew 5:9.

The Inchcape Rock, p. 126

1. **What picture did you see when you read the first stanza?**
   The first stanza paints a picture of a ship at perfect rest, motionless in the ocean, without a breeze or a sea wave to stir it.
   The second stanza?
   The second stanza describes the waves flowing over the rock so quietly the Inchcape bell was not moved.
2. **This story tells about a man who failed. You have read about Peter's heroism and the lives he saved, about the service a school boy rendered to a poor old woman, about a blacksmith who joyously made the tools by which men raised fruit and grain for food, and about a boy who was faithful to orders, even though it cost his life. Here you see how men sometimes try to make of no effect all the good deeds that others perform.**
3. **The Abbot of Aberbrothok was a man who lived up to the ideal of service; how did he do this, and why did men bless him?**
   The Abbot placed a bell, floating from a buoy, on the rock. When the storms came and the waves covered the rock, the bell would ring to warn seamen of the danger. The mariners blessed the Abbot for saving their lives.
4. **Ralph the Rover was a pirate; why did he destroy the bell?**
   Ralph wanted to annoy the Abbot; he gave no thought to the bell's purpose.
5. **All the others in the stories you have read, boys and men, thought less of themselves than of others; of what did Ralph think?**
   Ralph, who was perhaps jealous of the praises given to the Abbot, thought only of how he could discredit the Abbot and gain attention for himself.
6. **Is a merchant who raises the price of food as high as he can, who makes huge profits while others suffer or starve, any better than Ralph the Rover?**
   No, regardless of one's profession, one who withholds from

others for only personal gain, regardless of other's needs, is a poor example of citizenship.

7. **What test of loyalty to our country, mentioned on page 85, would prove such a man to be a "bad citizen"?**

Service is a test of loyalty. "The man or woman who thinks only of his own good time or his own fortune is a bad citizen."

8. **Ralph was a free man—what did "liberty" mean to him?**

Liberty to Ralph meant the freedom to do whatever he pleased at the expense of the safety and well-being of others.

9. **What happened to Ralph the Rover?**

His own ship struck the rock at night in a storm.

10. **Find in the glossary the meaning of: keel, abbot, perilous, joyance, breakers, methinks.**
11. **Pronounce: buoy, mariners, excess, scoured.**

Extended Activity:

Alliteration is a figure of speech that refers to the repetition of beginning sounds such as "merry mermaids make music." The poet in "The Inchcape Rock" sprinkles examples of alliteration throughout his poem. Have students identify as many examples as they can. Possible answers may include: stir in the sea, ship was still as she, sign or sound, Abbot of Aberbrothok, waves its warning, then they knew the perilous rock, buoy of the Inchcape Bell, Ralph the Rover, bubbles rose and burst, scoured the seas, swell is strong, shivering shock.

NAME______________________________ CLASS__________ DATE______

THE INCHCAPE ROCK, P. 126

Alliteration is a figure of speech that refers to the repetition of beginning sounds such as "merry mermaids make music." The poet in "The Inchcape Rock" sprinkles examples of alliteration throughout his poem. Identify as many examples as you can.

My Boyhood on the Prairie, p. 129

1. **Describe the boy's new home.**
His new home "was a mere shanty, a shell of pine boards, which needed reinforcing to make it habitable," a solitary cabin overlooking the vast, treeless plain.
2. **What work did the boy have to do?**
His father asked him to "run the plow team" to prepare the fields for planting.
3. **In what spirit did he start the plowing?**
"I drove my horses into the field that first morning with a manly pride which added an inch to my stature. I took my initial "round" at a "land" which stretched from one side of the quarter section to the other, in confident mood. I was grown up!"
4. **Why did his "sense of elation" soon disappear?**
Guiding a team of horses was hard work. Walking all day around the field, 15-18 miles a day, dragging the heavy equipment through the thick, wet stubble soon caused him to view the task as a job, not as a chore.
5. **Was his task harder than that of Peter or of the boy who helped "Somebody's Mother"?**
His task was harder because it went on day after day, week after week, unlike those of the other boys whose tasks were one-time events.
6. **Must a boy do some marvelous thing to be a hero?**
Heroic acts are not measured by greatness, but by courage and tenacity in spite of pain. One can do a very ordinary act of service with bravery and courage and be a hero.
7. **How did the boy try to keep himself in good cheer?**
He whistled, sang, and studied nature around him.
8. **On page 19 you are told that if you have eyes to see, "the world of nature is a fairyland." Why do you think this boy had "eyes to see"? Find your answer by reading the last two lines on page 131 and the first paragraph on page 132.**
"I whistled. I sang. I studied the clouds. I gnawed the beautiful red skin from the seed vessels which hung upon the wild rose bushes, and I counted the prairie chickens as they began to come together in winter flocks, running

through the stubble in search of food. I stopped now and again to examine the lizards unhoused by the share, and I measured the little granaries of wheat which the mice and gophers had deposited deep under the ground, storehouses which the plow had violated. My eyes dwelt enviously upon the sailing hawk and on the passing of ducks. The occasional shadowy figure of a prairie wolf made me wish for Uncle David and his rifle."

9. **What made him wish for freedom?**

The bitter cold wind, wild geese racing ahead of the coming winter, horses' tails, snow flurries, and mud-gummed boots that slowed him down made him wish "for the leisure of boyhood."

10. **Class reading: Page 131, line 8, to the end of the story.**
11. **Outline for testing silent reading. Tell the story briefly, using these topics: a) the region and the cabin; b) what plowing meant to a boy; c) how the boy was cheered.**

a. The region was bare and treeless. Houses were spread far apart, and the plain seemed to go on forever. The shanty was made of pine boards and in need of repair.

b. At first, plowing meant a boy was grownup and gave him a "manly pride." After awhile, plowing became tedious, hard work.

c. The boy was cheered in his hard work when people noticed him hard at work. He also whistled, sang, and studied nature to cheer himself.

12. **Find in the glossary the meaning of: marveled, scorched, skillet, ridges, reinforcing, habitable, commission, stature, implement, stubble, share, cross brace, judgment, tormentors, tolerable, unhoused, deposited, clogging, evaporated.**
13. **Pronounce: chore, tedious, loam, imaginable, gopher, leisure.**

Extended Activities:

1. Have students complete the follwing activity:

A new museum of history is opening up in your area. The museum is looking for actors who will accurately portray characters from the early American time period so visitors to the museum can visualize the life of the pioneers. To prepare for your interview with the employer, you must dress, act, and speak like this young pioneer in the story. After reading this story and any other research that would aid you, design your costume, your speech, and your presentation convincingly so you will be hired for the job.

2. The boy in this story had both positive and negative experiences while he was plowing. Have students create a list of his experiences in each category then choose one category and illustrate it. Possible images may include:

Suggested Answers:

Positive	Negative
neighbor Button's comment	walking miles a day
Harriet and Frank	dragging heavy equipment
cookie and milk	short stature
rich soil	savage flies
whistling	tortured horses
singing	bitter wind, coming winter
studying clouds	horses' tails
gnawing seed skins	snow flurries
counting prairie chickens	mud-covered boots
examining lizards	cold and loneliness
measuring granaries of wheat	
watching hawks and doves	

Name______________________________**Class**__________**Date**______

My Boyhood on the Prairie, p. 129

1. **A new museum of history is opening up in your area. The museum is looking for actors who will accurately portray characters from the early American time period so visitors to the museum can visualize the life of the pioneers. To prepare for your interview with the employer, you must dress, act, and speak like this young pioneer in the story. After reading this story and any other research that would aid you, design your costume, your speech, and your presentation convincingly so you will be hired for the job.**

Costume ____

____

____

____

____

Speech ____

____

____

____

____

Presentation ____

____

____

____

____

2. **The boy in this story had both positive and negative experiences while he was plowing. Create a list of his experiences in each category then choose one category and illustrate it.**

Positive	Negative

Woodman, Spare That Tree, p. 134

1. **To whom is the poet speaking in these verses?**
   The poet is speaking to the woodman who is preparing to cut down the tree.
2. **What does he wish to prevent?**
   The poet wishes to spare the tree from the woodman's axe.
3. **Why is the tree dear to him?**
   The tree sheltered him when he was young.
4. **Whom does he remember seeing under the tree?**
   He recalls seeing his sisters, his mother, and his father under the tree.
5. **What did they do there?**
   His sisters played, his mother kissed him, and his father "pressed" his hand.
6. **How will the poet protect the tree?**
   He will fight for the tree. "While I've a hand to save, Thy ax shall harm it not."
7. **How does the American Forestry Association protect trees?**
   The American Forestry Association works to educate the public about intelligent management and use of our natural resources including our forests, soil, and wildlife. They work to protect our forests and improve the environment to encourage healthy trees.
8. **Why should trees be cared for and protected?**
   Trees are essential to our environment. Their leaves absorb carbon dioxide from the air and produce oxygen, ingredients necessary to life. In addition, they help conserve soil and water, and they provide food, wood products, and shelter for wildlife.
9. **Why do we celebrate Arbor Day?**
   We celebrate Arbor Day to recognize the value of planting trees to improve our environment.
10. **Find in the glossary the meaning of: forefather, renown, towering, heart-strings.**

Extended Activity:

Have students complete the following activity:

You have been invited to participate in your community's Arbor

Day activities. You are to present a speech about the importance of trees. You want to contact the American Forestry Association to discover how your community can help protect their trees. Write a business letter to the association requesting information about how to protect this valuable natural resource. The association can be reached at 1516 P St. NW, Washington, DC 20005. Look up the association on the Internet to learn the name of the current director. Create a rough draft of your letter, revise and edit it for grammar, punctuation, and spelling so you have a well-organized business letter that clearly states your request. A business letter includes six parts: the heading includes your address and the date; the inside address includes the address of the business to which you are writing; the salutation addresses the person to whom you are writing (Dear Sir or Madam); the body of the letter includes a request for the information you need; the closing; and finally, your signature.

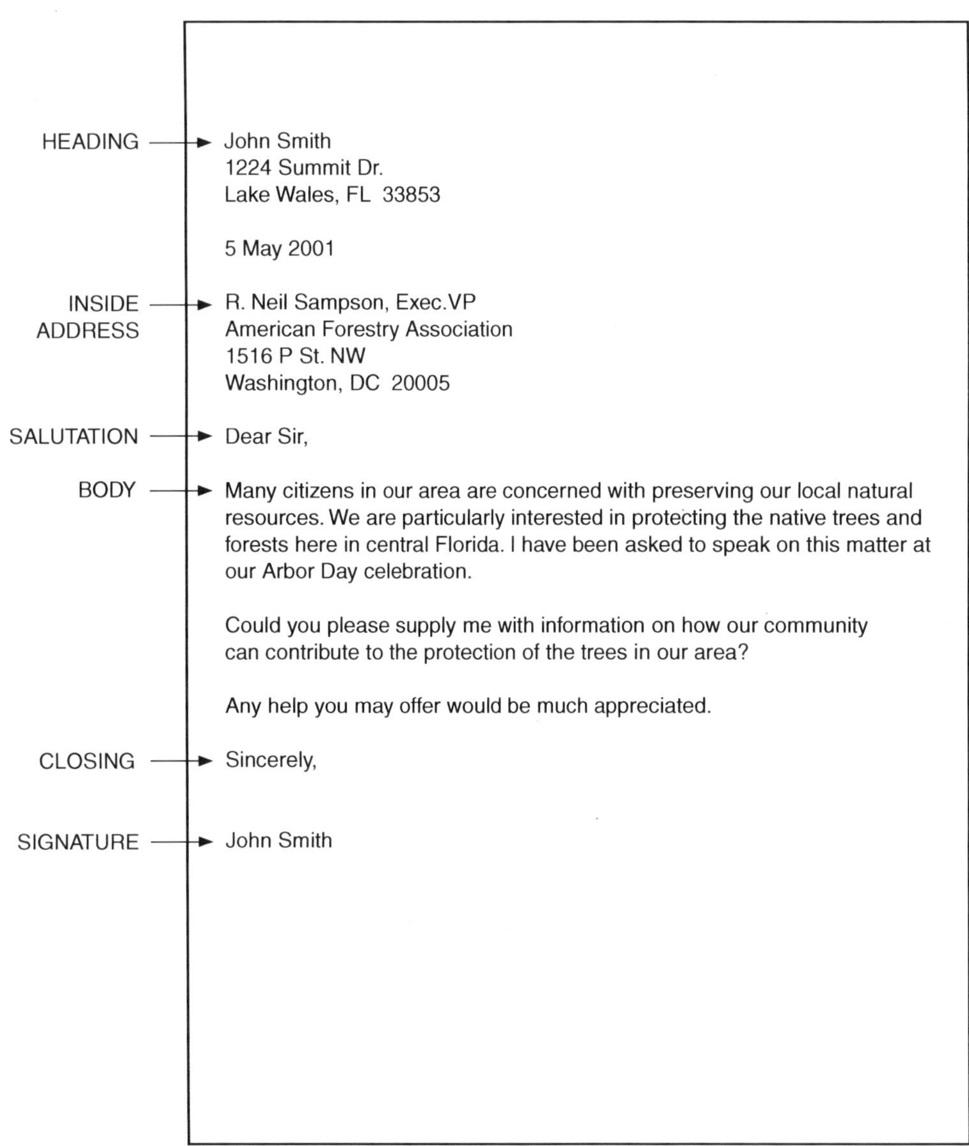

John Smith
1224 Summit Dr.
Lake Wales, FL 33853

5 May 2001

R. Neil Sampson, Exec.VP
American Forestry Association
1516 P St. NW
Washington, DC 20005

Dear Sir,

Many citizens in our area are concerned with preserving our local natural resources. We are particularly interested in protecting the native trees and forests here in central Florida. I have been asked to speak on this matter at our Arbor Day celebration.

Could you please supply me with information on how our community can contribute to the protection of the trees in our area?

Any help you may offer would be much appreciated.

Sincerely,

John Smith

NAME________________________________**CLASS**__________**DATE**______

WOODMAN, SPARE THAT TREE, P. 134

You have been invited to participate in your community's Arbor Day activities. You are to present a speech about the importance of trees. You want to contact the American Forestry Association to discover how your community can help protect their trees. Write a business letter to the association requesting information about how to protect this valuable natural resource. The association can be reached at 1516 P St. NW, Washington, DC 20005. Look up the association on the Internet to learn the name of the current director. Create a rough draft of your letter, revise and edit it for grammar, punctuation, and spelling so you have a well-organized business letter that clearly states your request. A business letter includes six parts: the heading includes your address and the date; the inside address includes the address of the business to which you are writing; the salutation addresses the person to whom you are writing (Dear Sir or Madam); the body of the letter includes a request for the information you need; the closing; and finally, your signature.

The American Boy, p. 136

1. **This selection sums up all the stories of service that you have been reading. You will get most out of it if you will think back over these stories and use them as illustrations of what Mr. Roosevelt tells you is his ideal of the American boy. What examples in these stories can you find to illustrate the sentence, "He must not be a coward or a weakling...He must work hard and play hard"?**

   In "Somebody's Mother" the young boy left his friends at play to help the old woman cross the street. Peter, the Dutch boy, plugged the leak in the dike and saved his country. The boy on the deck in "Casabianca" stood firm at his post when everybody around him fled for their lives. Tubal Cain turned his tools of war into tools of peace. The Abbot of Aberbrothok saved the lives of the mariners by placing a bell on the rocks to warn them. The pioneer boy kept plowing though the days were long and the work was hard. In "Woodman, Spare That Tree" the poet would have faced the woodman's ax in order to save his tree. Each of them were examples of bravery and courage who worked hard to help others.

2. **Illustrate, from the story of Lincoln, what Mr. Roosevelt says about study. What was Lincoln's attitude toward study?**

   Lincoln "read every book and newspaper he could get hold of" and was often the head of his class in school.

   What is yours?

   Answers will vary.

   Did Lincoln's studies have the effect on his character that Mr. Roosevelt speaks about?

   Yes, Lincoln was a man of character, courage, and honor. He did use his "strength on the side of decency, justice, and fair dealing."

3. **What story illustrates the sentence, "There is need that he should practice decency; that he should be clean and straight, honest and truthful, *gentle and tender*, as well as brave"?**

   The young boy in "Somebody's Mother" illustrates that sentence.

4. **How does the story about life on the prairie illustrate the paragraph that begins, "The boy can best become a good man by being a good boy"?**

   By sticking to the task without whining, he was learning the discipline needed to be a successful adult.

   What is the difference between being "a good boy" and "a goody-goody boy"?

   A good boy "is fine, straightforward, clean, brave, and manly." He does not brag about his goodness. A goody-goody boy may only be good when he thinks others are watching. He is good just to impress others, not for the sake of goodness itself.

5. **Was Ralph the Rover a brave man or a coward?**

   Ralph was a coward. He did not fit Mr. Roosevelt's description of a good man who is "incapable of submitting to wrong-doing."

6. **Apply the principle stated by Mr. Roosevelt at the end of the selection to the story about Washington and Braddock. To the story about the boy on the prairie.**

   Washington and the boy on the prairie both "hit the line hard;" they didn't foul or shirk when they faced hardships like an inexperienced general or a hard day plowing behind horses.

7. **Can you relate an instance in which a manly boy had a good influence upon another boy or upon his companions?**

   Answers will vary.

8. **Do you think the football slogan given in the last sentence on page 137 is a good principle of life?**

   Answers will vary but may agree that, if practiced, the slogan will develop strong character in those who practice it.

   Memorize the slogan.

9. **This selection is taken from *The Strenuous Life;* it first appeared in *St. Nicholas,* May, 1900.**

10. **Find in the glossary the meaning of: shirk, prig, resolutely, indifference, inability, horseplay, deems, indignation, bullies.**

11. **Pronounce: adage, neither, contemptible, ridiculous, stalwart, incapable, aught, incalculable.**

Extended Activity:

The American boy as described by Mr. Roosevelt may exhibit positive or negative characteristics. As the students read, have them list those images that are positive and those that are negative in the chart below.

Suggested Answers:

Positive	Negative
clean-minded	coward
clean-lived	weakling
decency	bully
clean	shirk
straight	prig
honest	shiftlessness
truthful	slackness
gentle	indifference
brave	mischief-doing
fine, straightforward	animal spirits
manly	
fearless	
stalwart	
hated by all that is wicked	
incapable of wrongdoing	
tender to the weak and helpless	
justice	
fair-dealing	

NAME______________________________**CLASS**__________**DATE**______

THE AMERICAN BOY, P. 136

The American boy as described by Mr. Roosevelt may exhibit positive or negative characteristics. As you read, list those images that are positive and those that are negative in the chart below.

Positive	Negative

NAME____________________________ **CLASS**__________ **DATE**______

Story	***Find in the glossary the meaning of:***
Reader p. 21	**alert**____________________
	mission____________________
	dejected____________________
	besmeared____________________
	brindled____________________
	docile____________________
	relaxed____________________
	crestfallen____________________
Reader p. 30	**unanimously**____________________
	unwittingly____________________
	sleight-of-mouth____________________
	tawny____________________
	muzzle____________________
	intruder____________________
Reader p. 34	**daybeds**____________________
	glade____________________
	skirted____________________
	yearling____________________
	trophy____________________
Reader p. 38	**acquainted**____________________
	explore____________________
	wary____________________
Reader p. 41	**peer**____________________
	glittering____________________
	trims____________________
	spray____________________
	blithe____________________
	measures____________________
Reader p. 43	**quoth**____________________
	publican____________________
	tax____________________
Reader p. 45	**drooping**____________________
	beaming____________________
	gauze____________________
	assembled____________________
	text____________________
	worship____________________
	expound____________________
Reader p. 48	**sedges**____________________

flaunt____________________

flutter____________________

Reader p. 50 **fragrant**____________________

twining____________________

aftermath____________________

haunts____________________

Reader p. 52 **fading**____________________

quail____________________

eaves____________________

Reader p. 59 **boar**____________________

encounter____________________

tusks____________________

riveted____________________

gigantic____________________

abyss____________________

severed____________________

whereupon____________________

exaggerations____________________

ramparts____________________

touchhole____________________

recoil____________________

repelling____________________

dismounted____________________

hold____________________

Reader p. 63 **learning**____________________

observation____________________

approached____________________

wonder____________________

resembles____________________

marvel____________________

grope____________________

disputed____________________

stiff____________________

Reader p. 65 **soaring**____________________

lank____________________

gimlet____________________

yore____________________

pinion____________________

tinkered____________________

mummies____________________

quirk____________________

crevice____________________

weasel____________________

cunning____

ancient____

helm____

ruefully____

Reader p. 77 **muttering**____

sledge____

wedge____

grim____

matchless____

blare____

Reader p. 87 **humble**____

hallow____

charm____

fond____

soothe____

beguile____

roam____

Reader p. 89 **creation**____

bonny____

reckless____

fretted____

wend____

pomp____

fame____

Reader p. 91 **sire**____

knight____

lady____

glens____

towers____

Reader p. 92 **store**____

sheaves____

clearings____

wrack____

dames____

mayhap____

befall____

slaughtered____

appointed____

summoned____

fervently____

sate____

braves____

brawny____

clatter ______

Reader p. 95 coursers ______

hurricane ______

obstacle ______

twinkling ______

tarnished ______

encircled ______

elf ______

gushing ______

Reader p. 98 rills ______

rugged ______

rear ______

vales ______

dells ______

lone ______

ween ______

rippling ______

Reader p. 100 reverence ______

bunting ______

proclaim ______

original ______

maintain ______

constituting ______

valor ______

cherished ______

faltering ______

Reader p. 101 thrilled ______

blast ______

driven ______

symbol ______

dawn ______

Reader p. 104 gleaming ______

host ______

discloses ______

beam ______

triumph ______

forlorn ______

Reader p. 106 shanty ______

princely ______

wilderness ______

epidemic ______

shiftless ______

ash-cakes ______

slab __________
guidance __________
ciphering __________
clapboard __________
pulp __________
advisers __________
Reader p. 110 **situation** __________
caution __________
ford __________
array __________
gallantly __________
huddled __________
collected __________
disaster __________
renown __________
prattle __________
Reader p. 115 **presence** __________
anxious __________
trickling __________
stoutest __________
save __________
astir __________
yester __________
stricken __________
chieftain __________
Reader p. 120 **unconscious** __________
booming __________
despair __________
fragments __________
pennon __________
fashioned __________
Reader p. 123 **handiwork** __________
wrought __________
anew __________
lust __________
brooding __________
forebore __________
plowshare __________
keel __________
Reader p. 126 **abbot** __________
perilous __________
joyance __________
breakers __________

methinks____________________________________
marveled____________________________________

Reader p. 129 **scorched**____________________________________
skillet____________________________________
ridges____________________________________
reinforcing____________________________________
habitable____________________________________
commission____________________________________
stature____________________________________
implement____________________________________
stubble____________________________________
share____________________________________
cross brace____________________________________
judgment____________________________________
tormentors____________________________________
tolerable____________________________________
unhoused____________________________________
deposited____________________________________
clogging____________________________________
evaporated____________________________________
forefather____________________________________

Reader p. 134 **renown**____________________________________
towering____________________________________
heart-strings____________________________________
shirk____________________________________

Reader p. 136 **prig**____________________________________
resolutely____________________________________
indifference____________________________________
inability____________________________________
horseplay____________________________________
deems____________________________________
indignation____________________________________
bullies____________________________________

Pronounce:
hearthrug, anecdote, guinea, toward, extraordinary, calm, blancmange, haunches, bison, boundary, frequented, knoll, melancholy, remnant, incline, strewn, partners, again, anemones, guileless, languidly, gentian, dusky, rival, vagrant, freighting, Munchausen, projected, harrowing, Monsieur, sturdy, wondrous, scope, Darius, aspiring, genius, awry, grimace, droll, Daedalus, Icarus, almanacs, phoebe, calked,

breeches, accoutered, pagans, jaunty, stanched, exile, solace, bayou, arching, laughing, therefore, franchise, wily, sachem, pumpkin, matrons, corselet, Massasoit, granaried, miniature, tiny, chimney, droll, hoary, fantastic, haunts, echo, symbolizes, sublimely, alternate, constellation, rapturous, christening, audible, haughty, vauntingly, pollution, hireling, desolation, Aesop, bade, Duquesne, Monongahela, mortally wounded, chafe, sluices, loosed, heroic, shroud, helm, hurrah, wield, carnage, smoldered, stanch, buoy, mariners, excess, scoured, chore, tedious, loam, imaginable, gopher, leisure, adage, neither, contemptible, ridiculous, stalwart, incapable, aught, incalculable.

Part II:
Stories of Adventure

In This Section—

Objectives—

By completing Part II, the following objectives will be met.

1. The student will use effective reading strategies to construct meaning and identify purpose of text including:
   a. defining unfamiliar words
   b. retelling and summarizing
   c. predicting possible events and outcomes
2. The student will determine the main idea or essential message and identify relevant supporting details and facts of a text.
3. The student will prepare for writing by focusing on the topic and organizing supporting details in a logical sequence.
4. The student will draft and revise writing in cursive.
5. The student will produce final documents that have been edited for correct spelling and punctuation.
6. The student will write a fictional narrative.
7. The student will identify the development of plot using the literary terms *exposition, climax* and *resolution.*
8. The student will identify the basic types of conflicts (man versus man, physical and/or verbal; man versus society; man versus himself; and man versus nature) and how those conflicts are resolved.
9. The student will understand the development of character and use the literary terms *dynamic* and *static.*
10. The student will identify and understand similarities and differences among the characters, settings, and events presented in various texts.
11. The student will recognize cause-and-effect relationships in literary texts.
12. The student will respond to a text by explaining how the motives of the characters or events compare with those in his or her own life.
13. The student will understand the qualities necessary for people to become good citizens and apply those qualities to his/her personal life.
14. The student will understand the qualities necessary to develop good character.

Part II: Stories of Adventure

The following collection of stories brings us tales of magic, adventure, and excitement. While each story is unique, they share common elements: characterization, setting, plot, and conflict; to name a few. Following are a variety of extended activities that can be used to enhance the learning experiences of students who read these stories of adventure. Any of the activities may be adapted to one or more of the stories.

Extended Activities:

1. Aladdin's wonderful lamp helps him realize all his wishes. Ali Baba's "Open Sesame" brings him riches for a lifetime. Have you ever wished for a magic lamp or phrase that gives you whatever you ask? Some wishes may bring positive as well as negative results. In the following chart list any three wishes you would ask for if you had Aladdin's lamp or Ali Baba's "Open Sesame." Then in the following boxes, list a "positive" result of that wish and a "negative" result of that wish.

Wishes	Positive Result	Negative Result
1.		
2.		
3.		

2. Characterization, the description of the person in a story, is usually presented in such a way that the reader can visualize his appearance, personality, and behavior. Often there will be a change in the character's personality from the beginning to the end of the story. Characters who change are considered dynamic. Characters who do not change throughout the story are considered static. Complete the following chart with characters from any of these stories. Be sure to support your answers with details from the story.

Name:
Age:
Position:
Dreams/Wishes:
Actions:
Change in character at the end of the story:

Suggested answers for teacher reference:

Name: Aladdin
Age: 15
Position: He was poor, lazy, and foolish and loved play more than work.
Dreams/Wishes: At the suggestion of his pretended uncle, he wanted to take over a shop and become a merchant.
Actions: He acquired a magic ring and lamp and used them to become wealthy.
Change in character at the end of the story: Dynamic—He spoke only with wise people; he became wise, courteous, and handsome. He married the princess, and together they ascended the throne, leaving behind noble sons and daughters at their deaths.

Name: Ali Baba
Age: He was a married man with a family to support.
Position: He was poor and hardworking.
Dreams/Wishes: He wanted to acquire the wealth of the cave.
Actions: He, along with the faithful servant, Morgiana, outwitted the robbers by killing them.
Change in character at the end of the story: Dynamic—He gave Morgiana her freedom and his son as a husband, and together they enjoyed the riches of the cave with happiness and comfort.

Name: Sindbad
Age: He was an old, grave, tall gentleman with a long white beard.
Position: He lived in a mansion with officers and servants to attend to his needs.
Dreams/Wishes: He wished to share his adventures and wealth with the poor.
Actions: He invited Hindbad, a poor man, to dinner and told him of his adventures at sea.
Change in character at the end of the story: Static—Sindbad was essentially the same at the story's end as at the beginning. Hindbad, however, though he was not a major character, may be considered dynamic. After listening to Sindbad's tales of adventure, he regretted his early anger and wished Sindbad a long and happy life with his riches.

Name: Robin Hood
Age: He was a young knight of England.
Position: Robin was the head of a band of outlaws living in the forest.
Dreams/Wishes: He wished to live freely and eat lavishly of the wild game in the king's forest. He also wished to bring justice to the poor.
Actions: He fought battles against the rich and powerful on behalf of the poor.
Change in character at the end of the story: Static—He remained the same Robin Hood, faithful to his friends, and kind and gentle to the poor.

Name: Gulliver
Age: He was a married man, a doctor and a sailor.
Position: He became the captive of the Lilliputs after a shipwreck.
Dreams/Wishes: He wished to return to his homeland after making the acquaintance of the Lilliputs and the Blefuscudians.
Actions: He befriended the Blefuscudians after the Lilliputians determined to kill him. From them he gained the needed supplies to return to his homeland.
Change in character at the end of the story: Static—No clear change emerged in Gulliver. Encourage the students to support their conclusions with details from the story.

Name: Robinson Crusoe
Age: He was a young adventurer.
Position: He was marooned on an island after his ship wrecked.
Dreams/Wishes: He longed for human companionship and his homeland.
Actions: He survived on the island for twenty-seven years, living off the land and making the tools he needed to survive.
Change in character at the end of the story: While the story does not state specific examples of change of character, one may suggest that his hard toil and isolation did, in fact, make him more sympathetic to the human condition. The students may be encouraged to determine Crusoe's changes based on their observations.

3. Plot tells the events as they occur in the story. It follows the design of a pyramid and usually consists of three main parts: the exposition explains the background and setting of the

STORY:

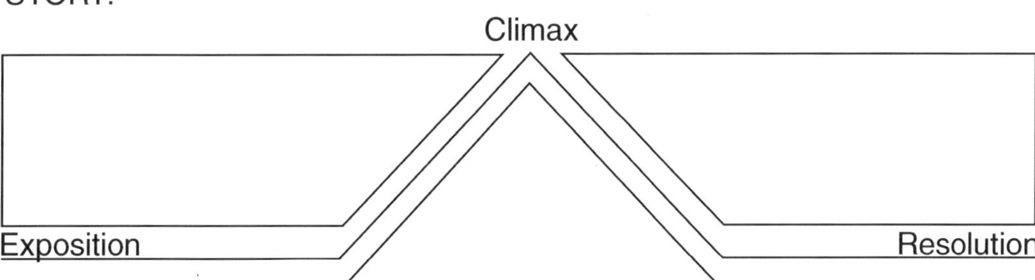

story including any of the following: who, what, where, when; the climax is the turning point, the height of the action, the highest part of the pyramid from which we can begin to predict accurately the end of the story; the resolution is the satisfying end of the story when the problems are all solved. Apply any of the stories to the pyramid diagram to identify the plot line of the story.

Possible answers are as follows:

STORY: Aladdin

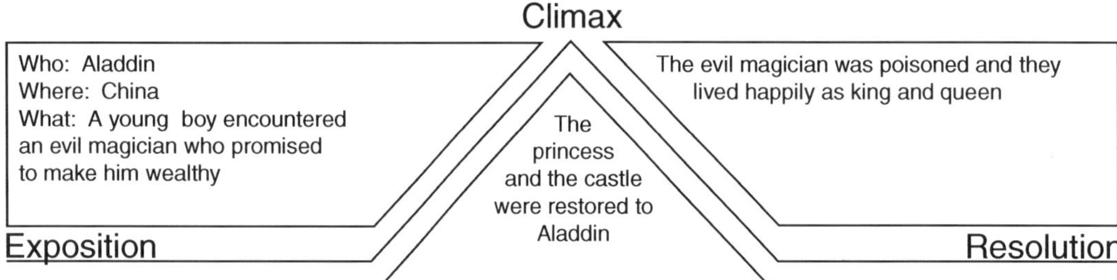

STORY: Ali Baba

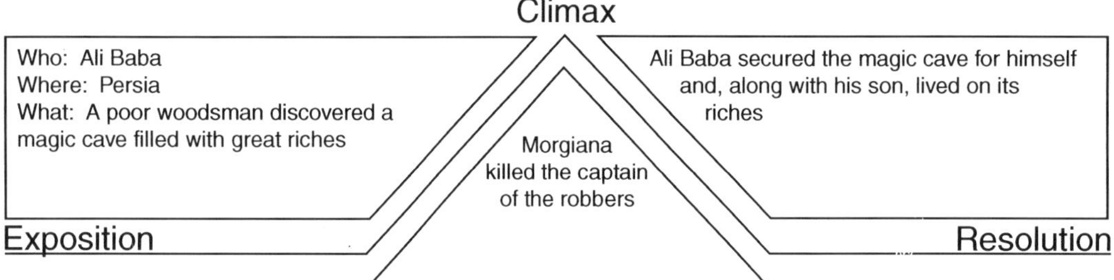

STORY: Sindbad

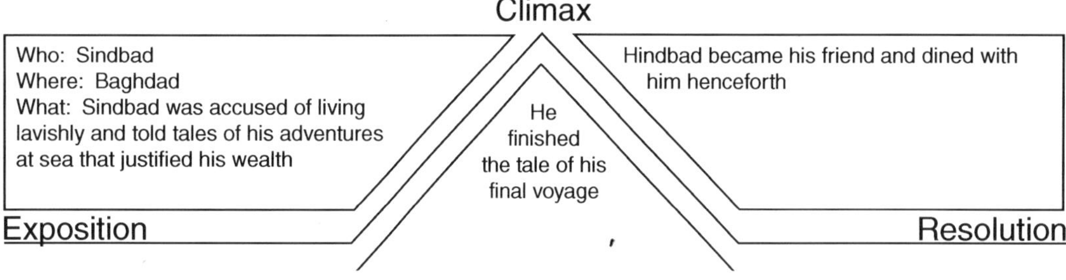

STORY: Robin Hood

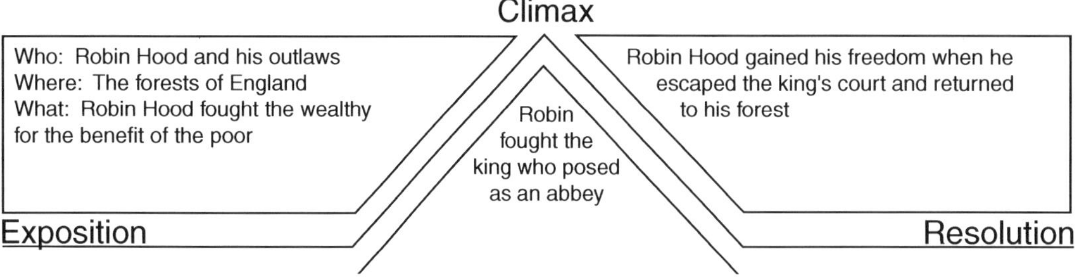

STORY: Gulliver's Travels

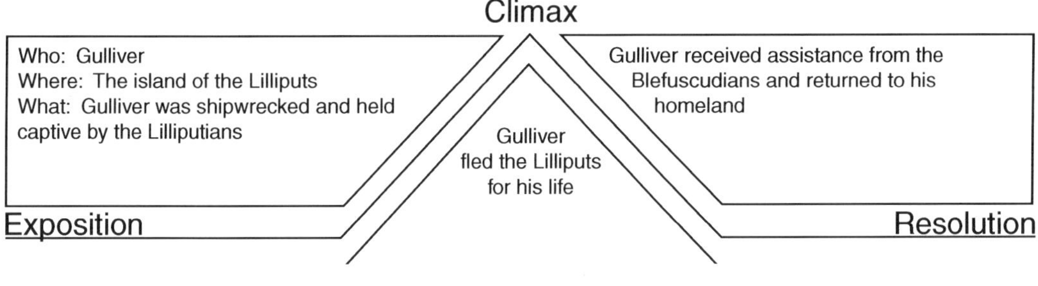

STORY: Robinson Crusoe

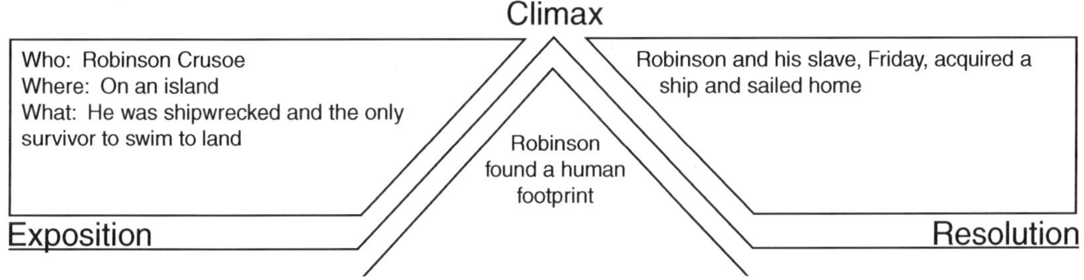

4. Conflicts in stories are the problems that cause the action to occur. The basic types of conflicts are: man versus man—physical and/or verbal; man versus society—the character may face a problem with the world around him; man versus himself—a character may struggle with a personal decision; man versus nature—the character may struggle with some element of nature such as storms or wild animals. Choose any of the stories and identify as many of the conflicts as you can, making sure you identify the conflict and its solution—who has won the conflict.

The following answers are given as a guideline only and highlight the major conflicts. Minor conflicts may be identified as well. Students are encouraged to justify additional conflicts and support their answers with details from the story.

Story	Conflict	Result
Aladdin	man versus man	Aladdin against the evil magician; Aladdin killed the magician

Aladdin—man versus man—Aladdin against the evil magician; Aladdin killed the magician

Ali Baba—man versus man—Ali Baba against the robbers; Ali Baba destroyed the robbers and claimed the magic cave for himself.

Sindbad—man versus nature—Sindbad against the dangers on his voyages; Sindbad survived all the dangers he encountered and came back a wealthy man.

Robin Hood—man versus man—Robin Hood against the rich and powerful; Robin Hood reclaimed his freedom from the king.

Gulliver—man versus society—Gulliver against the Lilliputians; Gulliver escaped and arrived safely at home.

Robinson Crusoe—man versus nature—he struggled to survive on a deserted island; Crusoe won by surviving and returning to his homeland.

5. In the discussion section of each of these stories of adventure, the students are encouraged to summarize the story in their own words using the topic headings of each section as their starting point. Have the students read each topic heading, predict the events in that section, then read it and see if their predictions were correct. Complete the following chart as they read.

Topic Heading	Prediction	Actual Result

6. As an alternative to predicting (see #5) and/or summarizing as directed in the discussion sections of each story, divide the class into small groups. Assign each group a section of the story. They must determine the main event or idea in that section and create a piece of art that communicates that main idea or event to the rest of the class. When put in sequence, the art work should adequately describe the major events in the story.

7. After reading these stories of adventure, choose one of the following writing prompts and create a short story using your imagination and vivid details to entertain your reader.

I finally got it, the wish I always wanted! But what a problem it caused!

It was the experience of my life!

I was lost and all alone!

The forest was deep and dark!

You'd never guess where I traveled last summer!

NAME________________________ CLASS________________ DATE__________

WISHES WITH POSITIVE/NEGATIVE RESULTS

Wishes	Positive Result	Negative Result
1.		
2.		
3.		

Wishes	Positive Result	Negative Result
1.		
2.		
3.		

NAME_______________ CLASS_______________ DATE_______________

CHARACTERIZATION

Name:
Age:
Position:
Dreams/Wishes:
Actions:
Change in character at the end of the story:

NAME______________________ CLASS______________ DATE__________

PLOT

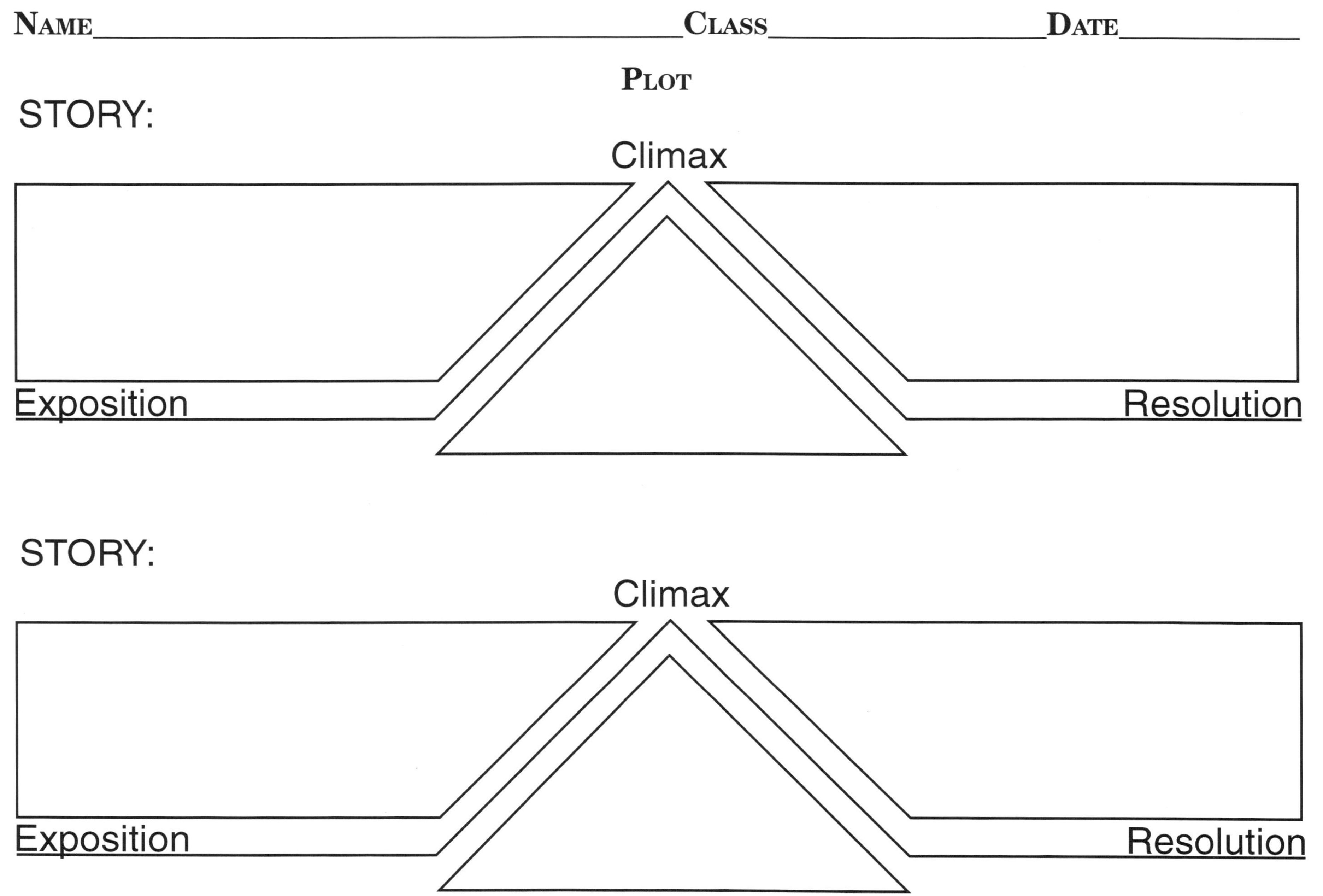

NAME________________________ CLASS________________ DATE__________

CONFLICT

Story	Conflict	Result

Story	Conflict	Result

Story	Conflict	Result

NAME______________________ CLASS______________ DATE__________

PREDICTING

Topic Heading	Prediction	Actual Result

ALADDIN, P. 147

ALADDIN, OR THE WONDERFUL LAMP

Aladdin is an Eastern legend of a young, idle boy from a poor family who meets an evil magician. The magician saw in him the potential for gaining his own wealth and convinced Aladdin that he was his uncle. He persuaded Aladdin and his mother to put Aladdin in his care, and he would make of him a great merchant. The magician led Aladdin to a hidden cave in the country to collect a lamp hidden there. In the cave Aladdin discovered many fine jewels, along with the desired lamp.

Upon his return to the cave entrance Aladdin refused to give up the lamp, so the angry magician shut up the cave with Aladdin inside. In desperation, Aladdin began to pray and accidentally rubbed the magic ring on his finger, a gift from the magician. A genius appeared to grant Aladdin's wishes, and he was immediately released from the cave. Finding nothing in the house to eat when he returned to his mother, they cleaned the lamp to sell for food. When his mother began to rub the lamp, the genius appeared again and granted their wishes with an elaborate feast.

At length, Aladdin, who had learned the value of the jewels gleaned from the cave, determined to marry the sultan's daughter. He sent his mother, along with the jewels from the cave, to request the hand of the princess for her son. The sultan, overcome by her elaborate offering of jewels, requested still more riches. The lamp was rubbed again to recall the genius to supply the sultan's requests. Their wishes were granted, and Aladdin married the princess. Together they lived in a palace prepared by the genius.

In the meantime, the angry magician heard of Aladdin's success and returned to retrieve the magic lamp for himself. He acquired the lamp from Aladdin's servants and whisked the princess and the palace to Africa. In his grief, Aladdin once more accidentally rubbed the ring on his finger. The genius reappeared and granted his wish to restore the princess and the palace to Aladdin. The two lived happily together with their riches.

1. **What kind of boy was Aladdin?**
   Aladdin was "an idle fellow, loved to play more than work, and spent his days playing in the public streets with other boys as idle as himself."
2. **What caused the magician to notice him?**
   Aladdin was playing in the streets with his friends, and when the magician saw him, he knew immediately by Aladdin's "whole manner and appearance that he was a person of small prudence" and very fit to be made a tool of.
3. **What did the magician do to make Aladdin and his mother like him?**

The magician claimed to be Aladdin's uncle returning from many years abroad. He gave Aladdin two pieces of gold to take to his mother and promised to come see her for supper that evening. At supper he promised to set up a shop, furnish it, and train Aladdin to be a merchant.

4. **How did he force Aladdin to obey him?**

The magician boxed him on his ears so hard it almost knocked him down and nearly knocked out some of his teeth. He told Aladdin, "Do you but obey me, and you will not repent of it."

5. **What did Aladdin see when he raised the stone?**

Aladdin saw "a small opening three or four feet deep, at the bottom of which was a little door, with steps to go down still lower."

6. **What directions did the magician give Aladdin before he descended the steps?**

He told Aladdin to go down into the cavern and through an open door that led to three halls. He was not to touch anything he saw. At the first hall, he was to wrap his robe around him and pass on to the second and third halls, not allowing his robe to touch even the walls or he would die instantly. At the end of the third hall he would find a door that led to a garden of beautiful fruit trees. He was to follow the path to the bottom of the flight of fifty steps where he would find a terrace. On the terrace Aladdin would see a niche with a lighted lamp. Aladdin was to take the lamp, extinguish the light, throw out the wick and liquid in it and bring the lamp back to Aladdin, picking as much fruit as he liked on his return.

7. **Explain the magician's anxiety to get the lamp before he helped Aladdin up from the cavern.**

The lamp was a magic lamp; with it came a genius who granted its owner his every wish. That was the treasure that the magician said would make the owner immensely rich. The magician wanted the lamp solely for himself, so if he could get it from Aladdin, he alone would be the sole owner of that wealth.

8. **How was Aladdin rescued from the cavern?**

In desperation, thinking that he was dying, Aladdin "clasped his hands in prayer." In joining his hands, he accidentally rubbed the magic ring on his finger. A genius appeared who rescued Aladdin from the cavern.

9. **How did he discover the power of his lamp?**
   Aladdin planned to sell the lamp for food, so his mother cleaned it so "perhaps it might sell for something more." When she began to scrub the lamp, the genius appeared to grant their wishes.
10. **What effect did his good fortune have upon him?**
   Aladdin was "sobered by his adventure and behaved with the greatest wisdom and prudence. He took care to visit the principal shops and public places, speaking only with wise and prudent persons; and in this way he gathered much wisdom and grew to be a courteous and handsome youth."
11. **What use did Aladdin make of the fruit he had gathered?**
   He used them as a gift to the sultan in exchange for the marriage of his daughter.
12. **How did Aladdin persuade his mother to see the sultan?**
   He told her that he had learned to know the value of the local merchants' gems and his gems were far superior to theirs. They would surely be a rich present for the sultan.
13. **Why did the sultan permit Aladdin to marry his daughter?**
   He agreed to the marriage only if Aladdin could fulfill this request: "forty large basins of massive gold, quite full of the same varieties of precious stones which you have already presented me with, brought by an equal number of black slaves, each of whom shall be led by a white slave, young, well-made, handsome, and richly dressed." When Aladdin heard this request, he went back to his lamp and genius and presented the sultan's request. Soon the genius returned with the gold and the slaves just as the sultan requested. Upon seeing them, the sultan immediately gave his permission for Aladdin to marry his daughter.
14. **How and where was Aladdin's palace built?**
   The sultan suggested that Aladdin build his palace on the open space before the sultan's palace. Aladdin summoned the genius and commanded that he instantly build "the most gorgeous palace ever seen, on the spot of ground given by the sultan."
15. **Where had Aladdin left the lamp when he went on his hunting trip?**

He had left the lamp "on the cornice of the hall of four-and-twenty windows."

16. **How did the magician gain possession of it?**
"The magician bought a dozen shining new lamps, put them in a basket, and set out for Aladdin's palace. As he came near it he cried, 'Who will change old lamps for new?'" Aladdin's slaves decided to see if what he said was true, and they traded the magic lamp for the best lamp the magician had.

17. **How did Aladdin regain the lamp?**
He bought poison and had the princess mix it in the magician's drink. When the magician fell to the floor, Aladdin took the lamp from the magician's bosom. He immediately summoned the genius and had them all transported back to the sultan.

18. **Class readings: Page 156, line 9, to page 160, line 4 (5 pupils).**

19. **Outline for testing silent reading. Tell in your own words the story of Aladdin, using the following topics: a) the boyhood of Aladdin; b) Aladdin's pretended uncle; c) the visit to the cave; d) Aladdin's return to his mother; e) Aladdin and the princess**

20. **Find in the glossary the meaning of: province, prudence, bewilderment, abashed, extinguish (pp. 147-151), transparent, enchantment, dungeon, genius (pp. 152-155), sultan, magnificence, bounties (pp. 156-159), cornice, transport (p 160).**

21. **Pronounce: dessert, nephew, niche (pp. 147-151), fatigue, hideous, imaginable (pp. 152-156), porcelain, vizier, gorgeous (pp. 156-159).**

Extended Activity:

For a reading check, have students answer true or false to the following statements:

F 1. Aladdin's family lived in a rich village in India.

T 2. Aladdin's pretended uncle was really a famous African magician.

T 3. The magician used fire, perfume, and magic words to open the cave.

T 4. Aladdin thought the fruit trees in the cave produced colored glass.

F 5. Aladdin's mother recognized the value of the colored glass as soon as she saw it.

F 6. The gigantic genius popped out of the lamp when Aladdin's mother rubbed it.

T 7. The sultan requested forty basins of gold, forty black slaves, and forty white slaves in exchange for the princess.

F 8. When Aladdin went to meet the sultan, he wore shining garments, rode a splendid horse, and had his slaves toss fruit to the crowds.

F 9. Asleep in bed, Aladdin was dreaming about his lost princess and palace when he rubbed the magic ring and the genius appeared.

T 10. Throughout the story, Aladdin changed from a lazy, irresponsible, young boy to a kindhearted, generous man.

NAME______________________________CLASS__________DATE______

ALADDIN, OR THE WONDERFUL LAMP P. 147

For a reading check, circle true or false to the following statements:

True False 1. Aladdin's family lived in a rich village in India.

True False 2. Aladdin's pretended uncle was really a famous African magician.

True False 3. The magician used fire, perfume, and magic words to open the cave.

True False 4. Aladdin thought the fruit trees in the cave produced colored glass.

True False 5. Aladdin's mother recognized the value of the colored glass as soon as she saw it.

True False 6. The gigantic genius popped out of the lamp when Aladdin's mother rubbed it.

True False 7. The sultan requested forty basins of gold, forty black slaves, and forty white slaves in exchange for the princess.

True False 8. When Aladdin went to meet the sultan, he wore shining garments, rode a splendid horse, and had his slaves toss fruit to the crowds.

True False 9. Asleep in bed, Aladdin was dreaming about his lost princess and palace when he rubbed the magic ring and the genius appeared.

True False 10. Throughout the story, Aladdin changed from a lazy, irresponsible, young boy to a kindhearted, generous man.

Ali Baba and the Open Sesame, p. 164

Ali Baba, another tale from *The Arabian Nights*, recounts the tale of a poor man who found great riches. Laboring in the woods one day, Ali Baba looked up to see a band of robbers coming his way. He climbed quickly up into a tree and watched as the robbers halted their horses, took their bags and, with the words, "Open Sesame," entered a cave in the rocks. At length they returned to their horses and left. Ali Baba, driven by curiosity, entered the cave using their phrase to gain entrance.

Upon entering the cave he found great riches. He gathered as much as he could, loaded them on his asses and returned to his house. His wife, overwhelmed with their good fortune, went to Cassim's house, Ali Baba's brother, to borrow a measure with which to measure her wealth. Suspicious of her actions, Cassim's wife put tallow on the bottom of the measure to collect any trace of what was measured. When Ali Baba returned the measure, a gold piece was stuck to the bottom of the measure.

Upon hearing of Ali Baba's good fortune, Cassim demanded to know how Ali Baba had acquired this great wealth, so Ali Baba told him about the cave. Cassim went to the cave, opened it as Ali Baba instructed him and gathered all the gold he could carry. But when he returned to the cave's entrance, he forgot the magic words and was locked inside. The robbers returned, found him there, and killed him. Ali Baba found him in the cave and took his body back for burial. However, he did not want anyone to know how Cassim had died, so he, along with Cassim's wife and slave girl, Morgiana, covered up his death by pretending he had become very ill and died.

Seeking revenge, the robbers found and marked Ali Baba's house so they could return and kill him. However, Morgiana sensed trouble and marked many houses so Ali Baba's house could not be identified. In frustration, the captain of the thieves presented himself to Ali Baba as an oil merchant and requested that Ali Baba house him for a night. He deposited his oil barrels, in which he had hidden his men, in the yard and went to bed, planning to release the men at night and attack Ali Baba. Once again, Morgiana came to the rescue. She ran out of oil in her lamp, so she went to the barrels in the yard to get some. To her dismay she discovered the men hiding in the barrels, so she gathered some oil, boiled it, and poured it over the men, killing them. The captain escaped with his life but decided to make another attempt on Ali Baba's life.

He befriended Ali Baba's son, a merchant, and attracted the attention of Ali Baba. Wanting to repay the captain for his kindness to his son, Ali Baba invited the captain to eat dinner with him. The captain arrived with a dagger hidden in his clothes. Upon seeing it, Morgiana figured out his plot and once again came to Ali Baba's rescue. She dressed up as a dancer and went in to entertain Ali Baba and the captain after dinner. As she approached the captain, she pulled out her own dagger and killed him. Ali Baba repaid her kindness by giving her his son in marriage and the code, "Open Sesame," to the cave of riches.

1. **How did Ali Baba make his living?**
   Ali Baba made his living by cutting wood in the forests and selling it in town.
2. **When did he first see the robber band?**
   One day as he was finishing up his wood cutting for the day, he noticed a cloud of dust that seemed to be heading toward him. Eventually, he saw the robber band approaching rapidly on horseback. To save himself, he climbed into a tree and hid in the leafy branches where he could see and not be seen.
3. **What words did the captain say to gain entrance to the cave?**
   The captain said, "Open Sesame," and the door in the rock opened.
4. **Why did Ali Baba wish to see the cave?**
   Ali Baba was curious to see what it was that the robbers did when they disappeared and reappeared through the door in the rock.
5. **How did he plan to hide his gold after he returned home?**
   Ali Baba planned to dig a pit and bury the gold.
6. **What aroused the suspicions of his brother?**
   His wife found a piece of gold stuck in the bottom of the measure that Ali Baba had borrowed to measure his gold.
7. **How did Cassim feel toward Ali Baba when he heard the story?**
   "Far from feeling glad at the good fortune which his brother had met with, Cassim grew so jealous of Ali Baba that he passed almost the whole night without closing his eyes."
8. **What did Cassim plan to do?**
   After learning from Ali Baba how he'd found the treasure, Cassim took his ten mules and went to the cave, "determined to seize the whole treasure."
9. **Why could not Cassim open the door after it closed upon him?**
   Cassim forgot the secret words, "Open Sesame," that opened and closed the door, so he tried to open the door by calling the names of other kinds of grains. Of course, the door would not open for him.
10. **Why did Ali Baba wish to conceal the fact that Cassim was killed by the robbers?**

If the town people or the robbers learned where and how Cassim had died, the secret of the cave would be found out, and Ali Baba's life would be in danger.

11. Why could not the robbers find Ali Baba's house after it had been marked with chalk?

Morgiana, Cassim's slave girl, saw the chalk mark on Ali Baba's door. Suspecting that it may mean trouble for him, she took chalk and marked several other doors around Ali Baba's door.

12. What plan did the captain of the robbers determine upon in order to have revenge upon Ali Baba?

The captain purchased mules and large oil jars in which he hid his men. Then, pretending to be an oil merchant, he arrived at Ali Baba's house requesting lodging. He intended to release the thieves after dark and attack Ali Baba.

13. How did Morgiana discover the plot and prevent it from being carried out?

Morgiana ran out of oil in her lamp, so she went to one of the oil pots of the robbers to get more oil. As she approached the first pot, the thief spoke to her, thinking she was the captain. She disguised her voice and answered as the captain would. Each thief in turn spoke to her as she approached each pot. Suspecting the captain's plot, she filled a large kettle with oil, boiled it, and poured the boiling oil into each jar, killing the robbers inside. Thus when the captain came to release his men to attack Ali Baba, he found them all dead.

14. How did Ali Baba reward her?

"I will reward you as you deserve before I die. I owe my life to you, and from this moment I give you your liberty and will soon do still more for you." Eventually, he presented Morgiana to his son to be his wife.

15. How did the captain manage to win the friendship of Ali Baba?

The captain set up a shop across from Ali Baba's son's shop to sell expensive wares from the cave. The captain became a friend to the son, invited him over for meals, and rewarded him with rich gifts. Ali Baba wanted to return his kindness, so he invited the captain to his house for a meal.

16. What was his object in doing this?

His object was to get revenge on Ali Baba and eventually kill him.

17. **The captain would not eat salt in Ali Baba's house because, according to an old Eastern custom, the use of salt at a meal was a sign of friendship and loyalty. How did Morgiana save Ali Baba's life?**
    She disguised herself as a dancer and in her costume hid a dagger. After supper she went in to entertain the captain, and as she approached him, she "plunged the dagger into his heart."
18. **Who is the cleverest person in the story?**
    Morgiana is the most clever person in the story.
19. **Did Ali Baba have a right to take the treasure from the robbers and keep it? Why?**
    Responses may vary.
20. **Class readings: Select passages to be read aloud in class.**
21. **Outline for testing silent reading. Tell in your own words the story of Ali Baba, using the following topics: a) the adventure in the forest; b) Ali Baba's return; c) the fate of Cassim; d) Morgiana's plans; e) how the thieves were caught; f) how Ali Baba used his good fortune.**
22. **Find in the glossary the meaning of: bridled, recalling, astonished, merchandise (pp. 165-166), retreat, hampers, resolved, uneasiness, utmost, invention, packet, reflected, suppressed, ceremony (pp. 168-171), related, confused (pp. 172-173), presently, enterprise, contrived, diminished (pp. 176-178); prevent; gilt; surpassed; moderation (pp. 179-182).**
23. **Pronounce: Ali Baba, sesame, brocades (pp. 164-166), inquiries, hearken, affliction, apothecary, lozenge, burial (pp. 168-171), comrades (p. 173), averted, corpse (pp. 177-178), Cogia Houssam, villain, curtsy, agility, poniard (pp. 179-181).**

Extended Activity:

For a reading check, have students answer true or false to the following statements:

F 1. This story takes place in China.

F 2. Ali Baba was digging for gold when he saw the robbers approach.

F 3. The magic cave was lit by a magic lamp hanging from the ceiling.

T 4. Cassim's wife was suspicious about why Ali Baba wanted to borrow her measure.

F 5. When he was ready to leave the cave, Cassim forgot the magic words that opened the door, so he kicked out the door to escape.

T 6. Cassim's family disguised his death at the hands of the robbers by pretending he was ill.

T 7. Two robbers were killed as a result of Morgiana's quick action in marking other houses just like the robbers had marked Ali Baba's house.

T 8. The captain of the thieves pretended to be an oil merchant when he first visited Ali Baba.

T 9. Morgiana single handedly killed all the robbers by pouring boiling oil on them.

T 10. Ali Baba rewarded Morgiana for her bravery by giving her his son in marriage and the magic words to open the cave.

NAME______________________________CLASS__________DATE______

ALI BABA AND THE OPEN SESAME, P. 164

For a reading check, circle true or false to the following statements:

True False 1. This story takes place in China.

True False 2. Ali Baba was digging for gold when he saw the robbers approach.

True False 3. The magic cave was lit by a magic lamp hanging from the ceiling.

True False 4. Cassim's wife was suspicious about why Ali Baba wanted to borrow her measure.

True False 5. When he was ready to leave the cave, Cassim forgot the magic words that opened the door, so he kicked out the door to escape.

True False 6. Cassim's family disguised his death at the hands of the robbers by pretending he was ill.

True False 7. Two robbers were killed as a result of Morgiana's quick action in marking other houses just like the robbers had marked Ali Baba's house.

True False 8. The captain of the thieves pretended to be an oil merchant when he first visited Ali Baba.

True False 9. Morgiana single handedly killed all the robbers by pouring boiling oil on them.

True False 10. Ali Baba rewarded Morgiana for her bravery by giving her his son in marriage and the magic words to open the cave.

Sindbad the Sailor, p. 183

The tale of Sindbad the Sailor, drawn from *The Arabian Nights,* begins in Baghdad where he resided in a mansion surrounded by many servants and great wealth. Upon seeing this wealth, a poor porter named Hindbad lashed out in anger comparing it to his own poverty. Sindbad, hearing his lament, invited him to his mansion and after hearing his complaint, prepared to tell Hindbad of his own terrible sufferings that had resulted in this wealth. Each day Sindbad invited Hindbad to his house for dinner and after each meal would describe a sea voyage. After each tale he would give to Hindbad a hundred sequins.

His first voyage included a short stop at an island that turned out to be the back of a large sea monster and an encounter with the Maharaja, coming home laden with treasures. On his second voyage, Sindbad was carried from deserts to mountains by rocs and eagles, collecting enormous diamonds in his travels. The third voyage took Sindbad through a violent storm, encounters with savage dwarfs and giants, trading for spices as he traveled. On his fourth voyage, Sindbad was shipwrecked and nearly starved until he met some people who rescued him. He came home once again with a great supply of goods. Sindbad's fifth voyage included stoning by rocs and slavery at the hands of the Old Man of the Sea. Once again he collected great riches of pearls, wood, and pepper on his homeward stops. The sixth voyage included a wrecked ship, a dark cavern, and the king of the Indies, along with additional riches. The seventh and final voyage, taken at the request of the caliph, included an attack from pirates and an encounter with elephants from which he gathered a vast quantity of ivory.

At the close of his tales, Hindbad repented of his complaints and wished Sindbad a long and happy life. And Sindbad in turn gave him another hundred sequins and an invitation to eat at his table henceforth.

1. **Why did Sindbad tell the story of his voyages?**
   The poor porter, Hindbad, complained loudly in the streets for all to hear that he worked hard and toiled long hours and could scarcely feed himself and his family while Sindbad lived in luxury. So Sindbad had him brought in and asked him to repeat his complaints. Then Sindbad replied that he had endured more sufferings than could be imagined; so extraordinary were his sufferings "that they would make the greatest miser lose his love of riches; and I will, with your leave, tell of the dangers I have overcome, which I think will not be uninteresting to you."
2. **What was the effect of these stories upon Hindbad?**
   Hindbad kissed his hand and said, "Sir, my afflictions are not to be compared with yours. You not only deserve a quiet life,

but are worthy of all the riches you possess. May you live happily for a long time."

3. **If Hindbad had desired to become as rich as Sindbad, what should he have done, and what price would he have paid?**

Responses may vary but should reflect the concept that Sindbad's riches came from his desire to follow the example of his father, "a wealthy merchant, much respected by everyone." Sindbad also remembered Solomon's wise saying, "A good name is better than precious ointment." So Sindbad decided to follow his father's ways. Had Hindbad used his gifts he had for others instead of complaining about what he didn't have, he may have acquired some of Sindbad's wealth, even if it meant hard labor and extreme suffering.

4. **Why did Sindbad give money to his guest at the end of each story?**

Sindbad wanted to prove to Hindbad that, though he had great wealth, he shared it with "the poor and lived honorably upon the vast riches I had gained with so many terrible hardships and so many great perils."

5. **Did he do other good deeds with his money?**

Sindbad shared his gifts of wealth with the people he met in his travels. He also gave a tenth of his profits to charity at the end of each voyage.

6. **In each of these three long stories, of Aladdin, Ali Baba, and Sindbad the sailor, what do you learn about the duty of men who have by chance or by their own hard work succeeded in acquiring riches?**

Aladdin, Ali Baba, and Sindbad all used their hard-won wealth to benefit other people in need. In "A Forward Look" we read, "The man who works hard, who seizes opportunities, who builds up a business or runs a farm, can find his treasure." Using that treasure responsibly to help others is a true test of our character.

7. **How many voyages did Sindbad make to satisfy his love of adventure?**

Sindbad made six voyages to satisfy his love of adventure.

8. **Which voyage was undertaken to please someone else?**

The seventh and final voyage was taken to please the caliph.

9. **Mention some things that Sindbad sold at great profit.**

He traded spices such as cloves and cinnamon, pepper,

precious wood, and pearls at great profit.

10. **Where are these articles most used or valued?**
These articles are highly valued in the countries and islands of the Middle and Far East such as Baghdad, India, and the islands of the Arabian Sea and the Indian Ocean.

11. **Why was it so difficult to travel by water at the time Sindbad lived?**
Sailors depended on the stars and favorable winds to help them reach their destinations. Their ships were not designed to withstand the storms at sea, so they were frequently tossed around and shipwrecked by storms.

12. **What do we learn about Sindbad's character from the story of his voyages?**
Sindbad had a creative, imaginative mind and exaggerated his tales of disaster and honor to promote his heroism.

13. **What do we learn about Sindbad's character from his treatment of Hindbad?**
Sindbad was generous with his wealth and wished Hindbad to remember him as a friend.

14. **What parts of the story show that people in Sindbad's time knew very little about geography?**
The merchants often wandered aimlessly from seaport to seaport, frequently getting lost or shipwrecked, finding themselves in unfamiliar places facing savages, giants, wild animals, and death.

15. **Which of Sindbad's seven voyages is the most interesting to you?**
Answers will vary.

16. **What have you learned of Eastern customs from this story?**
Answers will vary but references which we associate with Eastern customs may include: the maharaja, caliph and sultan, sea merchants, types of goods Sindbad collected, his turban, people riding elephants, dealing in ivory from elephant tusks, various jewels used in trade and clothing, and the custom of receiving guests with graciousness.

17. **On page 146 you were told why we read adventure stories of this kind; show why you think *The Arabian Nights* stories have the two values mentioned.**
"First of all, they are interesting, and are to be read for pure enjoyment." These stories are interesting and enjoyable.

"And next, these stories leave with you certain ideas that are worthwhile." These heroes used their great wealth to help their neighbors. They were just and responsible with their riches. Therefore, the stories from The Arabian Nights are valuable stories to read and learn from.

18. Class readings: Select passages to be read aloud.

19. Outline for testing silent reading. Tell in your own words the story of each of the voyages of Sindbad, using the topic headings given in the book. If possible, try to tell these stories to some child who cannot read them. (See summary at beginning of section.)

20. *The Arabian Nights* by Wiggin and Smith was illustrated by the famous American artist, Maxfield Parrish; you will enjoy looking at these pictures.

21. Find in the glossary the meaning of: mansion, grave, humor (pp. 183-184), ointment, sandalwood (pp. 185-186), repentance, turban, shipping (pp. 187-190), traffic (p. 193), azure (p. 197).

22. Pronounce: caliph, Harun-al-Rashid, savory, repast (pp. 183-184), becalmed, maharaja, rarities, aloes, sequin (pp. 185-186), roc, desert (p. 188), Arabic, sovereign (pp. 196-197), tradition (p. 200).

Extended Activity:

For a reading check, have students answer true or false to the following statements:

F 1. All of the events in this story occur in Baghdad.

T 2. In the setting of this story, Sindbad was a wealthy old gentleman living a life of ease in a great mansion with many servants.

T 3. Sindbad's first voyage included a ride on the back of a sea monster.

T 4. On Sindbad's second voyage, he was transported by rocs and eagles.

F 5. On Sindbad's third voyage savage dwarfs stoned them and sank all their rafts.

F 6. On Sindbad's fourth voyage meat and bread saved his life.

T 7. On Sindbad's fifth voyage his ship was stoned by rocs.

F 8. On Sindbad's sixth voyage he spoke to the inhabitants of the land in Chinese.

T 9. On Sindbad's final voyage he was captured by pirates and sold to a rich merchant.

F 10. Shipwrecks were a part of every voyage.

NAME______________________________**CLASS**__________**DATE**______

SINDBAD THE SAILOR, P. 183

For a reading check, circle true or false to the following statements:

True False 1. All of the events in this story occur in Baghdad.

True False 2. In the setting of this story, Sindbad was a wealthy old gentleman living a life of ease in a great mansion with many servants.

True False 3. Sindbad's first voyage included a ride on the back of a sea monster.

True False 4. On Sindbad's second voyage, he was transported by rocs and eagles.

True False 5. On Sindbad's third voyage savage dwarfs stoned them and sank all their rafts.

True False 6. On Sindbad's fourth voyage meat and bread saved his life.

True False 7. On Sindbad's fifth voyage his ship was stoned by rocs.

True False 8. On Sindbad's sixth voyage he spoke to the inhabitants of the land in Chinese.

True False 9. On Sindbad's final voyage he was captured by pirates and sold to a rich merchant.

True False 10. Shipwrecks were a part of every voyage.

THE STORY OF ROBIN HOOD, P. 203

Robin Hood, the legendary outlaw whose tales date back to the 1300s, lived in Sherwood Forest. He was famous for robbing the rich and protecting the poor of the country. "The Story of Robin Hood" highlights several of his adventures.

Little John, nicknamed for his seven-foot stature, was Robin's second in command and acted on Robin's behalf. When they encountered a poor knight whose land had been taken from him by a rich man, Robin Hood and Little John helped him regain his land by lending him money and clothes. Little John, well-known for his excellent marksmanship, was noted by the Sheriff of Nottingham and was asked to enter the sheriff's service. He did so, but because the sheriff was hated by the outlaws, Little John determined to cause him harm. He broke into the sheriff's treasure house and carried off as many of his treasures including dishes, silver, and gold as he could carry. Then he lured the sheriff to Robin Hood's dinner where the sheriff was forced to eat off his own valuable plates. Robin Hood released the sheriff from being his prisoner only because the sheriff promised never to harm him or his men again.

Friar Tuck, also known for his marksmanship, encountered Robin Hood by the river where, after a brief encounter, he dumped Robin into the water. Angry at being outsmarted, Robin shot an arrow at Friar Tuck. That began a duel between Robin Hood's men and Friar Tuck's dogs. At length they called a truce, struck a bargain, and Friar Tuck became another famous member of Robin Hood's men.

In time Robin Hood and Little John fell out, much to Robin's regret. When he went to the church to pray, he was accosted by the sheriff, taken prisoner, and eventually rescued by Little John, but not before he brought Robin Hood to the attention of the king. The king had long wanted to meet Robin Hood, so he dressed up in monk's clothes and rode to the forest. There he met Robin Hood who treated him honorably until he learned that he was really the king. Robin Hood pled for mercy, and at the king's invitation, went with his men to join the king's service. After a year of service, Robin's men became weary of court life and escaped to the forest. Robin Hood himself became homesick for his old life and returned to the forest where he resumed his life as "a faithful friend, kind to the poor, and gentle to all women."

1. **Why was Robin Hood obliged to live in the forest?**

   "We know very little about him, who he was, or where he lived, except that for some reason he had offended the king, who had declared him an outlaw, so that any man might kill him and never pay a penalty for it." From this and the historical notes, the reader can assume that Robin Hood lived in the forest where he would be safe from the king's officers.

2. **How did he win the friendship of Little John?**
Robin Hood met Little John on a narrow bridge. When Robin Hood demanded that little John back up so Robin could pass, Little John refused. Robin Hood became angry and drew his bow to shoot Little John, so he challenged Robin to a duel. The first to fall in the water would lose. Little John "planted a blow so well that Robin rolled over into the river." Robin Hood "declared Little John to be second in command to himself among the brotherhood of the forest."
3. **What did Robin Hood tell him about the Sheriff of Nottingham?**
Robin Hood told Little John, "...mark that you always hold in your mind the High Sheriff of Nottingham" because he was Robin Hood's bitterest enemy.
4. **Describe the appearance of the knight whom Little John met in the forest.**
"A sorrier man than he never sat a horse on a summer day. One foot only was in the stirrup; the other hung carelessly by his side. His head was bowed; the reins dropped loose, and his horse went on as he would."
5. **What foods were prepared for the dinner to which Robin Hood invited the knight?**
Bread, wine, deer, swans, and pheasants were prepared for the dinner.
6. **How had these provisions been obtained?**
They were obtained by shooting the wild game in the king's forests.
7. **What story did the knight tell to Robin Hood?**
The knight's son killed a knight of Lancaster and his squire. The knight had to pay a large sum of money for their deaths, money which he did not have, so he gave his land as a pledge that he would pay the money. If he could not raise the money by a certain day, his land would be lost to him forever. His friends had all left him, and he had little hope of finding the money to regain his land.
8. **How did Robin Hood help him?**
He gave the knight the price of his land, four hundred pounds, some new clothes, a horse, along with a new saddle, a good palfrey, and a pair of boots. Finally, Robin Hood lent the knight Little John as his squire.
9. **Where do you think the treasure chest was kept?**

Answers will vary, but the chest may have been hidden deep in the forest where only Robin Hood and Little John could find it. Using this question as a class discussion, have students support their responses with details from the story that would justify their opinions.

10. From whom had this treasure been taken?

Robin Hood took the treasure from rich men who passed through the forest.

11. How did the knight show his gratitude after he regained his lands?

He worked on his land until he had saved the four hundred pounds loaned to him by Robin Hood. Along with the money, he took "a hundred bows and a hundred arrows, and every arrow was an ell long, and had a head of silver and peacock's feathers." All of this he presented to Robin Hood for his kindness.

12. Why did the Sheriff of Nottingham want Little John in his service?

Little John competed in a shooting match arranged by the sheriff. Little John "split the slender wand of willow with every arrow that flew from his bow." The sheriff knew that Little John was the best archer he'd ever seen and offered him a position in his service.

13. What thought was constantly in Little John's mind?

He wanted to do the sheriff "all the mischief he could."

14. How did he accomplish his purpose?

While the sheriff was out hunting, Little John asked for food from the steward who refused him. He then went to the butler who locked the kitchen door in front of him, so Little John kicked open the door and ate all he wanted. Then he started a sword fight with the cook. The cook fought so well that Little John offered him a position with Robin Hood. Together they ate and drank all they wanted then broke into the treasure house and carried off all the silver and gold they could carry and left to go back to Robin Hood.

15. What explanation did he give to Robin Hood for what he brought from the sheriff's house?

"The proud sheriff greets you and sends you by my hand his cook and his silver vessels and three hundred pounds and three also."

16. How did he induce the sheriff to follow him to the place

where Robin Hood was?

Little John told the sheriff that he had seen a green hart and seven score deer feeding in the forest.

17. **What punishment did Robin Hood decide upon for the sheriff?**

Robin Hood decided that the sheriff would spend twelve months in the forest with Robin Hood and learn to be an outlaw.

Why did he not carry it out?

The sheriff begged to be free and promised to be the best friend that the foresters had ever had.

18. **How was Robin Hood captured by the sheriff?**

Robin Hood and Little John held a shooting match in which Little John won. Robin Hood became angry and hit Little John after which Little John fled and went back to the forest, saying that Robin Hood would never be his master again. Robin Hood was ashamed of his behavior and went to the Church of St. Mary and knelt down. One man in the crowd recognized him and ran to get the sheriff. When the sheriff returned with his men, Robin Hood killed twelve of them and broke his sword on the sheriff's head. The sheriff's men overpowered him and bound his arms.

19. **What reason do you think the king had for wanting to see Robin Hood?**

Answers may vary, but Robin Hood's reputation as a famous outlaw probably created the curiosity of the king. Robin Hood had also killed many of the king's wild game for which the king wanted revenge. Have students list their responses with details from the story that would support their answers.

20. **What did he determine to do after Robin Hood's escape?**

"I would I had this Robin Hood in my hands, and an end should soon be put to his doings."

21. **Find words in which Robin Hood expressed his love for his king.**

"I love no man in all the world so well as I do my king."

22. **What offer did the king make to Robin Hood and his men?**

He invited them to leave the forest and dwell with the king in his court.

Why did the king make them such an offer?

Answers may vary: perhaps he wanted Robin Hood and his men nearby so they could not destroy his hunting grounds; or perhaps he wanted them nearby so he could destroy them.

23. **Why did Robin dislike living at court?**

His men could not live in the town, and one by one they fled to the forests again. Robin Hood became homesick and begged the king for permission to go on a pilgrimage.

24. **How long did Robin Hood live in the greenwood after he left the court?**

He lived in the greenwood for twenty-two years after he left the court.

25. **Under what conditions do you think life in the forest would be pleasant?**

In a classroom discussion, have students identify the conditions for a pleasant life in the forest.

26. **What were these men obliged to give up when they went into the forest to live?**

Possible responses may include giving up family and a stable life. They had to scrounge for their food and always be on the lookout for the king's officers who wanted to harm them. Have students use this question and the following question to compare and contrast the value of life in the forest.

27. **What did they gain by living in the forest?**

They gained the freedom to come and go as they pleased, practice their hunting skills and help those whom they wanted to help. See #26 for a class discussion idea.

28. **When did Robin Hood show himself generous?**

In the king's court, "he had spent a hundred pounds, for he gave largely to the knights and squires he met, and great renown he had for his openhandedness."

29. **When did Robin show himself merciful?**

After leaving the kings' court, "he was ever a faithful friend, kind to the poor, and gentle to all women."

30. **What do you think of Little John's treatment of the Sheriff of Nottingham after he had lived in his house?**

Use this to generate a class discussion of Little John's actions.

31. **When did Little John show himself a loyal friend?**

He was a loyal friend to Robin Hood when he rescued Robin

Hood from the king's prison, even though Robin Hood had treated him rudely. He also stayed with Robin Hood in the king's court when others had fled.

32. When did he show himself hard and cruel?

He was hard and cruel to the sheriff's steward and butler when he overpowered them and broke into the sheriff's kitchen against their command.

33. What things mentioned in this story show that the manners and life of the people in England at this time were rough?

The story refers to low huts, peasants, charcoal-burners, and plowmen. It also indicates that travel was difficult—outlaws were plentiful in the forests, waiting to loot and destroy any man of means. The rich took advantage of the poor and neither trusted the other.

34. What qualities were most admired in men at the time of Robin Hood?

Men were admired for their chivalry, or noble character. They protected their land, gave freely to the less fortunate, protected women, and fought against injustice. They met their enemies with bravery and courage and were admired for their skill in hunting and fighting.

35. What was the reason for this?

Life was difficult and dangerous, and men who protected their families, friends, or fellow countrymen were considered heroes.

36. Make a list showing the good qualities of Robin Hood, such as his courtesy, his justice, his sense of fair play. Mention the incidents that illustrate each characteristic.

Student responses may vary; examples may include—

courtesy: Robin Hood befriended the knight and served him a fine dinner; he treated the king with respect, thinking he was the abbot.

justice: he gave the knight the money he needed to recover his land that the wealthy had taken from him; he forbade his men to attack the poor people in the forest paths.

fair play: even though Little John beat him in their first encounter, he invited him to become his second in command; even though he hated the sheriff, "for charity's sake, and for the love of Little John" he spared his life; though Friar Tuck seemed to be winning the fight with his dogs, Robin Hood recognized his skills and invited him to join his men.

37. Show that this story has the two values mentioned in the first paragraph of page 146.

The two values mentioned that make a good story are high interest and worthwhile ideas. The story of Robin Hood contains high interest and includes worthy ideas such as helping the oppressed people of his time.

38. Why did Robin dislike the sheriff?

The story refers to the sheriff as a proud man who was every outlaw's enemy.

39. Find, from the story, ways in which poor or unfortunate men were oppressed by the laws in those days.

The knight's land was taken until he could pay for his son's actions. The rich man decided he would never come back to reclaim it and was prepared to take over his land even though his time to pay the costs had not yet run out. He refused to grant the knight any extensions.

40. Did the laws seem made to give equal justice to all, or unfair advantages to the rich and powerful?

The rich and powerful took advantage of the weak and powerless. Use as a class discussion question.

41. How do you think Robin felt about these matters?

He hated the injustices and encouraged his men to use every opportunity to take from the rich to give to the poor.

42. How did he try to take the side of the poor men who were thus unfairly dealt with by the government?

He gave them money, food, and the services of his men to protect and fight for them.

43. Tell the story of Friar Tuck.

Friar Tuck was known for his marksmanship, so Robin Hood set out to find him. They met by the side of a river. Robin Hood asked the friar to carry him to the other side which he promptly did. The friar then asked Robin Hood to take him back to the other side. Robin complied, but when he asked the friar to return him to the other side again, the friar dumped him in the water. Robin Hood shot an arrow at him which he deflected with his shield. They fought a long time until Robin's strength was waning and he requested the favor of blowing his horn. Friar Tuck was amazed when he saw fifty men coming to Robin's aid, so he also asked for a favor. He blew his whistle and fifty dogs came to his aid. The dogs and men fought valiantly until Little John, seeing the men were losing, asked the friar to call off his dogs. Friar Tuck and Robin Hood made a bargain that the friar would leave his abbey and join Robin Hood for a year.

44. Why did the king take such an interest in Robin?

He blamed Robin for killing the herds of wild deer in the king's forests.

Do you think the king was glad to get away from the court? Why?

Answers will vary. Have students identify reasons for the king's actions.

45. What did he say about the way in which Robin was obeyed by his followers?

"They are quicker to do his bidding than my men are to do mine."

46. What does the "Forward Look," page 144, tell you about the source of this story?

Robin Hood was a popular English hero. The "Forward Look" reminds us that "many old ballads and tales, older than the first American colony, have come down to us with these stories of the famous outlaw."

47. Class readings: Little John's first adventure, omitting all but the dialogue, page 206, line 23, to page 209, line 27 (3 pupils); Robin and his archers with the king, page 224, line 25, to page 226, line 19; Robin at the king's court, page 226, line 20, to page 227, line 32.

48. Outline for testing silent reading. Tell the story of Robin Hood, using these topics: a) the home of Robin in Sherwood Forest; b) the coming of Little John; c) Little John's first adventure; d) the knight's recovery of his lands; e) Little John as the sheriff's servant; f) Robin's meeting with Friar Tuck; g) the disagreement between Robin and Little John; h) the king's visit to Robin Hood; i) Robin at court.

49. You will enjoy seeing the pictures in the edition of *Robin Hood* illustrated by N. C. Wyeth.

50. Find in the glossary the meaning of: abbey, battlements (p. 204), ell (p. 205), coffers (p. 209), tourneys (p. 211), hart (p. 216), broom, boon, noble (pp. 219-220).

51. Pronounce: Plantagenets, palfreys, pheasants, yeoman, toll (pp. 203-204), naught, hie, surety (pp. 207 -209), justiciar, gainsaid, justs, heir, tryst (pp. 210-213), steward, balked (p. 215), lea (p. 219), ado, liege, beguiled (pp. 221-223), buffet (p. 226).

Extended Activity:

For a reading check, have students answer true or false to the following statements:

T 1. The setting of this story takes place in England.

T 2. Though he was an outlaw, Robin Hood behaved honorably to poor people.

F 3. Robin Hood gave John Little the name of Little John because he was so short.

T 4. The knight's son's behavior caused the knight to give his land in pledge to a rich man.

F 5. The knight was able to reclaim his land by borrowing money from his neighbors.

F 6. Little John was a faithful, honest servant for the sheriff.

F 7. Friar Tuck used a bow and arrows to fight his battles.

F 8. Little John saved Robin Hood by persuading the king to release him.

T 9. The king's disguise was discovered when he lost his hat in a match with Robin Hood.

T 10. Upon his return to the green wood, Robin Hood's first act was to shoot a hart.

NAME_____________________________CLASS__________DATE______

THE STORY OF ROBIN HOOD, P. 203

For a reading check, circle true or false to the following statements:

True False 1. The setting of this story takes place in England.

True False 2. Though he was an outlaw, Robin Hood behaved honorably to poor people.

True False 3. Robin Hood gave John Little the name of Little John because he was so short.

True False 4. The knight's son's behavior caused the knight to give his land in pledge to a rich man.

True False 5. The knight was able to reclaim his land by borrowing money from his neighbors.

True False 6. Little John was a faithful, honest servant for the sheriff.

True False 7. Friar Tuck used a bow and arrows to fight his battles.

True False 8. Little John saved Robin Hood by persuading the king to release him.

True False 9. The king's disguise was discovered when he lost his hat in a match with Robin Hood.

True False 10. Upon his return to the green wood, Robin Hood's first act was to shoot a hart.

GULLIVER'S TRAVELS, P. 231

Gulliver, a surgeon and sailor from Nottinghamshire, became shipwrecked on the island of Lilliput. Upon waking from his terrible ordeal, he discovered his arms and legs were firmly fastened to the ground, and he was being attacked by tiny humans whose language he could not speak. He was visited, in time, by His Imperial Majesty of the island who decided that Gulliver should be moved to the capital city.

The people built a machine that would carry Gulliver, and at length he was transported to his new home, an old temple. There he was kept a prisoner, taught the language of the Lilliputians and provided with food and clothes. After swearing to abide by the conditions set down for his freedom, his chains were unlocked, and he was free to come and go.

In time the island of Lilliput was threatened by an invasion from a neighboring island, Blefuscu. The Lilliputians pled with Gulliver to save them. After designing his tools, he swam out to the Blefuscudian fleet, cut their anchors and towed them back to Lilliput. His Majesty, grateful for Gulliver's aid, determined that Gulliver should use his great strength to help the Lilliputs take over the Blefuscudians. Gulliver thought it selfish and greedy and refused to grant His Majesty's wishes. Therefore, His Majesty, along with his men, determined to kill Gulliver. Being warned of the plot by a faithful friend, Gulliver fled the island of Lilliput and escaped to Blefuscu where he was greeted warmly and treated generously.

Later Gulliver discovered an overturned old ship off the coast of Blefuscu. He recovered the ship, rebuilt and supplied it with the aid of the Blefuscudians, and sailed for his homeland again where he made money by showing the tiny animals he had brought back with him.

1. **How did Gulliver arrive at the land of the Lilliputians?**
   Gulliver was on a ship that wrecked in a violent storm. He and six sailors escaped in a small boat, only to be overturned by another gust of wind. Only Gulliver survived and swam for his life. Finally his feet touched bottom, and he made his way to shore where he promptly fell asleep. When he awoke he was in the land of the Lilliputians.
2. **How was he treated by the inhabitants?**
   They bound him with strings fastened to pegs in the ground so he could not escape. They shot at him with arrows and brought him meat and bread. They transported him to the capital city where they gave him an old temple for his home but kept him in chains.

What did they call him?

They called him the Man-Mountain.

3. **How did Gulliver prove that he did not wish to hurt them?**

   One of the soldiers left to guard him shot an arrow at him, narrowly missing his eye. The other guards grabbed the soldier and turned him over to Gulliver for punishment. After threatening to eat him, Gulliver cut the strings with which he was bound and set him free. The people were pleased with his show of mercy.

4. **What arrangements did they make for his comfort?**

   They provided him with food, soldiers as guards, a bed to sleep on, servants to do his bidding, and a suit of clothes like those worn by the Lilliputians.

5. **What rules were set for him when he was given his liberty?**

   One: he could not leave without permission; Two: he could not enter their chief city without their consent; Three: he could walk only on main roads, not in the pastures; Four: he could not walk on nor carry any of the people or their horses and carriages; Five: he was obliged to carry all their messages; Six: he must not join the armies of their enemies and must work to destroy their fleets of ships; Seven: he must always help the workmen lift heavy weights; Eight: he must walk around the island and tell them how much it measured; Last: he would have a daily food allowance equal to 1,724 of the people.

6. **How did Gulliver capture the fleet from Blefuscu?**

   He designed hooks and ropes and swam out to the ships. He fastened a hook to each ship, cut their anchors and walked off with most of the fleet.

7. **What did the emperor of Lilliput wish to do when Gulliver had won the victory?**

   He wanted to take over the whole island and reign over it himself.

8. **What evil thing about war does this incident show?**

   It shows that power can lead to greed; because the Lilliputian king had the advantage of Gulliver's power on his side, he thought he could take over other lands as his own.

9. **Can a nation fight a great war without desire to add to its territory?**

Student responses may vary. History will show that frequently wars were fought with the desire to add to their territory.

Was this true of the United States in World War One?

The major goal of the United States in World War One was to protect and maintain its democracy and its people, not to gain more territory. They fought to assist their allies in the war against Germany.

10. What was Gulliver's feeling about the proposal of the emperor?

"I did not think this at all fair, but very selfish and greedy of His Majesty. I tried to tell him so as politely as I could, and I said I could not help to bring a free and brave people into slavery."

Was he right?

Answers will vary. Based on the American ideal of freedom and independence, Gulliver was right to disagree with the king's proposal to take captive the island of Blefuscu. However, student responses that reflect other opinions may surface.

11. How did the emperor feel toward him after his refusal?

"From this time His Majesty and some of his court began to bear me ill will, which nearly ended in my death...he became ungrateful when he found he could not get all he wanted."

12. How did Gulliver learn of the plot against him?

A Lilliputian noble came to him privately at night and warned him of the plot against him.

13. Why did he not use his strength against his enemies?

"But I put the idea away as unfair and dishonorable, because I had given my oath not to harm the island and its inhabitants. And even though the emperor was so unjust and cruel to me, I did not consider that his conduct freed me from the promise I had made."

14. What did he decide to do?

Having received the emperor's permission to visit the island of Blefuscu, Gulliver made plans to go there at once. When he arrived, the people greeted him with pleasure.

15. What fortunate discovery did Gulliver make at Blefuscu?

He found a big, overturned boat which had likely been driven there in a storm.

16. How did Gulliver get back to England?

With the emperor's consent and assistance, he recovered the

boat, rebuilt it, stocked it, and sailed for England.

17. **Name two or three things that you think he learned on his travels.**

Have students list on the board their responses using details from the story to support their opinions. Some possible answers may reflect that Gulliver learned that kindness is valuable in any culture; power can become abusive; greed can blind men to freedom and human rights.

18. **What are we told about the education of children in Lilliput?**

"In Lilliput there are large public schools to which parents are bound to send their children. Here they are educated and fitted for some position in life, for no one is allowed to be idle. All the children are brought up very well indeed and taught to be honorable, courageous, and truthful men and women. The nurses are forbidden to tell the children foolish or frightening stories, and if they are found to do so, they are soundly whipped and sent to a most lonely part of the country."

19. **Why did the people consider deceit worse than stealing?**

Deceit and cunning are considered worse than stealing "for the people say that a man can take means to protect his goods and money, but he cannot prevent another man's deceiving him."

20. **What did they think of a person who returns evil for good?**

They thought "anyone who returns evil for good is judged not fit to live."

21. **Name some of the laws of the Lilliputians.**

A man caught lying about another man is severely punished. If a man makes a promise and breaks it or loses another's money he is guilty of a crime. The emperor does not bestow favors on the clever or the learned but on the brave and true. Ingratitude is a crime, as is returning evil for good.

Which of these laws do you like, and why?

Answers will vary.

22. **Why were not all the people of Lilliput good when they had such good laws?**

Good laws alone cannot create good people. People must make responsible decisions to respect the rules that guide society. Students should be encouraged to form their own responses to the question.

23. Compare Gulliver's adventures with those of Baron Munchausen.

Students should be familiar with the story of Baron Munchausen on page 59 of the reader. He, like Gulliver, tells tall tales of his travels in a book first published in England in 1785. His name is associated with one who exaggerates or brags of his feats.

24. How does this story differ as to its source from *The Arabian Nights* tales?

Tales from *The Arabian Nights* originated in the tents of the deserts and cities of the East and were passed along among the common people. Gulliver's Travels, however, was composed by a single author who wrote and printed the tales for all to enjoy.

25. Show that it has the two values mentioned on page 146.

The two values mentioned that make a good story are high interest and worthwhile ideas. Gulliver's Travels contain high interest and include worthy ideas such as kindness, returning good for evil, and honesty.

26. Class readings: Select passages to be read aloud in class.

27. Outline for testing silent reading. Tell the story briefly in your own words, following the topic headings given in the book.

28. Find in the glossary the meaning of: keep, human (pp. 231-233), engines, bandages, turret (pp. 235-236), carriages (p. 237), merchantmen (p. 255).

29. Pronounce: ruined, drowned, waistcoat (pp. 232-233), Imperial, courtiers (p. 234), theater, reigned, learned (pp. 237-239), Lilliput, graciously, fortnight (pp. 240-241), Lilliputians (p. 244).

Extended Activity:

For a reading check, have students answer true or false to the following statements:

T 1. Gulliver was a husband, a doctor, and a sailor living in England.

F 2. After his shipwreck, Gulliver was washed up on the shores of a country with customs and language like his.

T 3. The Lilliputians were skillful builders of machines.

F 4. As soon as he was moved into his new home, Gulliver was free to come and go as he pleased.

F 5. His Majesty invited the people from miles around to come see Gulliver as much as they pleased.

T 6. While sitting in Gulliver's hands, Reldresal sought Gulliver's help in fighting the Blefuscudians.

F 7. Gulliver used thread and knitting needles to steal the fleet of the Blefuscudians.

T 8. Gulliver had 600 dishes of food at his meals.

T 9. To get rid of Gulliver, His Majesty planned to slowly starve him to death.

F 10. The Lilliputians sent Gulliver back to his homeland with an enormous going-away party.

NAME______________________________CLASS__________DATE______

GULLIVER'S TRAVELS, p. 231

For a reading check, circle true or false to the following statements:

True	False	1. Gulliver was a husband, a doctor, and a sailor living in England.
True	False	2. After his shipwreck, Gulliver was washed up on the shores of a country with customs and language like his.
True	False	3. The Lilliputians were skillful builders of machines.
True	False	4. As soon as he was moved into his new home, Gulliver was free to come and go as he pleased.
True	False	5. His Majesty invited the people from miles around to come see Gulliver as much as they pleased.
True	False	6. While sitting in Gulliver's hands, Reldresal sought Gulliver's help in fighting the Blefuscudians.
True	False	7. Gulliver used thread and knitting needles to steal the fleet of the Blefuscudians.
True	False	8. Gulliver had 600 dishes of food at his meals.
True	False	9. To get rid of Gulliver, His Majesty planned to slowly starve him to death.
True	False	10. The Lilliputians sent Gulliver back to his homeland with an enormous going-away party.

Robinson Crusoe, p. 257

The story of Robinson Crusoe describes the tale of a man deserted on an island after being shipwrecked. After salvaging all the goods he could transport from the wrecked ship to his island on a raft, he set out to build his home and create a new life for himself. His only companions were the four pets he had taken from the ship, two cats, a dog, and a parrot. He supplied his needs by planting grain found on the ship with which he made bread, designing tools to use for food and work, and building a boat with which to scout out his island.

One day during his explorations, he discovered a human footprint. Filled with terror he hid in his house until hunger and curiosity forced him out. Eventually he discovered the source of the footprint and acquired a new friend, Friday, an escaped slave from a ship which had stopped at his island.

They spent many days becoming acquainted and exploring together. Their exit from the island occurred when they overpowered the crewmen on a ship that had stopped at the island. They left the crewmen behind to care for the animals and set sail for their homeland, twenty-seven years, two months, and nineteen days after being abandoned.

1. **Why was an ocean voyage so difficult and dangerous at the time when *Robinson Crusoe* was written?**
   Pirates attacked their ships, and storms blew them off course or wrecked completely.

Note to the teacher: the following questions may have a variety of answers depending on the students' prior experiences. They are not intended to elicit one correct answer but attempt to have the students identify with Robinson Crusoe's dilemmas. Use these questions as a class or small group discussion to encourage your students to think about the qualities of perseverance, hard work, courage, and bravery.

2. **Find the lines that describe what you think was the most difficult work undertaken by Robinson Crusoe.**
3. **What undertaking required the most perseverance? Find lines that show this.**
4. **At what time did Crusoe show the greatest courage? Find lines that seem to you to prove your answer is correct.**
5. **What was the greatest disappointment that he had to bear while on the island?**
6. **What do you think was the greatest happiness he had?**

7. Find lines that tell how Robinson Crusoe studied to make something which was very necessary to him.
8. Mention something he made that you have tried to make.
9. How did your result compare with his? What reason can you give for this?
10. This story shows how dependent we are upon the tools, the inventions, and the means of protection that men have devised for making life happy. Crusoe had to make for himself under great difficulties things that we think nothing of. Show from the story how dependent we are upon the cooperation and assistance of others. Imagine the cooperation that has been necessary to give you milk, oranges or bananas, sugar for your dessert, meat for your dinner. What has been done to give you the stove on which your dinner is cooked, the fuel that it burns, the light that you use at night, the telephone that you use? Crusoe had to get along without such assistance.
11. Do you owe anything, any return service, for what you receive and use? If Crusoe's hut had taken fire, what would have happened? What would happen if your home should catch fire? Who would pay for the help given you? If Crusoe had been attacked by robbers, what would have happened? What keeps you safe at night? If Crusoe had wished to go on a long journey, what would have been necessary? Who would help you if you had to take such a journey?
12. Tell a story about your debt to someone for an invention or discovery that makes your life pleasanter or safer. Tell a story about your debt for the sugar you use as your dessert. Tell a story to illustrate what the government does for you.
13. Class readings: Select passages to be read aloud in class.
14. Outline for testing silent reading. Tell the story briefly in your own words, using the topic headings given in the book.
15. You will enjoy seeing the pictures in the edition of *Robinson Crusoe* that is illustrated by N. C. Wyeth.
16. Find in the glossary the meaning of: stern (p. 258), bulge, spikes (pp. 260-261), adz (p. 265), limes, mute, thongs (pp. 266-269), league, fowling piece (pp. 278-279).

17. Pronounce: pursuit, swoon (pp. 257-259), spars (p. 260), drought, sieve, launch, cruise, shoal, tour (pp. 266-269), jib (p. 277), gestures, formidable, sheathe, sprites (pp. 278-281).

Extended Activity:

For a reading check, have students answer true or false to the following statements:

F 1. Robinson Crusoe's father sent him on his voyage.

T 2. He was dashed ashore by waves five times before he landed safely.

F 3. The birds on land were accustomed to the sound of loud noises.

F 4. One of Robinson Crusoe's valuable finds on the ship was a gold coin.

T. 5. His greatest desire was to have human companionship.

T 6. Robinson Crusoe kept goats to provide for light, clothes, food, and milk.

F 7. Robinson Crusoe was ecstatic when he found signs of human life on the island.

F 8. He used his gold coin to purchase Friday from the sailors.

T 9. Robinson Crusoe feared for his own life when he thought Friday wished to return to his tribe.

T 10. Robinson Crusoe's escape from the island ended peacefully.

NAME______________________________CLASS__________DATE______

ROBINSON CRUSOE, P. 257

For a reading check, circle true or false to the following statements:

True False 1. Robinson Crusoe's father sent him on his voyage.

True False 2. He was dashed ashore by waves five times before he landed safely.

True False 3. The birds on land were accustomed to the sound of loud noises.

True False 4. One of Robinson Crusoe's valuable finds on the ship was a gold coin.

True False 5. His greatest desire was to have human companionship.

True False 6. Robinson Crusoe kept goats to provide for light, clothes, food, and milk.

True False 7. Robinson Crusoe was ecstatic when he found signs of human life on the island.

True False 8. He used his gold coin to purchase Friday from the sailors.

True False 9. Robinson Crusoe feared for his own life when he thought Friday wished to return to his tribe.

True False 10. Robinson Crusoe's escape from the island ended peacefully.

NAME______________________________ **CLASS**__________ **DATE**_______

Story	***Find in the glossary the meaning of:***
Reader p. 147	**province**____________________
	prudence____________________
	bewilderment____________________
	abashed____________________
	extinguish____________________
	transparent____________________
	enchantment____________________
	dungeon____________________
	genius____________________
	sultan____________________
	magnificence____________________
	bounties____________________
	cornice____________________
	transport____________________
Reader p. 164	**bridled**____________________
	recalling____________________
	astonished____________________
	merchandise____________________
	retreat____________________
	hampers____________________
	resolved____________________
	uneasiness____________________
	utmost____________________
	invention____________________
	packet____________________
	reflected____________________
	suppressed____________________
	ceremony____________________
	related____________________
	confused____________________
	presently____________________
	enterprise____________________
	contrived____________________
	diminished____________________
	prevent____________________
	gilt____________________
	surpassed____________________
	moderation____________________
Reader p. 183	**mansion**____________________

grave______________________________
humor______________________________
ointment______________________________
sandalwood______________________________
repentance______________________________
turban______________________________
shipping______________________________
traffic______________________________
azure______________________________
Reader p. 203 **abbey**______________________________
battlements______________________________
ell______________________________
coffers______________________________
tourneys______________________________
hart______________________________
broom______________________________
boon______________________________
noble______________________________
Reader p. 231 **keep**______________________________
human______________________________
engines______________________________
bandages______________________________
turret______________________________
carriages______________________________
merchantmen______________________________
Reader p. 257 **stern**______________________________
bulge______________________________
spikes______________________________
adz______________________________
limes______________________________
mute______________________________
thongs______________________________
league______________________________
fowling piece______________________________

Pronounce:

dessert, nephew, niche, fatigue, hideous, imaginable, porcelain, vizier, gorgeous, Ali Baba, sesame, brocades, inquiries, hearken, affliction, apothecary, lozenge, burial, comrades, averted, corpse, Cogia Houssam, villain, curtsy, agility, poniard, caliph, Harun-al-Rashid, savory, repast, becalmed, maharaja, rarities, aloes, sequin, roc, desert, Arabic, sovereign, tradition, Plantagenets, palfreys,

pheasants, yeoman, toll, naught, hie, surety, justiciar, gainsaid, justs, heir, tryst, steward, balked, lea, ado, liege, beguiled, buffet, ruined, drowned, waistcoat, imperial, courtiers, theater, reigned, learned, Lilliput, graciously, fortnight, Lilliputians, pursuit, swoon, spars, drought, sieve, launch, cruise, shoal, tour, jib, gesture, formidable, sheathe, sprites.

Part III:
Great American Authors

In This Section—

Objectives

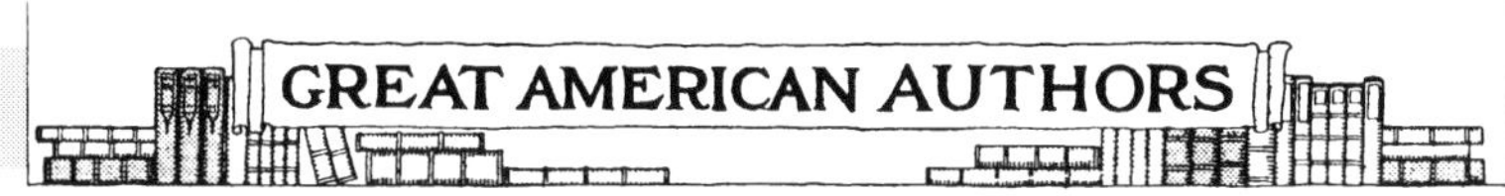

By completing Part III, the following objectives will be met.

1. The student will use effective reading strategies to construct meaning and identify the purpose of a text including:
   a. using illustrations
   b. defining unfamiliar words
   c. retelling and summarizing
2. The student will determine the main idea or essential message and identify relevant supporting details and facts of a text.
3. The student will read and organize facts from the text and other sources to make a report and perform an authentic task.
4. The student will prepare for writing by focusing on the topic and organizing supporting details in a logical sequence.
5. The student will draft and revise writing in cursive.
6. The student will produce final documents that have been edited for correct spelling, punctuation, and grammar.
7. The student will write for a variety of audiences and purposes.
8. The student will write in a variety of genres including narrative and expository writing.
9. The student will use reference materials (dictionaries, encyclopedias, maps, charts, photos, and electronic reference) to gather information.
10. The student will write a business letter.
11. The student will identify the development of plot and how conflicts are resolved in a story.
12. The student will identify and understand similarities and differences among the characters, settings, and events presented in various texts.
13. The student will identify author's purpose and point of view.
14. The student will identify and use literary terminology such as rhyme scheme and personification.
15. The student will respond critically to fiction and poetry.
16. The student will recognize cause-and-effect relationships in literary texts.
17. The student will respond to a text by explaining how the motives of the characters or events compare with those in his/her own life.
18. The student will understand the qualities necessary for people to become good citizens and apply those qualities to his/her personal life.
19. The student will understand the qualities necessary to develop good character.

BENJAMIN FRANKLIN—

THE WHISTLE, P. 293

1. **Why did Franklin say that he paid too much for his whistle?**
   Franklin paid too much for his whistle because he bought it on a whim. Rather than carefully considering his purchase, he hastily spent too much money on the whistle.
2. **How was this incident of use to him afterwards?**
   This incident was useful to Franklin afterwards because any time he was tempted to buy some unnecessary thing, he said to himself, "Don't give too much for the whistle." He saved his money.
3. **How does it apply to a man too fond of popularity? To the miser? To the man of pleasure? To the one who cares too much for appearance?**
   This story applies to the man too fond of popularity because that man neglected his own affairs and ruined them by that neglect. The miser spent too much by forsaking "every kind of comfortable living, all the pleasure of doing good to others, all the esteem of his fellow citizens, and the joys of benevolent friendship for the sake of accumulating wealth." The man of pleasure sacrificed "every laudable improvement of the mind or of his fortune to mere corporal sensations, and ruining his health in their pursuit." The one who cares too much for appearance contracts debts and ends his career in prison. All these men spent too much for their whistle.
4. **Can you think of other incidents that illustrate what Franklin had in mind?**
   Answers will vary.
5. **Extravagance has been called the great fault of America. During World War One what efforts were made by our people to correct this fault? Why were the efforts successful?**

To help raise money for the war effort, the government sold Savings Bonds. This allowed people to invest their money and helped curb their extravagance. Other efforts to curb extravagance were made by the Industries Board. They fixed prices, established priorities on production, and helped reduce waste. For example, the Industries Board eliminated extravagance by standardizing products. One of the standardizations was the production of tires where 232 kinds of buggy wheels were decreased to four. In addition, Daylight Savings Time, invented by Benjamin Franklin, was implemented to help save electricity. People were also urged to use all their food left-overs. Slogans such as "Food will win the war—don't waste" were popular.

6. **Why is it necessary to continue these efforts now? If all Americans would practice what Franklin advises, what would be the effect on the cost of living, and why?**

Answers will vary. Possibly if Americans were more thrifty, there would be less poverty and fewer people in debt.

7. **In what ways can you save some of the pennies you might spend foolishly?**

Answers will vary.

8. **What do you know about Savings Bonds? About savings accounts?**

Saving Bonds are bonds one purchases from the government, then trades them in for money at a later date for more than was originally paid. For example, if a person pays $20, when he cashes the bond, he might receive $25. A savings account is an account one sets up to put money into which he does not use on a regular basis. This money is money saved for emergencies and other unexpected expenses. Normally, the money will acrue interest for the length of time the money remains in the account.

9. **Write a letter to your teacher, proposing that the children in your class save as many pennies as possible for opening a savings accounts or for buying Saving Bonds, pointing out some ways in which children may save their pennies; bring in a part of Franklin's story in the most interesting way you can.**

10. **Tell what you can about the author.**

Refer to pages 292-293 for information about the author.

11. Find in the glossary the meaning of: coppers, voluntarily, vexation, ambitious, esteem, contracts.

12. Pronounce: directly, chagrin, sacrificing, levee, accumulating, laudible, equipage.

Extended Activity:

1. For question 9, have students write a formal business letter using the format from "Part I" (see page 100).

2. To coordinate with math, have students learn the formula for simple interest and work several problems.

NAME______________________________CLASS__________DATE______

THE WHISTLE, P. 293

1. **For question 9, write a formal business letter using the format from "Part I."**

2. **To coordinate with math, learn the formula for simple interest and work several problems.**

An Ax to Grind, p. 295

1. **In this story Franklin advises you to be on your guard against flatterers who wish to make use of you in order to gain their own ends. What made Franklin do as the man wanted him to? What do you think of the man?**
   Franklin did as the man asked because he was "pleased with the compliment of 'fine little fellow.'" Answers will vary concerning what the students think of the man, but they should realize that the man used insincere flattery for his own gain.
2. **How would you have sought the boy's help?**
   Answers will vary.
3. **In what ways was this incident of use to Franklin afterwards?**
   This incident was of use to Franklin afterwards because it made him cautious of those who use flattery for personal gain.
4. **What is meant when we say of a person that he has "an ax to grind"?**
   When a person has "an ax to grind", it means he has a problem or issue he wishes to discuss or dispute.
5. **How do you think Franklin valued sincerity?**
   Answers will vary; although, it is obvious Franklin highly valued sincerity and thought it was a good character quality.
6. **How do you value it?**
   Answers will vary.
7. **Tell the story as the man would have told it to a friend.**
8. **Pronounce: accosted.**

Extended Activity:

Have students write a paper describing a time when they had "an ax to grind" or someone had "an ax to grind" with them. Before students write, they should plan their writing. Use the following chart for planning.

Students should write a draft and edit it for spelling and punctuation. A final draft should be written in cursive.

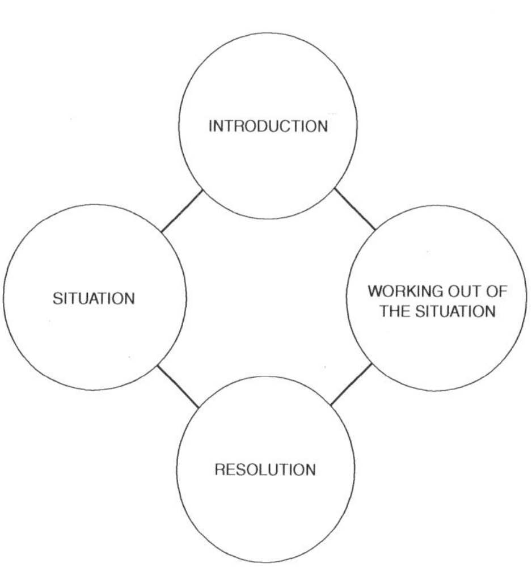

NAME________________________________CLASS__________DATE______

AN AXE TO GRIND, p. 295

Write a paper describing a time when you had "an ax to grind" or someone had "an ax to grind" with you. Before you write, you should plan your writing. Use the following chart for planning:

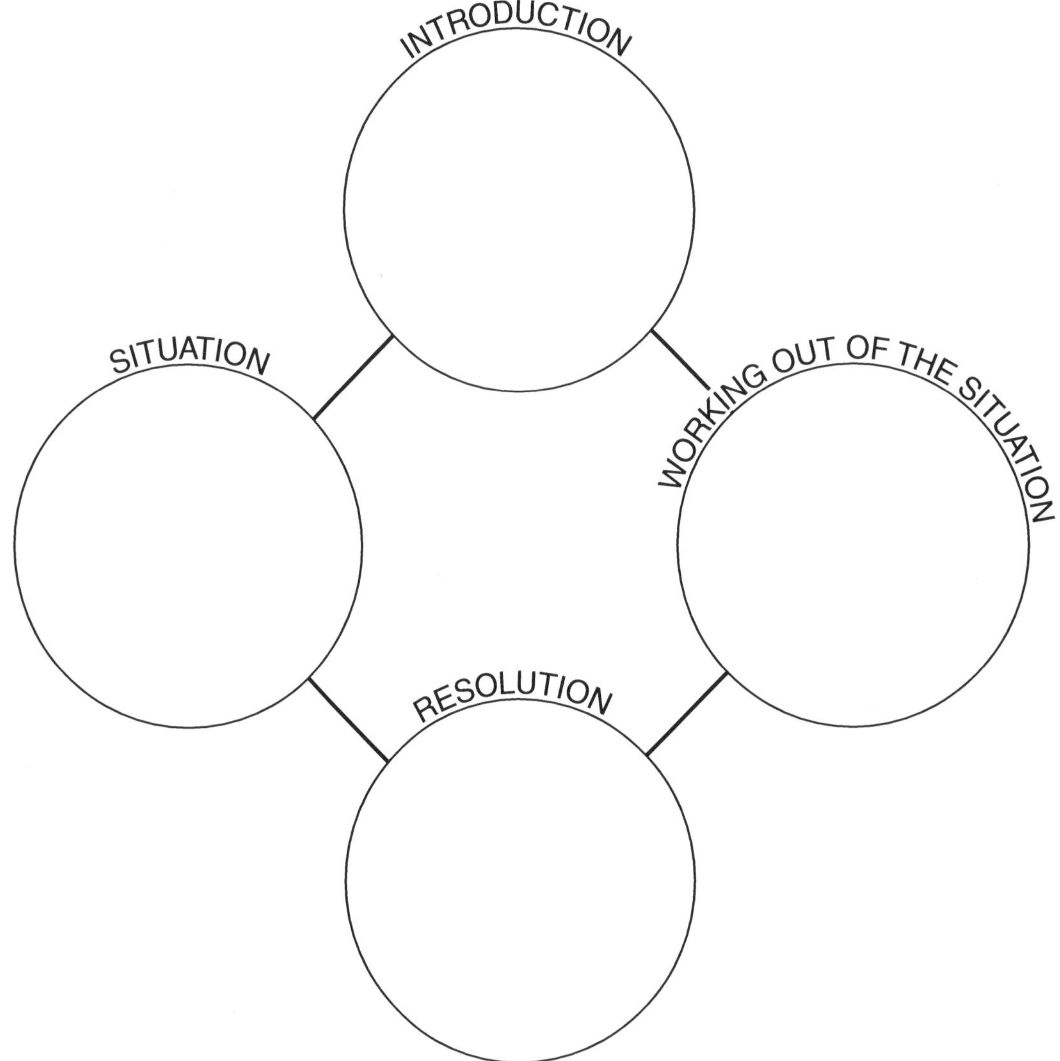

You should write a draft and edit it for spelling and punctuation. A final draft should be written in cursive.

William Cullen Bryant—

The Yellow Violet, p. 298

1. **When does the poet say the violet makes its appearance?**
   The violet makes its appearance in early spring when there is still snow on the ground:

   The yellow violet's modest bell
   Peeps from the last year's leaves below.
   And I have seen thee blossoming
   Beside the snow-bank's edges cold.

2. **Why is the violet called a "modest" flower?**
   The violet is called "modest" because it hangs and does not make a grand appearance. It "peeps" and often goes unnoticed.
3. **Why does the violet make glad the heart of the poet? When the woods and fields are *full* of flowers, does he notice the violet?**
   The violet makes glad the heart of the poet because she appears in "sunless April" days. The violet is there when the spring is still yet to come. When the woods and fields are full of flowers, the poet does not notice the violet.
4. **What does "alone" add to the meaning of line 8, page 298?**
   The word "alone" adds to the humility and beauty of the violet who is alone, blooming this time of year.
5. **What is meant by "her train," line 9, page 298?**
   Her train is "those in a company" with her. Her train is all the other violets and flowers beside her.
6. **What are "the hands of Spring"?**
   "The hands of Spring" are all the changes that begin to occur as winter ends and spring begins.
7. **In what sense is the sun the "parent" of the violet?**
   The sun is the "parent" of the violet because it nurtures and watches over the violet just as a parent does her child.
8. **Why does Bryant say the violet's seat is low?**
   The violet is not as high or bold as the other flowers, so Bryant says the violet's seat is low.

9. **What does the poet say the violet's "early smile" has often done for him?**
The violet's "early smile" has "stayed" the author's walk. This means the author has stopped to look at the beauty of the violet as he is walking.

10. **Point out the stanzas in which the poet tells you where he finds the violet.**
Stanzas 1, 2, and 3 tell where he finds the violet.
The stanzas in which he tells you about the appearance and character of the flower
Stanzas 4, 5, and 6 tell about the appearance and character of the flower.
The stanzas in which he rebukes himself for passing it by, and makes a promise.
Stanzas 7 and 8 tell when the author rebukes himself and makes a promise.

11. **Why does Bryant stop to view the violet in April and pass it by in May?**
Bryant stops to view the violet in April because it is the first flower to bloom, but in May other "gorgeous blooms" can be seen.

12. **With what does the poet compare this treatment of the violet?**
The poet compares this treatment of the violet to those "who climb to wealth" and forget "The friends in darker fortunes tried."

13. **What does the poet say he regrets?**
The poet regrets that he "should ape the ways of pride."

14. **What other flowers come very early in the spring? How do you feel when you see them?**
Other flowers that come early in the spring are the tulip and the daffodil. Answers will vary.

15. **Which stanza of the poem do you like best?**
Answers will vary.

16. **What other poem on the violet have you read?**
Answers will vary.

17. **Tell what you can about the author.**
Refer to pages 297-298 for information about the author.

18. **Find in the glossary the meaning of: beechen, russet, train, jet, unapt.**

19. **Pronounce: ere, parent, gorgeous, humble, genial.**

Extended Activity:

Research and find a picture of a violet. Make your own illustration of the violet and copy your favorite lines from the poem. Display your work.

NAME______________________________CLASS__________DATE______

THE YELLOW VIOLET, P. 298

Research and find a picture of a violet. Make your own illustration of the violet and copy your favorite lines from the poem. Display your work.

The Gladness of Nature, p. 300

1. **What season is described here?**
   Spring is the season described.
2. **What are the signs that Nature is glad? How do all these things affect the poet? How do you sometimes feel on a rainy day.**
   The signs that nature is glad can be found in these lines:
   "Mother nature laughs around," "the deep blue heavens look glad," "There are notes of joy from the hangbird and wren," "The ground squirrel gayly chirps," "The clouds are at play," "There's a smile on the fruit, and a smile on the flower."
   These affect the poet by taking his "gloom away."
   Answers will vary on how students feel on rainy days.
3. **What signs of gladness are mentioned in the first two stanzas?**
   "Mother nature laughs around", "deep blue heavens look glad", "notes of joy from the hangbird and wren", "The ground squirrel gayly chirps", and "the wilding bee hums merrily" are signs of gladness.
4. **Which of these have you seen in springtime?**
   Answers will vary.
5. **Have you ever seen clouds that seemed to chase one another?**
   Answers will vary.
6. **What is meant by "a laugh from the brook"?**
   A brook runs quickly making gurgling noises that sound like laughs.
7. **What does the poet say the sun will do for us?**
   The sun will "smile thy gloom away."
8. **Do you think spring is "a time to be cloudy and sad"?**
   Answers will vary. Spring is often thought of as a time of rebirth and renewal. It should not be "a time to be cloudy and sad."
9. **Why do city boys and girls like to visit the country?**
   City boys and girls like to visit the country because in the city one does not see the rolling hills, forests, and other beauties of nature that one might see in the country.
10. **Read again "A Forward Look," pages 19-20, and then point out fancies that Bryant uses in this poem to help us see the beauty and wonder of nature.**

Fancies are images a poet uses to help us understand his thoughts and ways the poet uses his imagination. Some of the fancies in this poem are "Mother Nature laughs around" and "The clouds at play".

11. Commit to memory the stanza that you like best.

12. Pronounce: wilding, azure, isles, ay.

JOHN GREENLEAF WHITTIER—

THE HUSKERS, P. 303

1. **What is the difference between the sunshine of October and that of May?**

   The sunshine of October is "broad and red," but is "chastened and subdued." The sun of May is bright and hot.

2. **Why does it seem to the poet as if the sun wove with golden shuttle the yellow haze?**

   It seems as if the sun wove with golden shuttle the yellow haze because he "slanted through the painted beeches" and moved brightening the land.

3. **What had the frost done that made the woodlands gay?**

   The frost left the woodlands gay by making "the hues of summer's rainbow" appear on the ground.

4. **What words in the second stanza make you feel that the wood was some distance away?**

   It seems as if the wood is some distance away because Whittier describes it as "softly pictured." Normally, things at a distance have a softer look to them and detail cannot be easily seen.

5. **To whom does "he" in the third stanza refer?**

   In the third stanza "he" refers to the sun.

6. **What words in the second stanza explain the word "haze" in the third stanza?**

   "A thin, dry mist" in the second stanza explains the word "haze" in the third stanza.

7. **What gave the beeches the appearance of being painted?**

   The beeches appeared painted because the sun shone through the mist on the beeches bringing out the colors of the rainbow.

8. **What are the colors of the woods and sky in this poem? What colors are they in the poem, "The Yellow Violet"? Find the words and phrases that tell you.**

How many times, in this poem, does the poet use the words *golden* and *yellow*, or speak of things that suggest these colors.

The colors of the woods and sky in this poem are green, yellow, and red. The poet uses the words golden and yellow six times in "The Huskers."

9. **What do you think was the reason the boys laughed when they looked up to the sky?**

   Answers will vary. People often laugh when they feel good. A bright beautiful sky often helps people feel free and happy.

10. **What "summer grain" is mentioned in line 11, page 304?**

    The "summer grain" that is mentioned is most likely rye since rye is named in line 12.

11. **What crop was still ungathered?**

    Corn was the crop that was still ungathered.

12. **Where were the harvesters at work?**

    The harvesters were at work on the "gentle hill-slopes, in the valleys fringed with wood."

13. **What was it that set the sky "all afire beyond"?**

    The sun setting made the sky "all afire beyond."

14. **Where did the husking take place?**

    The husking took place in the barn. The lines "There wrought the busy harvester, and many a creaking wain, Bore slowly to the long barn-floor its load of husk and grain" tell you this.

15. **How did the old men spend the evening?**

    The old men spent the evening "talking their old times over."

16. **What things that we eat depend on the work of the huskers?**

    All kinds of cereals and food such as tortillas are things we eat for which we depend on the work of the huskers.

17. **Tell what you can about the author.**

    Refer to pages 302-303 for information about the author.

18. **Find in the glossary the meaning of: shuttle, spire, sear, verdant, wain, lapsed.**

19. **Pronounce: autumnal, chastened, beneath, sphere, wrought, radiance, tranquil, mow, serene, psalm.**

THE CORN-SONG, P. 307

1. **In a "Forward Look," pages 19 - 20, you read that poets help you to see beauty in things that might otherwise seem common. The yellow violet is less showy than the chrysanthemum, but the poet writes of the violet. The pineapple, the orange, the grape, seem more interesting than the yellow corn of the fields, but here is a poem about one of the commonest of farm crops. To whom is the poet speaking in the first two stanzas? Point out some of the poet's fancies in this poem.**

   The poet is speaking to God in the first two stanzas. Some of his fancies are "Autumn's horn," "April plays," "robber crows," "corn's hair."

2. **Is all corn "golden"? What other kinds have you seen?**

   No, not all corn is "golden." There is white and purple corn. Other kinds of corn are popcorn, field corn, sweet corn and millet.

3. **Name other gifts autumn brings us.**

   Other gifts autumn brings us are pineapples, oranges, and grapes.

4. **Why is the corn a "hardy gift"? What other words and phrases in the poem suggest the same idea?**

   Corn is a "hardy gift" because it is filling, can be used to make many types of foods, and does not rot as easily as the other autumn gifts. Other words and phrases that suggest the same idea are: "We better love the hardy gift," "All through the long, bright days of June its leaves grew green and fair," "We pluck away the frosted leaves and bear the treasure home."

5. **What do we call the "apple from the pine"?**

   The "apple from the pine" is pineapple.

6. **What clusters are picked from vines?**

   Grapes are clusters picked from vines.

7. **In what "other lands" do these fruits grow?**

   Pineapple and oranges grow in warmer, tropical climates such as Hawaii and Florida. Grapes grow abundantly in California and in European countries such as France.

8. **Where was Whittier's home?**

   Whittier's home was in Massachusetts.

9. **What do you know of the soil and climate of New England?**

New England has very cold winters and mild summers. They rarely are affected by tornadoes, but since the New England states border the Atlantic, they can be affected by hurricanes.

10. Find the line that tells when we plant corn.

The line that tells us when corn is planted reads: "We dropped the seed o'er the hill and plain, Beneath the sun of May."

11. Find the lines that tell when we harvest the corn.

The lines that tells us when corn is harvested read: "And now with Autumn's moonlit eves, It's harvest time has come."

13. What is the "yellow hair" the corn waves in summer?

The "yellow hair" is the silk of the corn.

14. What does he think of those who scorn the blessings of the corn?

The poet thinks that those who scorn the blessing of the corn are proud and vain.

15. What wish does the poet express in the last stanza?

The poet expresses adoration and thanksgiving for the corn.

16. What service did our farmers and boys and girls on the farms perform during World War One?

Farmers and boys and girls grew food for the war effort. They grew Victory Gardens in their backyards and in empty fields.

17. On page 291 you were asked to notice the way in which these American authors have expressed their thoughts. Does Whittier's use of rhyme add to the beauty of his "song" about corn? Point out some of the lines that rhyme.

The use of rhyme adds to the beauty of Whittier's song about corn. Lines that rhyme are the first and third line and the second and fourth line of each stanza. The rhyme scheme for this poem is ABAB:

Heap high the farmer's wintry hoard! A
Heap high the golden corn! B
No richer gift has Autumn poured A
From out her lavish horn! B

18 . Find in the glossary the meaning of: glean, hardy, meads, furrows, frosted, mildew, adorn.

20. Pronounce: hoard, lavish, glossy, root.

WASHINGTON IRVING—

CAPTURING THE WILD HORSE, P. 311

1. **What picture do the first three paragraphs give you?**
The first three paragraphs describe a beautiful meadow on the edge of rugged hills. Irving describes it as being designed "by the hand of art." There were horses and buffalo in the valley.
2. **Tell how "ringing the wild horse" is accomplished.**
The "ringing of the wild horse" is accomplished by men circling the horses. As the horses run in any direction, they are diverted back by the men. Eventually the horses tire and the hunters can ride beside them and throw a lariat over their heads.
3. **What preparations did Irving's party make for the hunt?**
Irving's party prepared for the hunt by taking the packhorses into the woods and firmly tying them. Several groups of 25 men were positioned around the wild horses.
4. **Who broke the rules of the chase?**
Tonish, the Frenchman, broke the rules of the chase.
5. **What was the effect of this?**
Tonish's furious pursuit of the wild horses caused them to run, and the other men joined in the chase.
6. **Tell all you can learn about Tonish, the little Frenchman.**
One should learn from Tonish that it is important to follow the plan set forth and work together as a group.
7. **What does Irving say about the ease with which the wild horses were tamed?**
Irving says it surprised him how easily the wild horses were tamed.
8. **List the words that give ideas of thrilling action in the paragraph beginning, "The whole troop joined in the headlong chase." What words tell the difference between the buffaloes and the horses in flight?**
The words that give ideas of thrilling action are "hair flying about," "heaved," "tempest," "heavy-rolling flight," "pell-

mell, hurry-scurry," "wild," "clang and clatter," "whoop and halloo."

The buffaloes are described as being "heavy rolling" compared to the "scouring" of the horses. These words show that the buffaloes were not as quick footed and graceful as the horses.

9. **Tell what you can about the author.**

Refer to pages 310 -311 for notes about the author.

10. **Class readings: Select the passages you like best.**
11. **Outline for testing silent reading. Tell the story in your own words, using the following topics: (a) the scene of action; (b) the method of approach; (c) the preparations; (d) the mistake of Tonish; (e) the excitement of the chase; (f) the two captures.**
12. **Find in the glossary the meaning of: toilsome, gullies, diversified, circumference, prime, skirted, fugitives, brake, defile.**
13. **Pronounce: diminutive, ruminating, herbage, maneuver, kept, lariat, circuit, reappeared, rangers, handkerchiefs, rearing, marred.**

Extended Activity:

For a reading check, have students answer true or false to the following statements:

F. 1. The story takes place in the hills of New England.

F. 2. The men were trying to capture wild buffalo.

T. 3. The men decided to try the hunting maneuver called "ringing the wild horse."

T. 4. To prepare for the capture, men were stationed in a large circle around the valley.

T. 5. Tonish was rash and pursued the animals.

NAME______________________________CLASS__________DATE______

CAPTURING THE WILD HORSE, P. 311

For a reading check, circle true or false to the following statements:

True False 1. The story takes place in the hills of New England.

True False 2. The men were trying to capture wild buffalo.

True False 3. The men decided to try the hunting maneuver called "ringing the wild horse."

True False 4. To prepare for the capture, men were stationed in a large circle around the valley.

True False 5. Tonish was rash and pursued the animals.

The Adventure of the Mason, p. 316

1. **What condition led the mason to undertake the stranger's task?**
   The mason was immensely poor and needed work; thus, he accepted the job.
2. **Why was the mason blindfolded?**
   The mason was blindfolded because his employer wanted to keep secret the vault's location.
3. **How long did it take him to complete the vault?**
   It took the mason two night's work to complete the vault.
4. **What was buried in it?**
   Three or four jars of money were placed in the vault.
5. **How did the mason find his way home?**
   The mason was led to the banks of the Xenil, from whence he made his way home.
6. **Was the mason's poverty relieved by the pay he received from the stranger?**
   The mason's poverty was not relieved by the pay he received from the stranger.
7. **What work did the grasping landlord propose to the mason?**
   The landlord asked the mason to restore the house at little cost.
8. **What stories had brought a bad name upon the landlord's house?**
   Stories of the miser clinking his gold at night gave a bad name to the landlord's house.
9. **What was the "dreamy recollection"?**
   The "dreamy recollection" was when the mason recognized the fountain under which the vault laid.
10. **How did the mason show his quick wit?**
    The mason showed his quick wit by offering to live in the house rent-free and restore the house as well as rid it of the ghostly noises.
11. **Why did he say that he was not afraid of the devil in the shape of a bag of money?**
    The mason said he was not afraid of the devil in the shape of a money bag because he claimed to be a good Christian, and he knew the truth about the location of the money.

12. What differences do you notice between this story of how the mason came upon great wealth and the stories of Aladdin and Ali Baba?

The stories of Aladdin and Ali Baba each contain elements of fantasy or magic. Aladdin has a genius who grants riches and Ali Baba uses a magic word to enter the cave. All of the main characters in the three stories attain riches they did not earn.

13. Read again pages 289-291 and tell what makes Irving a real author. Can you tell why you enjoyed this story?

Answers will vary.

14. Class reading: The second part of the story, page 318, line 21, to the end.

15. Outline for testing silent reading. Tell the story in your own words, using the following topics: (a) how the mason built the vault in the mysterious house; (b) how he unexpectedly came into possession of this vault many years later.

16. Find in the glossary the meaning of: hoodwinked, vault, maze, cathedral, pest, ducat.

17. Pronounce: Granada, señor, ponderous, ghastly, obliterated, route, gaunt, hovel, curmudgeon, daunted.

Extended Activities:

1. For a quick reading check, have students answer true or false to the following statements:

T. a. The mason was a religious man who kept all the saints' days and holidays.

F. b. The mason was paid poorly for making a vault for the stranger.

T. c. The Landlord's house was thought to be haunted and thus, had a bad reputation.

F. d. The Landlord offered the mason money from the vault in exchange for his work to restore the old house.

T. e. The mason became one of the richest men in Granada.

2. For class discussion have students answer and defend their answer to these questions:

a. Do you think the mason was demonstrating good character by not telling the landlord about the money in the vault?

b. Do you think the mason had a right to keep the money? If not, why? What should he have done with the money?

NAME______________________________CLASS__________DATE______

THE ADVENTURE OF THE MASON, P. 316

1. For a reading check, circle true or false to the following statements:

True False a. The mason was a religious man who kept all the saints' days and holidays.

True False b. The mason was paid poorly for making a vault for the stranger.

True False c. The Landlord's house was thought to be haunted and thus, had a bad reputation.

True False d. The Landlord offered the mason money from the vault in exchange for his work to restore the old house.

True False e. The mason became one of the richest men in Granada.

2. For class discussion answer and defend:

a. Do you think the mason was demonstrating good character by not telling the landlord about the money in the vault?

____

____

____

____

b. Do you think the mason had a right to keep the money? If not, why? What should he have done with the money?

____

____

____

____

HENRY WADSWORTH LONGFELLOW—

THE ARROW AND THE SONG, P. 322

1. **What became of the arrow? Of the song?**
   Both the arrow and the song fell to earth and the poet did not know where.

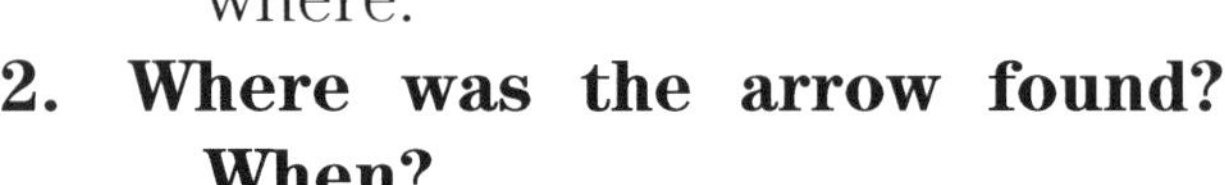

2. **Where was the arrow found? When?**
   The arrow was found in an oak tree "long, long afterwards."

3. **Where was the song found?**
   The song was found "again in the heart of a friend."
4. **Point out lines that rhyme.**
   In each stanza the first and second lines rhyme (air, where; air, where; oak, unbroke) and the third and fourth lines rhyme (sight, flight; strong, song; end, friend.)
5. **What is Longfellow's purpose in this poem?**
   The author's purpose could be to show how happiness is contagious.
6. **Why is the poet's song compared to the flight of an arrow?**
   The poet's song is compared to the swift flight of an arrow because like the arrow a song can travel fast and far and affects others.
7. **A poet once said, "Let me make the songs of a nation, and I care not who makes the laws." What did he mean?**
   The poet might have meant that writing songs of a nation do more for peace than making laws by inspiring people to be good citizens.
8. **What was the song doing "in the heart of a friend."?**
   The song was bringing happiness to a friend.

The Children's Hour, p. 323

1. **What is the time "Between the dark and the daylight" usually called?**
   It is usually called twilight.
2. **What do you suppose Longfellow had been doing in his study before the children came down to him?**
   Answers will vary. Longfellow may have been reading or working.
3. **What reasons can you give for the "pause in the day's occupations"?**
   Reasons for the "pause in the day's occupations" vary. Many people take time in the early evening to reflect on the day's events and to rest from their work.
4. **Who were the children whom the poet saw "Descending the broad hall stair" to enter "his castle wall"?**
   The children the poet saw "Descending the broad hall stair" were "Grave Alice, and laughing Alegia, and Edith with golden hair."
5. **What were these children whispering about?**
   The children were "plotting and planning together" to take the author by surprise.
6. **What does Longfellow mean by his "turret"?**
   The author is comparing his chair to a turret, a small tower. He writes that the children "climbed up into my turret o'er the arms of and back of my chair."
7. **To what does he compare the rush made by the children?**
   He compares the children's rush to that of an army attack.
8. **What wall did they scale in order to reach him?**
   They scaled the wall of his castle in order to reach the author.
9. **Where does Longfellow say he will put the children now that he has captured them?**
   Longfellow says he will put the children in his dungeon now that he's captured them.
10. **Which stanza of this poem do you like best?**
    Answers will vary.
11. **Tell what you know about the life of Longfellow.**
    Refer to pages 321 and 322 for information about the author.
12. **Find in the glossary the meaning of: raid, match.**
13. **Pronounce: lower, banditti, dungeon.**

The Song of Hiawatha, p. 326

Introduction, p. 326

1. **Where did these stories come from? Read lines which tell.**
   These stories came from "the forests and the prairies,
   From the great lakes of the Northland,
   From the land of the Ojibways,
   From the land of the Dacotahs,
   From the mountains, moors, and fenlands."
2. **Name the Great Lakes.**
   Lake Michigan, Lake Heron, Lake Erie, Lake Superior, and Lake Ontario.
3. **Who was Nawadaha?**
   Nawadaha was a singer who sang the song of Hiawatha.
4. **What word tells the sound of the pine trees?**
   The word that tells the sound of the pine trees is "singing."
5. **Read five lines that tell what the singer sang of Hiawatha.**
   The five lines that tell what the singer sang of Hiawatha are:
   Sang his wondrous birth and being,
   How he prayed and how he fasted,
   How he lived, and toiled, and suffered,
   That the tribes of men might prosper,
   That he might advance his people!
6. **Find in the glossary the meaning of: reverberations, fenlands.**
7. **Pronounce: legends, wigwams, aerie.**

Hiawatha's Childhood, p. 329

1. **What body of water is called Gitche Gumee?**
   Lake Superior is called Gitche Gumee.
2. **Where did the wigwam of Nokomis stand?**
   The wigwam of Nokomis stood "by the shining Big-Sea- Water."
3. **What is meant by the "beat" of the water?**
   The "beat" of the water was the waves lapping on shore.
4. **Why does Longfellow call the pine trees "black and gloomy"?**
   Longfellow calls the pine trees "black and gloomy" because they are tall and shaded.
5. **Who was Nokomis?**

Nokomis was Hiawatha's mother.

6. **Why did she call Hiawatha "my little owlet"?**
Hiawatha was her "little owlet" because as a baby he made small hooting noises such as an owl makes.

7. **What do we call the "broad, white road in heaven"?**
The "broad, white road in heaven" is the Milky Way.

8. **What word tells the sound of the water?**
"Lapping" is the word that tells the sound of the water.

9. **Read lines that tell what Hiawatha learned of the birds and the beasts.**
Page 331 lines 29-33:
Learned of every bird its language,
Learned their names and all their secrets
How they built their nests in summer,
Where they hid themselves in winter
Talked with them whene'er he met them,"
Page 332 lines 1-7:
"Called them 'Hiawatha's Chickens'
Of all beasts he learned the language,
Learned their names and all their secrets—
How the beavers built their lodges,
Where the squirrels hid their acorns,
How the reindeer ran so swiftly,
Why the rabbit was so timid;

10. **Of what was Hiawatha's bow made? His arrows? The cord?**
Hiawatha's bow was made of a branch of ash. The arrows were made of oak-bough, and the cord was made of deerskin.

11. **Why was a tip of flint used on the arrows?**
Flint is a rock that can be sharpened to pierce what it strikes.

12. **What is meant by "the ford across the river"?**
The "ford across the river" was a shallow place where Hiawatha could cross.

13. **Read lines which tell that Hiawatha was excited when hunting.**
Lines that tell Hiawatha was excited about hunting are:
But he heeded not, nor heard them,
For his thoughts were with the red deer
On their tracks his eyes were fastened,

14. **Find in the glossary the meaning of: linden, frolic, nostrils.**

15. Pronounce: moss, sinews, warrior, haunches, alder, palpitated, exulted.

Hiawatha's Friends, p. 335

1. What two friends had Hiawatha "Singled out from all the others"?

Hiawatha's two friends were Chibiabos, the musician, and Kwasind, the strong man.

2. What were they "contriving"?

They were contriving "How the tribes of men might prosper,"

3. Read lines that tell of Chibiabos.

Lines that tell of Chibiabos can be found on page 335 lines 10-23, page 336 lines 1-34 and page 337 lines 1-4.

4. With what is he compared? Read lines that tell.

Chibiabos is compared to a brave man, a soft woman, the wand of a willow, and a deer. The lines that tell are on page 335 lines 13-15.

5. From what did he make his flutes?

He made his flute from hollow reeds.

6. Read lines that tell how musical they were.

That the brook, the Sebowisha,
Ceased to murmur in the woodland,
That the wood-birds ceased from singing,
And the squirrel, Adjidaumo,
Ceased his chatter in the oak-tree,
And the rabbit, the Wabasso,
Sat upright to look and listen.

7. What did the brook say to Chibiabos? The bluebird? The robin?

The brooks said, "O Chibiabos,
Teach my waves to flow in music,
Softly as your words in singing!"
The bluebird said, "O Chibiabos,
Teach me tones as wild and wayward,
Teach me songs as full of frenzy!"
The robin said, "O Chibiabos,
Teach me tunes as sweet and tender,
Teach me songs as full of gladness!"

8. Of what did Chibiabos sing?

Chibiabos sang "of peace and freedom,
Sang of beauty, love, and longing;

Sang of death, and life undying"

9. **Why did Hiawatha love him more than all others?**
Hiawatha loved him more than all the others because of his gentleness and "the magic of his singing."
10. **For what did Hiawatha love Kwasind?**
Hiawatha loved Kwasind "For his very strength."
11. **What did Kwasind's mother say to him? His father?**
Kwasind's mother said, "Lazy Kwasind!" and, "In my work you never help me."
His father said, "Lazy Kwasind!" and, "In my hunt you never help me."
12. **What is meant by the line, "every bow you touch is broken"?**
Kwasind was so strong that just his touch on the bow would break it.
13. **Read lines that tell of Kwasind and the beaver.**
Lines that tell of Kwasind and the beaver can be found on page 339 lines 15-33.
14. **Which of Hiawatha's two friends do you like the better? Why?**
Answers will vary.
15. **Find in the glossary the meaning of: reeds, frenzy, listless, cowering, clamber, ponder, sported.**
16. **Pronounce: pliant, wand, pathos, allied, asunder, quoit, triumphant.**

Hiawatha's Sailing, p. 341

1. **Of what did Hiawatha make his canoe?**
Hiawatha made his canoe with the bark of a birch tree, the boughs of the cCedar, the roots of the larch tree, and the balm of the fir tree.
2. **Why does Hiawatha call the bark of a birch tree a cloak?**
Hiawatha calls the bark of the birch tree a cloak because the bark covers the tree like a cloak (coat) would.
3. **What other name does he give the bark of the birch tree?**
The other name Hiawatha calls the bark of the birch tree is "white-skin wrapper."
4. **What word tells the sound made by the leaves of the birch tree?**

The word that describes the sound of the birch tree is "rustled."

5. **What word tells that Hiawatha cut all around the birch tree?**
The word that tells Hiawatha cut all around the birch tree is "girdled."

6. **Why did Hiawatha ask the cedar tree for its boughs?**
Hiawatha asked the cedar tree for its boughs so he could make his canoe more steady.

7. **Read lines that tell why he asked the larch tree for its roots.**
The lines that tell why Hiawatha asked the larch tree for its roots are:
My canoe to bind together,
So to bind the ends together,
That the water may not enter,
That the river may not wet me!

8. **What other name does he give the larch tree?**
The other name he gives the larch tree is "Tamarack."

9. **Why does Hiawatha call the drops of balsam "tears"?**
Hiawatha calls the drops of balsam "tears" because like tear drops that run down one's face, so balsam runs down the trunk of a tree.

10. **Can the hedgehog really shoot his quills "like arrows"?**
No, the hedgehog cannot shoot its quills.

11. **What is meant by "my beauty"?**
"My beauty" means Hiawatha is going to decorate himself with a necklace.

12. **Read lines that tell how Hiawatha decorated his canoe.**
The lines that tell how Hiawatha decorated his canoe are page 343 lines 18-25:
From the ground the quills he gathered,
All the little shining arrows;
Stained them red and blue and yellow,
With the juice of roots and berries;
Into his canoe he wrought them,
Round its waist a shining girdle,
Round its bows a gleaming necklace,
On its breast two stars resplendent.

13. **What did he use for paddles for the canoe?**
Hiawatha used his thoughts for paddles:

"Paddles none he had or needed,
For his thoughts as paddles served him."

14. What did Kwasind do to aid the canoeing?

Kwasind helped Hiawatha canoe by clearing the river "of its sunken logs and sandbars" making it easier to navigate.

15. Why is the fir tree spoken of as "somber"?

The fir tree is spoken of as "somber" because it "sobbed through all its robes of darkness."

16. Find in the glossary the meaning of: stately, larch, channel.

17. Pronounce: horror, hewed, tamarack, fibrous, forehead, balm, balsam, resin, fissure, crevice, bosom, resplendent, supple, veered, swam.

Hiawatha's Wooing, p. 346

1. Why did Nokomis wish Hiawatha to wed a maiden of his own people?

Nokomis wanted Hiawatha to marry a maiden of his own people because the people of the Dacotahs had been feuding with Hiawatha's people, and their ways were unfamiliar.

2. Whom did Hiawatha say he would wed?

Hiawatha said he would wed Minnehaha, Laughing Water, from the Dacotahs.

3. Find the Falls of Minnehaha on your map.

Minnehaha is a waterfall near the city of Minneapolis.

4. Read lines that tell of Hiawatha's journey "To the land of the Dacotahs."

The lines that tell of Hiawatha's journey are on p. 347 lines 25-33 and page 348 lines 1-7:

Thus departed Hiawatha
To the land of the Dacotahs,
To the land of handsome women,
Striding over moor and meadow,
Through interminable forests,
Through uninterrupted silence.
With his moccasins of magic,
At each stride a mile he measured;
Yet the way seemed long before him,
And his heart outran his footsteps;
And he journeyed without resting,
Till he heard the cataract's laughter,
Heard the Falls of Minnehaha
Calling to him through the silence.

5. **Of what was the Arrow-maker thinking when Hiawatha appeared?**

When Hiawatha arrived, the Arrow-maker was thinking about the past of hunting and war-parties.

6. **Read lines that tell of what the maiden was thinking.**

Lines that tell what the maiden was thinking are on page 349 lines 5-17:

She was thinking of a hunter,
From another tribe and country,
Young and tall and very handsome,
Who one morning, in the springtime,
Came to buy her father's arrows,
Sat and rested in the wigwam,
Lingered long about the doorway,
Looking back as he departed.
She had heard her father praise him,
Praise his courage and his wisdom;
Would he come again for arrows
To the Falls of Minnehaha?

7. **Read the words of Hiawatha when he asked the father for his daughter.**

"After many years of warfare
Many years of strife and bloodshed,
There is peace between the Ojibways
And the tribe of the Dacotahs."
Thus continued Hiawatha,
And then added, speaking slowly,

"That this peace may last forever,
And our hands be clasped more closely,
And our hearts be more united,
Give me as my wife this maiden,
Minnehaha, Laughing Water,
Loveliest of Dacotah women!"

8. **In what words did the Arrow-maker give his consent?**
   The Arrow-maker gave his consent, "Yes, if Minnehaha wishes."
9. **What was Minnehaha's answer?**
   Minnehaha answered, "I will follow you, my husband."
10. **Read lines that tell of the journey homeward.**
    Lines that tell of the journey homeward are page 352, lines 1-33 and page 353, lines 1-5.
11. **Why did Hiawatha "check" his pace on this journey?**
    Hiawatha checked his pace on the journey so Minnehaha could keep up.
12. **What greeting did the bluebird give them?**
    The greeting the bluebird gave them was "Happy are you, Hiawatha, Having such a wife to love you."
13. **What was the greeting of the robin? The sun? The moon?**
    The greeting of the robin was, "Happy are you, Laughing Water, Having such a noble husband." The sun said, "O my children, Love is sunshine, hate is shadow; Life is checkered shade and sunshine; Rule by love, O Hiawatha." The moon said, "O my children, Day is restless, night is quiet, Man imperious, woman feeble; Half is mine, although I follow; Rule by patience, Laughing Water."
14. **Read the lines that you like best.**
15. **Find in the glossary the meaning of: cord, nimble, moor, fallow, swerve, jasper, flags, rushes, basswood, flaunting.**
16. **Pronounce: dissuading, feuds, wounds, chalcedony, plaiting, bade, spacious, benignant, mystic, imperious.**

The White-Man's Foot, p. 355

1. **Read lines that tell Iagoo's story of adventures.**
   The lines that tell of Iagoo's story of adventures are on page 355 lines 14 -18 and page 356 lines 1-25.
2. **Where do you think he had seen these things?**
   He saw these things in the eastern states near the Atlantic Ocean.

3. **What was the "bitter" water Iagoo told about?**
The "bitter" water was the saltwater from the ocean.
4. **What were the "lightning" and the "thunder" that came from the "canoe with pinions"?**
The "lightning" and "thunder" were the cannons and weapons from the ships.
5. **Why was his story laughed at as false by the Indians?**
His story was laughed at because Iagoo often told exaggerated stories and this one seemed too unreal for the Indians.
6. **How did Hiawatha know it was all true?**
Hiawatha knew it was all true because he had seen it in a vision.
7. **How did Hiawatha say they should receive the white man when he came?**
Hiawatha said they should welcome the white man and "Hail them as our friends and brothers."
8. **What secrets came to Hiawatha in the vision?**
Secrets of the future came to Hiawatha in the vision.
9. **What "darker vision" did he see?**
The darker vision he saw was:
"I beheld our nations scattered,
All forgetful of my counsels,
Weakened, warring with each other;
Saw the remnants of our people
Sweeping westward, wild and woeful,"
10. **Has Hiawatha's vision come true?**
Yes, Hiawatha's vision has come true.
11. **What do you think of Hiawatha's character?**
Answers will vary.
12. **Which of all the stories in this poem do you like best?**
Answers will vary.
13. **Give the reason for your answer.**
Answers will vary.
14. **You no doubt enjoyed reading this poem. Can you tell why?**
Answers will vary.
15. **Read "A Forward Look," pp. 289-291, and tell why you think Longfellow was a real author.**
Answers will vary.
16. **You will enjoy reading Eastman's *Indian Legends Retold.***
17. **Find in the glossary the meaning of: tittered, hither, counsels.**

18. Pronounce: pinions, derision, vision, regions, vague, warring.

Extended Activities:

1. A narrative poem is one that tells a story. Choose one of the following topics to write an original narrative poem.
   a. The story of your birth
   b. Your best friend
   c. Your greatest adventure
   d. The dream of your future
2. Make a Zig-Zag book about Hiawatha (refer to directions from Part I, page 22). Each page should be dedicated to: Hiawatha's Childhood, Hiawatha's Friends, Hiawatha's Sailing, Hiawatha's Wooing, and The White Man's Foot. Illustrate the main idea of each of these subtitles. On the last page write a short biography of Longfellow.
3. Research one of the following topics and write a paper to present to the class. Include at least one visual. Visuals can be pictures, maps, or objects.
   a. Minnesota
   b. Dakota Sioux
   c. Ojibway Indians
   d. Iroquois Indians
   e. The Milky Way

At the end of the essay, the student should prepare a "Works Cited" page that acknowledges his or her sources. The MLA (Modern Language Association) style is commonly used when citing works of literature. The list of resources are alphabetized by the author's last name or, if there is no author, by the first main word in the title:

Elson,William H. and Christine M. Keck. "Henry Wadsworth Longfellow." *The Elson Readers, Book 6*, Lake Wales, FL: Lost Classics Book Co., 2001, 346-347

Hoffman, Kathryn. "A Family That Digs Together..." *Time for Kids*. 1 May 2001: 4-5

Lukes, Bonnie L. *Henry Wadsworth Longfellow: America's Beloved Poet (World Writers)*. Greensboro, NC: Morgan Reynolds, Inc., 1998

Rabe, Roberto. "Henry Wadsworth Longfellow." 28 June 2001 http://eclecticesoterica.com/longfellow_bio.html

Robbins, J. Albert. "Henry Wadsworth Longfellow." *The World Book Encyclopedia*. 1985 ed

(Note: Titles of books are italicized if possible. If it is not possible to italicize as, for instance, when using a typewriter, then underlining should be used to denote italics.)

NATHANIEL HAWTHORNE—

THE PARADISE OF CHILDREN, P. 360

The Paradise of Children is a story taken from Greek mythology. The story takes place before children grew to adults when there was no labor and no troubles. An only child, Pandora, was brought to Epimetheus, also an only child, by Quicksilver to be his playmate. Prior to her arrival, Quicksilver had allowed Epimetheus to keep a beautifully carved box on the condition that he never open it. Pandora was constantly enthralled with the box and curious as to its contents. For quite a while, Epimetheus refused to answer any of Pandora's questions about the box until he gave in to help appease her curiosity. Pandora would spend hours studying the box and its gold rope binding. She imagined she heard murmurs from inside the box. Eventually, she could not stand not knowing what was in the box any longer, for she imagined all kinds of beautiful riches just for her locked inside. When Epimetheus was out playing, she opened the box and horrible creatures flew from it. These creatures were the Troubles of the earth. Epimetheus was angry with Pandora, but he too had been curious about the contents of the box. While despairing as to what to do, Pandora heard another voice from inside the box. Epimetheus agreed Pandora could open the box once again. This time, Hope came out to help ease people of the Troubles of the earth.

1. **How long ago did Pandora and Epimetheus live?**
   "Long, long ago when this old world was in its tender infancy" is when Pandora and Epimetheus lived.
2. **Find the lines that tell how different the world was then from what it is now.**
   Lines that tell how different the world was then from now can be found on page 361 lines 13-33 and page 362 lines 1-5.
3. **Where did the box come from?**
   The box was delivered to Epimetheus by Quicksilver "who looked very smiling and intelligent, and who could hardly forbear laughing".
4. **On what conditions was it given to Epimetheus?**
   The condition of Epimetheus keeping the box was that he should never open it.
5. **Find lines that describe the box.**
   Lines that describe the box are on page 365 lines 1-26.
6. **Why was Pandora interested in it?**
   Pandora was interested in the box because she thought it possibly contained pretty dresses, toys, or very nice things to eat.

7. **In what way was it a blessing to Pandora?**
It was not a blessing to Pandora when she let out the Troubles of the earth; only when she let out Hope did it become a blessing.
8. **What led her to open the box?**
Pandora's insatiable curiosity led her to open the box.
9. **Do you think Epimetheus was at fault? Why?**
Answers will vary. The author thinks Epimetheus was also at fault.
10. **What happened when Pandora raised the lid of the box?**
All the Troubles of the world escaped when Pandora raised the lid of the box.
11. **How did this affect the Paradise of Children?**
This affected the Paradise of Children because the children grew older and had to labor.
12. **What happened when Pandora opened the box a second time?**
Hope escaped when Pandora opened the box a second time.
13. **Why was Hope put into the box with the Troubles?**
Hope was packed in the box "to make amends to the human race for that swarm of ugly Troubles."
14. **Why are the wings of Hope like the rainbow?**
The wings of Hope are like a rainbow so that when people think Hope has left them, they might see the glimmer of her wings and know she is there.
15. **What does Hope do for us?**
Hope "spiritualizes the earth, Hope makes it always new; and, even in the earth's best and brightest aspect, Hope shows it to be only the shadow of an infinite bliss hereafter."
16. **What qualities in Epimetheus do you like?**
Answer will vary.
17. **What did Hope mean by saying she was partly made of tears?**
Hope meant that she is partially made of tears because Troubles accompany Hope.
18. **How does Hope "spiritualize" the earth, i.e., make it purer?**
Hope "spiritualizes" the earth by giving people better times for which to look forward.
19. **Tell what you can about the author.**
Refer to pages 359 and 360 for information about the author.

20. **On page 291 you were asked to notice the way in which these authors tell their stories. You have no doubt noticed that Hawthorne uses humor and fancy to add interest.**
21. **Point out examples of his humor.**
    Answers will vary.
22. **What quaint fancy has he about the way food was provided when the world was young, page 361?**
    The author talks about the trees bearing the children's dinner. In the morning they would see the bud of lunch getting ready to bloom. The children could just pick their meals from the trees.
23. **By what fancy does he increase our interest in the mystery of the box, page 368, lines 12 - 19?**
    To increase our interest in the box the author has Pandora hearing "murmurs" from inside the box.
24. **Class readings: Select passages to be read aloud in class.**
25. **Outline for testing silent reading. Tell the story briefly in your own words using the topic headings given in the story.**
26. **You will enjoy seeing the pictures in the editions of *The Wonder-Book* that is illustrated by the well-known artist, Maxfield Parrish.**
27. **Find in the glossary the meaning of: caroling, mysterious, whence, pettishly, intelligent (pp. 361-363), babble, combine (pp. 364-365), pried, restore (pp. 368-369), constant, intent, pestered (pp. 371-374), witchery, personage, glimmer, lightsome (pp. 375-378).**
28. **Pronounce: Epimetheus, either, Pandora, threshold, livelong, disquietude, merry, forbear (pp. 360-363), accompany, perseveringly, vexations, profusion, mischievous, contrivance (pp. 364-367), ingenious, merest (pp. 368-369), lamentable, gigantic, molested, calamity (pp. 370-373), grievously, intolerable, hovered, destined, venomous, spiritualizes, aspect, infinite (pp. 374-378).**

Extended Activity:

1. For a quick reading check, have students answer true or false to the following statements:

F a. Pandora and Epimetheus were married.
F b. Epimetheus purchased the box from Quicksilver.
F c. Epimetheus tried to open the box, but couldn't.
T d. Pandora was always curious about the contents of the box.
T e. The children would play all day and never had to work or go to school.
T f. Pandora studied how to untie the knot around the box.
F g. Epimetheus agreed to allow Pandora to open the box.
T h. Swarms of Troubles flew out of the box and one stung Pandora.
T i. Hope was the last thing to come out of the box.

2. Have students read the account of Adam and Eve from Genesis 2-3. In a class discussion compare and contrast the story from Genesis with "The Paradise of Children." Draw a Venn Diagram on the board or on chart paper. Record the students' responses. A Venn Diagram is a visual way to represent similarities and differences between two things. The part of the circles that overlap should contain the similarities and the outer circles the differences.

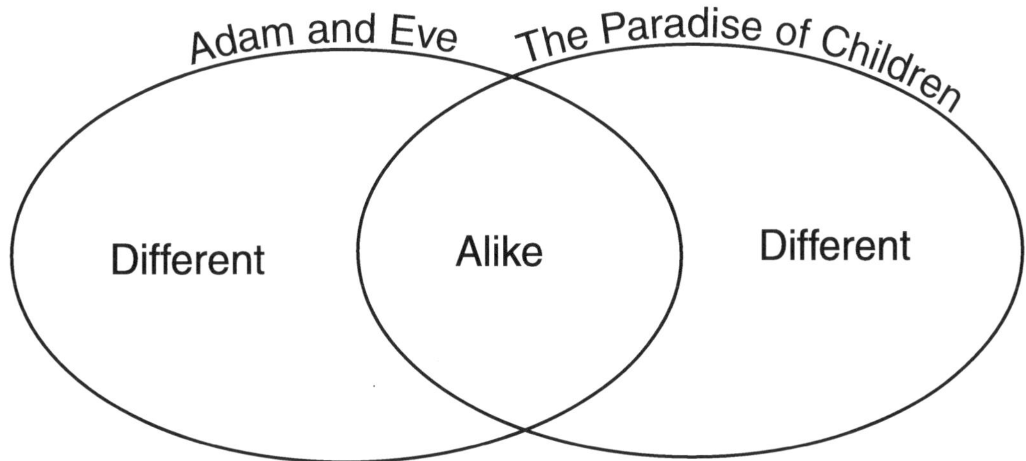

NAME______________________________CLASS__________DATE______

THE PARADISE OF CHILDREN, P. 360

1. For a reading check, circle true or false to the following statements:

True False a. Pandora and Epimetheus were married.

True False b. Epimetheus purchased the box from Quicksilver.

True False c. Epimetheus tried to open the box, but couldn't.

True False d. Pandora was always curious about the contents of the box.

True False e. The children would play all day and never had to work or go to school.

True False f. Pandora studied how to untie the knot around the box.

True False g. Epimetheus agreed to allow Pandora to open the box.

True False h. Swarms of Troubles flew out of the box and one stung Pandora.

True False i. Hope was the last thing to come out of the box.

2. Compare and contrast the story from Genesis with The Paradise of Children using the Venn Diagram below.

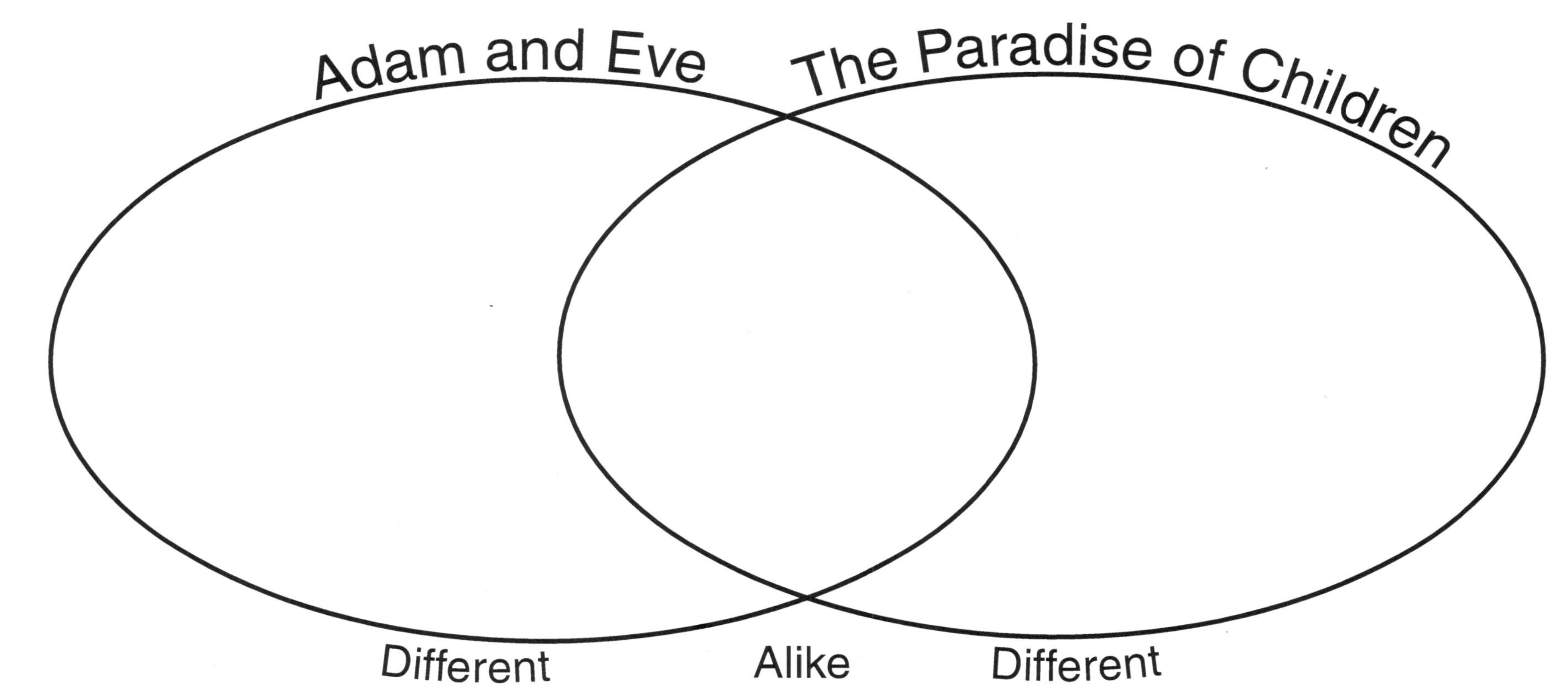

The Golden Touch, p. 380

The Golden Touch is a story about a man who in the beginning loved gold more than anything else. King Midas had a daughter, Marygold, whom he also loved dearly. He thought the best thing he could do for her is have more gold. Marygold, however, cared more for the fragrant flowers and nature's beauty than she did gold. One day a little man visited King Midas while he was admiring his treasures. The man asked the king the one thing that would satisfy him. The king answered that he wished whatever he touched be turned to gold. Sure enough, the next morning things he touched turned to gold. During breakfast he turned his daughter's bowl into gold as well as some roses. Marygold was not happy. When the king went to console her, Marygold turned into gold. This saddened the king greatly. The little man appeared again and asked King Midas if he had learned a lesson. To reverse the effects the king had to wash in the river and fill a pitcher with the water. He was to sprinkle the water on anything that was gold that he wished turned back. Of course, he first regained his daughter.

1. **How did Midas think he could best show his love for his daughter?**
   He thought he could best show his love by giving her more gold.
2. **What was his chief pleasure?**
   His chief pleasure was going through his treasures.
3. **Describe the visitor who appeared to Midas in his treasure room.**
   "It was a young man with a cheerful and ruddy face" and he threw a yellow tinge over everything.
4. **What did the stranger ask him?**
   The stranger asked Midas what would most satisfy him.
5. **Find the sentence that tells what Midas wished.**
   King Midas said, "I wish everything that I touch to be changed to gold."
6. **When did he receive his new power?**
   He received his new power with the first sunray of the morning.
7. **What use did he make of it?**
   King Midas touched his sheets and clothes and the roses in the garden.
8. **What did Marygold think of the gold roses?**
   She did not like the gold roses because they had lost their color and scent.

9. **Why was not Midas's breakfast a success?**
His breakfast wasn't a success because he could not eat it. Everytime he went to put food in his mouth, it turned to gold.
10. **When did Midas first doubt whether riches are the most desirable thing in the world?**
He first doubted whether riches were the most desirable thing when he decided he might get hungry.
11. **How did he drive this thought away?**
He drove this thought away by thinking of the pleasure the gold brought him.
12. **What made him realize that his little daughter was dearer to him than gold?**
He realized his daughter meant more to him than gold when she, herself, turned into gold.
13. **Find lines that tell what he realized when it was too late.**
He said, "My precious, precious Marygold."
14. **What did the stranger ask when he came again?**
The stranger asked him, "How do you succeed with the golden touch?"
15. **What was the discovery that Midas had made since the stranger's first visit?**
He discovered that gold was not the most important thing in life.
16. **How was Midas cured of the Golden Touch?**
Midas was cured of the Golden Touch by washing in the river.
17. **What was he told to do in order to restore Marygold to life?**
He was told to plunge in the river, fill a vase with water, and sprinkle it over every object he wanted to be turned "from gold into its former substance."
18. **What was the only gold he cared about after he was saved from the Golden Touch?**
The only gold he cared about after he was saved from the Golden Touch was the golden highlights in his daughter's hair.
19. **Find examples of humor; of fanciful expressions, such as "day had hardly peeped over the hills," page 384, lines 17, 18; of descriptions that you like.**
20. **Class readings: Select passages to be read aloud in class.**

21. Outline for testing silent reading: Tell the story briefly in your own words, using the topic headings given in the story.

22. Find in the glossary the meaning of: purpose, mortal, inhaling, induce (pp. 380-384); flexibility, balustrade, burnished, afflicted (pp. 385-387); affright, consideration, perplexity, fatal, agony, infinitely (pp. 390-392); desperate, earthen, conscious, molten (pp. 393-394).

23. Pronounce: Midas, calculate, particularly, obscure, tinge, extraordinary, meditated, lustrous (pp. 380-383), composure, blighted (pp. 386-387); hue, cupboard, molten, aghast, admirably, metallic, frothy, pitiable, ravenous, indigestible, victuals, phrase (pp. 388-391); recognized, parched, avarice (pp. 392-393).

Extended Exercise:

F 1. King Midas named his little girl Marygold.

T 2. As a king, Midas spent most of his day in his dark, gloomy basement.

F 3. When Midas awoke the first morning after meeting the stranger, the very first object he touched turned to gold.

F 4. Marygold was thrilled to find the gold roses.

T 5. Marygold feasted on bread and milk for breakfast.

F 6. King Midas's rich breakfast was the best he had ever tasted.

T 7. Midas would rather give up breakfast than lose the Golden Touch.

T 8. Midas only regretted the Golden Touch after Marygold turned to gold.

F 9. Midas could only get rid of the Golden Touch by taking a swim.

T 10. The sparkle in the sand and the golden glow in Marygold's hair were all that remained to remind Midas of the Golden Touch.

NAME______________________________**CLASS**__________**DATE**______

THE GOLDEN TOUCH, P. 380

For a reading check, circle true or false to the following statements:

True False 1. King Midas named his little girl Marygold.

True False 2. As a king, Midas spent most of his day in his dark, gloomy basement.

True False 3. When Midas awoke the first morning after meeting the stranger, the very first object he touched turned to gold.

True False 4. Marygold was thrilled to find the gold roses.

True False 5. Marygold feasted on bread and milk for breakfast.

True False 6. King Midas's rich breakfast was the best he had ever tasted.

True False 7. Midas would rather give up breakfast than lose the Golden Touch.

True False 8. Midas only regretted the Golden Touch after Marygold turned to gold.

True False 9. Midas could only get rid of the Golden Touch by taking a swim.

True False 10. The sparkle in the sand and the golden glow in Marygold's hair were all that remained to remind Midas of the Golden Touch.

NAME______________________________ **CLASS**__________ **DATE**______

Story	***Find in the glossary the meaning of:***
Reader p. 293	**coppers**________________________
	voluntarily________________________
	vexation________________________
	ambitious________________________
	esteem________________________
	contracts________________________
Reader p. 298	**beechen**________________________
	russett________________________
	train________________________
	jet________________________
	unapt________________________
Reader p. 303	**shuttle**________________________
	spire________________________
	sear________________________
	verdant________________________
	wain________________________
	lapsed________________________
Reader p. 307	**glean**________________________
	hardy________________________
	meads________________________
	furrows________________________
	frosted________________________
	mildew________________________
	adorn________________________
Reader p. 311	**toilsome**________________________
	gullies________________________
	circumference________________________
	prime________________________
	skirted fugitives________________________
	brake________________________
	defile________________________
Reader p. 316	**hoodwinked**________________________
	vault________________________
	maze________________________
	cathedral________________________
	pest________________________
	ducat________________________
Reader p. 323	**raid**________________________
	match________________________

Reader p. 326 **reverberations** ______

fenlands ______

linden ______

frolic ______

nostrils ______

reeds ______

frenzy ______

listless ______

cowering ______

clamber ______

ponder ______

sported ______

stately ______

larch ______

channel ______

cord ______

nimble ______

moor ______

fallow ______

swerve ______

jasper ______

flags ______

rushes ______

basswood ______

flaunting ______

tittered ______

hither ______

counsels ______

Reader p. 360 **caroling** ______

mysterious ______

whence ______

pettishly ______

intelligent ______

babble ______

combine ______

pried ______

restore ______

constant ______

intent ______

pestered ______

witchery ______

personage ______

glimmer ______

Reader p. 380

lightsome_______________________________________
purpose_______________________________________
mortal_______________________________________
inhaling_______________________________________
induce_______________________________________
flexibility_______________________________________
balustrade_______________________________________
burnished_______________________________________
afflicted_______________________________________
affright_______________________________________
consideration_______________________________________
perplexity_______________________________________
fatal_______________________________________
agony_______________________________________
infinitely_______________________________________
desperate_______________________________________
earthen_______________________________________
conscious_______________________________________
molten_______________________________________
purpose_______________________________________

Pronounce:

directly, chagrin, sacrificing, levee, accumulating, laudable, equipage, accosted, ere, parent, gorgeous, humble, genial, wilding, azure, isles, ay, autumnal, chastened, beneath, sphere, wrought, radiance, tranquil, mow, serene, psalm, hoard, lavish, glossy, root, diminutive, ruminating, herbage, maneuver, kept, lariat, circuit, reappeared, rangers, handerchiefs, rearing, marred, Granada, señor, ponderous, ghastly, obliterated, route, gaunt, hovel, curmudgeon, daunted, lower, banditti, dungeon, legends, wigwams, aerie, moss, sinews, warrior, haunches, alder, palpitated, exulted, pliant, wand, pathos, allied, asunder, quoit, triumphant, horror, hewed, tamarack, fibrous, forehead, balm, balsam, resin, fissure, crevice, bosom, resplendent, supple, veered, swam, dissuading, feuds, wounds, chalcedony, plaiting, bade, spacious, benignant, mystic, imperious, pinions, derision, vision, regions, vague, warring, Epimetheus, either, Pandora, threshold, livelong, disquietude, merry, forbear, accompany, perseveringly, vexations, profusion, mischievous, contrivance, ingenious, merest, lamentable, gigantic, molested, calamity, grievously, intolerable,

hovered, destined, venomous, spiritualizes, aspect, infinite, Midas, calculate, particularly, obscure, tinge, extraordinary, meditated, lustrous, composure, blighted, hue, cupboard, molten, aghast, admirably, metallic, frothy, pitiable, ravenous, indigestible, victuals, phrase, recognized, parched, avarice.

Appendix I
Instructional Aids

The first section of this appendix, "Silent and Oral Reading," appears in the original *Elson Readers, Book Seven* and offers the teacher and parent a useful method of assisting the student(s) in attaining the objectives in this guide. The remaining aids have been written specially for this guide by the authors as additional resources for the teacher and parent.

Silent and Oral Reading

Silent Reading. This book includes abundant material for both silent and oral reading. Some stories and poems must be read thoughtfully in order to gain the author's full meaning; such reading cannot be done rapidly. In other selections the meaning can be grasped easily, and the reading can be rapid; in such cases we read mainly for the central thought, for the story element.

You read silently more often than you read aloud to others; you should, therefore, train yourself in rapid silent reading, concentrating your mind on the thought of the selection. You will soon discover that as you give closer attention to a story you will not only understand it better, but you will also remember more of it. In previous grades your training in silent reading has enabled you to gather facts from individual paragraphs and to hold in mind the thread of the narrative in shorter selections. But you are to extend this power steadily until you can gather facts and follow the unfolding plot in selections of considerable length. A number of stories in this book are long enough to train you to read with intelligence a newspaper, a magazine article, or a book. And this is precisely the ability you most need, not only in preparing lessons in history and other school subjects, but in all your reading throughout life. As you train yourself to grasp swiftly and accurately the meaning of a page, you increase your capacity to enjoy books—one of the most pleasurable things in life. Theodore Roosevelt trained himself to be such a rapid reader that he was able to grasp the central thought of a page almost as quickly as he could turn the leaves of the book.

In preparing lessons in geography and history and in the use of geographical and historical stories, you have a splendid opportunity to increase your ability to gather facts quickly from the printed page. These informational studies, however, do not take the place of the reading lesson in literature. They merely offer additional opportunity for you to increase your ability in rapid silent reading.

Notice that the rapid silent readers in your class generally gain and retain from their reading more facts than the slow readers do. Notice, too, that you read more rapidly when you are looking for the answer to some particular question or looking for a certain passage than you do when you read merely to follow the thread of the story. Moving your lips or pointing to the words with your finger retards your speed. In the selections in this book suggested for silent reading you may test your ability at thought-getting in any of the following ways:

1. By using a list of questions covering the most important ideas of the selection
2. By telling the story from a given outline
3. By making a list of questions yourself, allowing some classmate to use them to test his or her ability at thought-getting, while you make similar use of his or her questions.
4. By telling the story from an outline that you have made. Telling the substance of the story from your own outline is an excellent kind of test because you test not only your understanding of the story, but also your memory and your power to express the thought of what you have read.

In all your reading, both at home and at school, you should read as rapidly as you can, but not so fast that you fail to get the thought. In preparing your lessons on selections in this book, test yourself by seeing how many of the questions, under "Discussion," that develop the most important thoughts of the story, you can answer after one reading. You may have to read parts of the story more than once in order to gain the full meaning. If, from time to time, you record your reading speed and your thought-getting ability, comparing your standing with that of your classmates and with the standard for seventh grade pupils, you will be able to see whether or not you are making satisfactory progress. The standard for seventh grade boys and girls is 250 words per minute, with the ability to reproduce after one reading 50% of the ideas in a 400-word passage.

The following form will suggest a way to record the results of your test:

INDIVIDUAL RECORD

Date	Titles	Speed		Comprehension
		No. of minutes required to read story	No. words per minute	Ten points for each of ten test questions*
	Hunting the Grizzly Bear Total No. Words, 1957			
	The Great Stone Face... Total No. Words, 7475			

*Questions to be selected by the teacher.

CLASS RECORD

Date	Speed			Comprehension			
	No. words per minute			Ten points for each of ten test questions			
	Lowest	Highest	Median	Lowest	Highest	Median	

Oral Reading. In the prose selections suggested for silent reading, you will wish to read aloud certain passages because of their beauty, their dramatic quality, or the forceful way in which the author has expressed his thoughts. In these selections, "Class Readings" are listed for this purpose. Sometimes these readings are intended for individual pupils; sometimes, particularly in dialogue, they are intended for groups. "Class Readings" include also supplementary poems and stories suggested for oral presentation.

In general, all poetry should be read aloud, for much of the beauty of poetry lies in its rhythm. The voice, with its infinite possibilities of change, is an important factor in interpreting a poem. As you listen to your teacher or some other good reader, you will appreciate how much pleasure one who has learned the art of reading is able to give others. Oral reading trains the ear of the listener to become sensitive to a pleasing voice, to correct pronunciation, and to distinct articulation. The sympathetic reading of many of the poems in this book will reveal to you the beauty of the language that we speak and by which we express our thoughts. Longfellow says, "Of equal honor with him who writes a grand poem is he who reads it grandly."

Outline for Oral Presentations

The following rubric is a general guideline to consider when critiquing student oral presentations. As the teacher, you may want to assign a point value to each of the items which you consider to be pertinent to the assignment.

General Guidelines

	Points Possible	Points Earned
Completed on time		
Fulfilled the guidelines of the assignment		
Message: **Clear and pertinent**		
Appealing and detailed		
Research: **Current and varied**		
Properly cited		
Technology: **Used technical materials, i.e., computer, puppets, tools appropriately**		
Used art materials i.e. wood, paint, paper creatively		
Presentation: **Good posture**		
Eye contact with the audience		
Voice control, volume, rate and expression		
Body language shows enthusiasm		

Presentation Checklist:

The following checklist is designed to assist the student in gathering materials and information for an oral presentation. The student should be encouraged to complete the proposal and review it with the teacher to ensure a well-organized presentation.

Proposal

Topic on which I'll speak

____

Supporting facts I plan to use

____

____

____

____

Supporting anecdotes or stories to interest my listeners

____

____

____

____

Visual aids to enhance my speech

____

____

Musical background to accompany my speech

____

____

Technological equipment I will need

____

____

What do I want my listeners to learn from this presentation

____

____

My concluding punch line

____

The Stages of the Writing Process

Throughout the reader, students are encouraged to write essays on a variety of topics for a variety of audiences and purposes. The following general guideline for the stages of the writing process will assist the student in producing a meaningful, well-organized, well-crafted essay. The writing process includes four stages: prewrite, draft, edit/revise, final copy.

Prewrite Planning Guide:

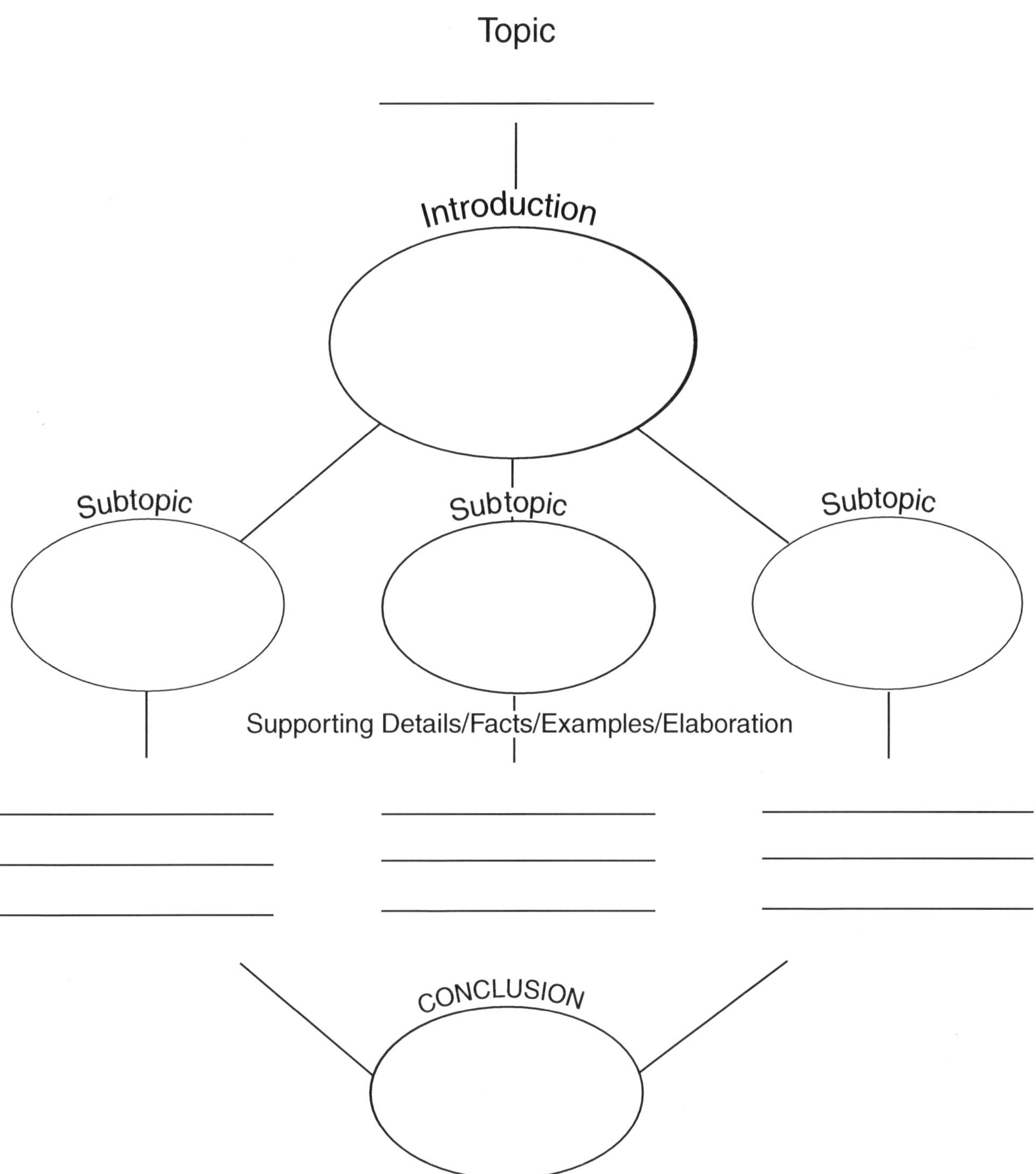

1. Introduction:

I. Students should develop their paper with the following elements:

A. Introduction:

a. Hook sentence—This sentence "hooks" the interest of the reader. A hook sentence can be a quote, a question, an interesting fact, or anecdote.

b. Thesis sentence—This sentence must include the subject about which the paper is written and an opinion. For example: Those living near the Mississippi River need to be prepared for floods. NOT: I'm going to write about floods along the Mississippi River.

c. Map sentence—This sentence lists the three main points of the body of the paper.

2. Body:

Develop the main reasons, one paragraph for each reason, using vivid sensory details. As appropriate use statistics, quotations, stories, and examples to support the reason. Use transitions appropriately at the beginning and within each body paragraph.

TREEES paragraphs

Topic
Reason
Elaboration
Example
Elaboration
Summary

3. Conclusion:

Restate the thesis and summarize your main reasons. Challenge the reader with a closing thought, action, or recommendation. In the conclusion, do not use exact words or phrases from the introduction.

Edit/Revise:

Review the essay to make sure it is organized with vivid details and examples that support the thesis, the tone is appropriate for the audience, and word choice is precise and lively. Sentences should be complete and varied in length and structure. Grammar should be appropriate, and spelling and punctuation are generally correct.

Final Draft:

Rewrite the essay to include the revisions made in the editing stage.

Evaluation Rubric (Checklist):

At right.

	Points Possible	Points Earned
Planning:		
Draft:		
Revision/ Editing:		
Final Copy: **Conventions** spelling, punctuation, grammar		
Supporting Details		
Neatness		
Introduction		
Conclusion		
Organization		

Appendix II

A Brief Description of World War One

by Andy Jameson

World War One had ended just a few years before the original *Elson Readers* appeared. This event was fresh in the mind of Americans and profoundly changed the way they looked at themelves and their role in the world. This changed outlook is reflected in *The Elson Readers*, in both the literature that was included and in the study questions. This brief description of that great event is provided as both a source of background information and a starting point for parents, teachers, and students to begin discussions on this turning point in American history.

World War One (also known as the Great War) lasted for four years—from 1914 to the end of 1918. The war was fought between Germany and its allies (Austria-Hungary of the Hapsburg Empire and Turkey of the Ottoman Empire) known as the Central Powers (or the Triple Alliance), and Great Britain, France, Russia, Italy, Japan, and, from 1917, the United States called the Allies. Germany was forced to fight the war on two fronts: the Western Front against the Allies and the Eastern Front against Russia. It was the first international conflict in which the United States participated.

The leading causes of the war were the alliance system of the late nineteenth century, which divided European states into two contending camps; the German victory over France in the Franco-German War (1870-71); the unification of Germany under Chancellor Otto von Bismarck and its rapid industrialization; the nationalist and ethnic agitation in the Balkans; and the fact that by 1900, European states were engaged in an escalating arms race and building vast military and naval forces in peacetime. The alliance system was symptomatic of the tension in European society between the growth of an international economy—the competition for goods and markets—and the political outlook of European states based on their own narrow national interests.

Bismarck set out to build a German empire based on the nationalistic premise that Germany also deserved a "place in the sun"—which meant an international political, economic, and military position like that of the British Empire. In Europe, the Germans claimed that they were being encircled by France and Russia. The entrance of Germany into the world scene exacerbated the intense rivalry for power and colonial markets in Africa, the Near East, and the Far East, as well as control of the seas. When the Germans decided to build a navy in 1891, they began the Anglo-German naval race.

The "race for empire" led to crises in Morocco, where Germany sent a gunboat to protect German interests, and in the Balkans, where Germany supported its Austrian ally against the national liberation movements which threatened the integrity of the Austro-Hungarian Empire. The three Balkan Wars (1912-1913), which were a prelude to World War One, also involved the Turks, whose Ottoman Empire had been disintegrating under the liberation movements of the Greeks and the southern Slavic peoples (Serbs, Croats, Bulgarians), and the Russians, who intervened in the Balkans as the "big Slavic" protectors of the Orthodox Christians—thus posing a threat to the Central Powers.

It was the nationalist movements in the Balkans which provided the "spark" that began World War One. On June 29, 1914, the heir to the Hapsburg Empire, Archduke Franz Ferdinand, was assassinated in Sarajevo (the capital of Bosnia). The Germans supported their Austrian ally, while the French supported the Russians. Protected by their navy, the British tried to maintain their policy of "splendid isolation," but the threat to the British naval forces in the North Sea from the German fleet, and with the French coast of the Channel open to German naval attack, the British were forced to protect their sea lanes and defend their French ally. When the Russians refused a German demand to stop their mobilization on the eastern border, Germany declared war (August 1, 1914), and France followed with its declaration (August 3). And when the Germans launched their Schlieffen Plan—a military strategy which involved a rapid thrust through Belgium to crush the French forces (in violation of the treaty which guaranteed the neutrality of Belgium)—Great Britain also declared war on Germany (August 4).

To supply their Russian ally, the British and French launched a disastrous naval attack on Turkey via the Dardanelles (1915), but the campaign was called off when the Allies lost 143,000 killed or wounded in the Gallipoli campaign.

On the Eastern Front, the early Russian offensive of 1914, which had driven into German territories in Prussia, Poland, and Galicia, was stopped and driven back by the Austro-German offensive of 1915.

By 1916, the war of maneuver on the Western Front ground to a halt, and it became a war of position and attrition—the massive armies were deadlocked in trench warfare. The machine gun—a new weapon—immobilized the troops which could advance only with staggering losses, while the tank, which was to become the antidote to the machine gun, and the airplane, the future antidote to the tank, were still in the experimental stages of development as weapons of war. The stalemate on the Western Front, however, ended when the Russians withdrew from, and the Americans entered, the war. The imperial Russian armies, plagued by poor military leadership and inadequate supplies, collapsed, and Czar Nicholas II was forced to abdicate from the internal pressure of the socialists (Marxists), especially from the leader of the Bolsheviks, the extreme faction of the Russian Marxists, V. I. Lenin (who formed the Communist party). When the czar abdicated, Lenin seized power in November, 1917, and the Bolsheviks signed the treaty of Brest-Litovsk with the Germans (December 3, 1917). At this point the war shifted to the Western Front, where the German High Command, under its Generals Hindenburg and Ludendorff, planned an offensive against the Allies. The Germans moved their army from the Russian front to the west via the railroad.

The German policy of unrestricted submarine warfare led United States President Woodrow Wilson to break off diplomatic relations with Germany, and when the British ship Lusitania was sunk with American passengers on board, and American ships were lost to U-boat action, he asked Congress for a declaration of war "to make the world safe for democracy,"(April 2, 1917). But it would be one year before the American military force and industrial production were prepared for war, and American soldiers arrived on the Western Front. With conscription administered by a Selective Service system, the armed services built a force of over four million. The government undertook the massive task of converting producers in the lumber, steel, automobile, and other industries to war production. Shipping tonnage increased from one million to ten million tons. The war effort encouraged citizens to conserve food (sugar was rationed and meatless Tuesdays were introduced) and fuel (daylight-saving time was adopted to save coal), and to purchase government Liberty bonds—the Treasury Department staged rallies at which Hollywood stars appeared to promote bond sales. At the same time, farmers were induced to grow more crops, and the production of civilian goods was cut (75,000 tons of tin were diverted to military production from children's toys and 8,000 tons of steel from the manufacture of women's corsets to munitions). The United States also provided loans to the Allies, which they used to purchase food and supplies.

While American military and economic power were geared up, the French and British suffered great losses in holding the line on the Western Front. When asked about an allied offensive, French General Pétain said, "I am waiting for the Americans and the tanks." In June, 1918, American troops under the command of General John J. Pershing, engaged the Germans at the Battles of Château-Thierry, Belleau Wood, and the Argonne, as 250,000 Americans were landing in France each month. Faced with this allied buildup, the German command realized that Germany could not win the war, and the government of Kaiser Wilhelm II began peace negotiations. By the time the armistice was signed (November 11, 1918), there were two million American soldiers in France and another million were heading for Europe. The Allies suffered ten million killed and twenty million casualties in the war, and the United States lost 115,000 dead and 315,000 casualties. While the allied losses far surpassed those of the Americans, it was the specter and the reality of American military and economic power that were decisive in ending the war.

In military history, World War One is notable for the brutal conditions under which the war was fought and for the incompetent leadership of the commanders—and the effect on the morale and discipline of the troops. The idea that soldiers were "manipulated from above" subject to the traditional military concept of obedience based on punishment resulted in revision of the military code of conduct.

Among the legacies of the war, which affected the course of the twentieth century, were the creation of the League of Nations (an international consortium), the rise of totalitarianism, and the imperial partition of the Near East (which resulted in the future states of Iraq, Syria, and Jordan).

GLOSSARY

a as in mat
e as in bed
i as in tip
ȯ as in saw

ə as in banana
ər as in further
ā as in day
ȯi as in coin
ᵊ as in eaten

ä as in father
aů as in loud
ē as in need
ü as in rule
th as in heather

Ø as in side
ŋ as in sing
ō as in snow
ů as in pull

A

a bashed (ə-'basht) ashamed

ab bey ('a-bē) the home of monks

ab bot ('a-bət) head of an abbey

above his for tune ('fȯr-chən) more than he can afford

ab so lute ly (ab-sə-'lut-lē) positively

ab surd in ven tions (əb-'sərd; in-'ven-shənz) made-up stories not believable

a byss (ə-'bis) a space so deep as not to be easily measured

ac com pa ny (ə-'kəmp-nē) go with

ac cost ed (ə-'kȯst-ed) spoken to

ac cout ered (ə-'kü-tərd) dressed

ac cu mu lat ing (ə-'kyü-mə-la-tiŋ) piling up

ac quaint ed (ə 'kwānt ed) friendly with each other

ad age ('a-dij) saying

Ad ji dau mo (äd-ji-'dȯ-mō)

ad mi ra bly ('ad-mə-rə-blē) well

a do (ə-'dü) fuss

a dorn (ə-'dȯrn) decorate

ad vance his people (əd-'vans) help his tribe of Indians to be better

ad vis ers (əd-'vØz-erz) men with whom he talked

adz ('adz) tool for trimming wood

ae rie ('ar-ē) high nest

Ae sop (ē-säp) a Greek slave who wrote many little stories

af flict ed (ə-'flikt-ed) distressed

af flict ed the souls (ə-'flikt-ed) made people do wrong

af flic tion (ə-'flick-shən) trouble

af fright (ə-'frØt) alarm

aft er math ('aft-ər-math) second crop

a gain (ə-'gen) once more

against all com ers ('kə-merz) with anyone he meets
age of doubt time when people are not ready to believe
a ghast (ə-'gast) startled
a gil i ty (ə-'ji-lə-tē) quickness
ag o ny ('a-gə-nē) grief
Ah meek (ə-'mek)
Ah mo ('ə-mo)
A lad din (ə-'la-dən)
al der ('ȯl-der) a kind of tree
a lert (ə-'lərt) watchful
A li Ba ba (a-lē-'bä-bə)
al lied ('a-lØd) joined
all in their best dressed in their best clothes
all its en dear ments (in-'dir-mənts) everything that makes it dear
al lot ted time ('ə-lät-ed) time granted for doing anything
al ma nacs ('ȯl-mə-naks) small books containing a yearly calendar with little stories
al oes ('a-lōz) a precious wood
al ter nate ('ȯl-tər-nāt) first one, then the other
am bi tious (am-'bi-shəs) eager for
am bush in the oak tree ('am-bu̇sh) hiding place in the oak
am e thyst ('a-mə-thəst) a clear purple or bluish violet; a precious stone
an cient ('ānt-shənt) old; of old time
an ec dote ('a-nik-dōt) a story
a nem o nes (ə-'ne-mō-nēz) wild flowers of pale, dainty colors
a new (ə-'nü) again
animal spirits loud, rough play
An ne mee kee (ən-ə-'mē-kē)
An toine ('an-twan)
anx ious ('ank-shəs) troubled
ape the ways of pride try to copy the actions of proud people
a poth e ca ry (ə-'pä-thə-ker-e) druggist
ap peared con cerned (ə-'pird; kən-sərnd) seemed anxious
apple from the pine pineapple
ap point ed (ə-'pȯint-ed) chosen beforehand for the feast
ap proached (ə-'prōcht) went near to
ap proach the bounds (ə-'prōch) come near the edge
Ar a bic ('ar-ə-bik) language of Arabs
arch and laughing tone (ärch) merry, teasing voice
ar cher y ('är-chər-ē) shooting with bow and arrow
arch ing (ar-chiŋ) curving

arching blue sky
arch of the sun lit bow (ärch; 'sun-lit; 'bō) curve of the rainbow
arch way of rock ('ärch-wā) meeting place overhead of two rock walls
ar ray (ə-'rā) order
ar tif i cer (är-'ti-fə-sər) skilled worker
ash-cakes unsweetened cakes baked on a hot shovel laid on the ashes
as pect ('as-pekt) outlook; state
as pen bow er ('as-pən; 'bau̇-er) thicket of trees, the leaves of which are easily moved by the wind
as pir ing gen ius ('a-spØr-iŋ; 'jēn-yəs) clever person who is trying to rise
as sem bled (ə-'sem-bəld) collected
as sumed the ap pear ance of (ə-'sumd; ə-'pir-əns) looked like
as ters in the brook ('as tərz) reflection of the asters in the water
a stir (ə-'stər) moving around
as ton ished (ə-'stän-isht) surprised
a stride the traces (ə-'strØd) having one leg over one of the straps which fastened the plow to the horses
a sun der (ə-'sun-dər) apart
at ten dance on lev ees (ə-'ten-dəns; 'le-vēz) going to receptions
attend his pleas ure ('ple-zhur) do his bidding
at their glit ter ing best ('gli-tər-iŋ) shining as bright as possible
au di ble ('ȯ-də-bəl) that can be heard
aught but tender any way except kind
au tum nal (ȯ-'təm-nəl) of autumn
av a rice ('a-və-rəs) greed
a vert ed (ə-'vərt-ed) turned aside
a wak en ing of the woods (ə-'wāk-niŋ) the budding of the forest trees
a wry (ə-'rØ) crooked
ay (Ø) yes
az ure ('a-zhər) sky-blue; the air
az ure space blue air above

B

bab ble ('ba-bəl) chatter
bade (bād) told; told to
bal as ('ba-ləs) a kind of ruby
balked (bȯkt) stopped balm
balm (bälm) sticky dried juice
bal sam ('bȯl-səm) same as balm
bal us trade ('ba-ləs-trād) railing

band ag es ('ban-dij-ez) strips of cloth
ban dit ti (ban-'di-tē) robbers
bar ter it all ('bär-tər) trade all that I have gained
bass wood ('bas-wůd) wood of the linden tree
bat tle ments ('ba-təl-mənts) irregular top of the high walls of a castle
bay ou ('bØ-ü) inlet
ba zaars (bə-'zärz) shops; market-place
beam ray of light
beaming ('bē-miŋ) shining
bear me ill-will dislike me
bear no mal ice ('ma-ləs) have no ill-will
beast of prey (prā) flesh-eating animal
Beat te ('bē-tə)
beat us holler do things we cannot do
beau te ous summer glow ('byü-tē-əs) lovely brightness of summer time
be calmed (bi-'kalmd) prevented from sailing because of lack of wind
beech en ('bēch-en) of the beech tree
be fall (bi-'fȯl) happen to
be guile (bi-'gØl) charm
be guiled (bi-'gØld) tricked
behold it a fore time (ə-'fōr-tØm) see it before it arrived
be lated thriftless va grant (bi-'lāt-təd; 'vā-grənt) tardy, lazy wanderer
bel fry ('bel-frē) tower for a bell
be moan himself (bi-'mōn) groan softly
be neath (bi-'nēth)
be nev o lent friendship (bə-'nev-ə-lənt) kind and generous acts of a friend
be nig nant (bə-'nig-nənt) kindly
be seems his qual i ty (bə-'sēmz; 'kwä-lə-tē) fits his rank
beside himself with joy so happy he did not know what to do
be smeared (bi-'smird) covered
best of cheer things that make one most happy
be trayed (bi-'trād) given me to my enemy by a trick
be wild er ment (bi-'wil-dər-mənt) perplexity
be witch ing ly per sua sive (bi-'wi-chiŋ-lē; pər-'swā-siv) charmingly coaxing
Big-Sea-Water Lake Superior
bil lowed like a rus set ocean ('bi-lōd; 'rə-sət) reddish grass blew like waves
Bish op of Bing en ('bi-shəp; 'bing-ən) Hatto, who starved the poor and was shut up in a tower, where mice devoured him
bi son ('bØ-sən) American buffalo
blanc-mange (blə-'maŋ) a dessert of starchy substances and milk
blare ('blar) blow harshly

blast ('blast) hard wind; loud, long sound
blazing in the sky showing bright against the sky
Ble fus cu (ble-'fəs-cū)
blend ed ranks ('blen-dəd) mixed lines
blight ed ('blØ-təd) withered
blithe ('blØth) happy; joyous
blossoming ground earth covered with flowers
blue day day when the sky is clear
blur in the eye tear
boar (bōr) wild hog
bon ny ('bä-nē) gay
boom ing ('bü-miŋ) hollow-sounding
boon ('bün) favor
borne their part ('bȯrn) done their share
born to rule the storm naturally able to do anything
bos om ('bu-zəm) front part
bound a ry ('baủn-də-rē) marking a division; separating
bound boy boy hired out to work by the year for his board and a small wage
bound by a spell charmed so that I could not move
boundless space the endless extent of the regions of the air
bound to him made them love him
boun ties ('baủn-tēz) generous gifts
boun ti ful trav e ler ('baủn-tē ful; 'trav-əl-ər) generous traveler
Bow doin ('bō-dən)
bow ers ('bau-ərz) lovely rooms
boul ders ('bōl-dərz) large stones
brake ('brāk) valley enclosed by hills
braves Indian men ready to fight
brawn y ('brȯ-nē) strong
break ers ('brā-kərz) big waves striking the shore
break my fast eat my meal
breathed a song sang a song softly
breech es ('brē-chəz) short trousers
bri dled ('brØ-dəld) put the headpiece on
brig ('brig) sailing ship with two masts
bright ened as he sped ('brØ-tənd) grew brighter as he mounted up into the sky
brightest as pect ('as-pekt) look that is most attractive
brin dled ('brin-dəld) having dark streaks or spots on a gray or yellowish brown ground; streaked
bring the hunting homeward carry home what I shoot

broad-faced sun round, cheerful sun.
bro cades (brō-'kādz) heavy silk woven with a raised figure or flower
brood ing ('brü-diŋ) thinking sadly
broom a shrub with yellow flowers
brought to bale ('bāl) made trouble for
buf fet ('bə-fət) slap
bulge ('bəlj) place bent in
bul lies ('bu̇-lēz) teases
bul wark ('bu̇l-wərk) protection; defense
bun ting ('bən-tiŋ) cloth for flags
buoy ('bü-ē) float
bur i al ('ber-ē-əl) act of placing in a grave
bur nished ('bər-nisht) shining
Bus so rah ('bus-ō-rä)
by dint of great quickness ('dint) by acting very fast
by way of sat is fy ing ('sat-əs-fØ-iŋ) in order to quiet the prickings of

C

ca lam i ty (kə-'la-mə-tē) misfortune
cal cu late ('kal-kyə-lāt) figure up
ca liph ('kā-ləf) an Eastern title
calked ('kȯkt) stopped up
calls but the warders ('wȯr-dərz) only calls the watchmen
calm (kälm) a period of quiet
came into the knowledge of was told
came into the world took part in the business, political, social, etc., activities of the world
can oe with pin ions (ka-'nü; 'pin-yənz) sailboat
cap i tal crime ('ka-pə-təl) a sin so bad that it is punished by death
care is sowing worry and work are making grow
car nage ('kär-nij) killing
car ol ing ('ka-rə-liŋ) singing
car riag es ('kar-ij-ez) carts
Ca sa-bian ca ('ka-zə-'byän-ka)
cast yourself free unroll
cat a ract's laugh ter ('ka-tə-rakts; 'laf-tər) laughing sound made by water falling from a height
catches the gleam reflects the light
ca the dral (kə-'thē-drəl) large church
cau tion ('kȯ-shən) carefulness

ceased their calling ('sēst) stopped singing because they have migrated
cer e mo ny ('ser-ə-mō-nē) formal act
chafe ('chāf) rub, trying to get through
cha grin (shə-'grin) annoyance
chal ce do ny (kal-'se-dᵊ-nē) a beautiful, very hard stone
change ful April ('chānj-fəl) April has sudden changes of weather
chan nel ('cha-nəl) bed of the stream
charg er ('chär-jər) fine horse
charm something with magic power
chas tened ('chā-sənd) with a softer light
Chee maun (chē-'mon)
cheering power of spring how spring makes one glad
cher ished ('cher-isht) lovingly cared for
cherished pos ses sions (pə-'ze-chənz) dearest things he had
Chib i a bos (chi-bə-'ä-bōs)
chief tain ('chēf-tən) one who gave orders
chim ney ('chim-nē)
chore ('chōr) light task
chris ten ing ('kris-niŋ) naming
ci pher ing ('sØ-fə-riŋ) working examples
cir cuit ('sər-kət) round-about trip
cir cum fer ence (sər-'kəm-fern(t)s) distance around the edge of a circle
clam ber ('klam-bər) climb
clap board ('kla-bərd) narrow board
clatter rattling noise
clearings ground where the trees have been cut
cleft the bark a sun der (ə-'sən-dər) split the bark
clog ging ('klä-giŋ) hindering
close couch ing ('kaúch-iŋ) crouching so as to be hidden
close the seams together make the cracks tight
cloud-rack of a tempest flying, broken clouds after a storm
cof fers ('kò-fərz) treasure chests
Cog ia Hous sam ('kō-gyä; 'hü-säm)
col lect ed (kə-'lek-təd) thoughtful
collected her thoughts thought quickly
com bine (käm-'bØn) form themselves
come what may no matter what happens
Com mand er of the Faith ful (kə-'man-dər; 'fāth-fəl) leader of those true to the Mohammedan religion. The title is given to the caliphs.
com mand ing look out (kə-'man-diŋ; 'lùk-aùt) place from which the surrounding neighborhood can be seen

com mis sion (kə-'mi-shən) thing to be done
com par a tive ly a new af fair (kəm-'pār-ə-tiv-lē; ə-'fār) a world that had been made only a short time
com po sure (kəm-'pō-zhər) calmness
com rades ('käm-radz) mates
con cealed (kən-'sēld) hidden
con fi dent mood ('kän-fə-dent; 'müd) feeling sure I could do it
con found ed with as ton ish ment (kän-'faùn-ded; ə-'stä-nish-mənt) so surprised that they could not think
con fused (kən-'fyüzd) bothered
con joined of them all (kən-'jȯind) made of all together
con nect ed with himself (kə-'nek-təd) have reference to him
con scious ('kän-shəs) aware
con se quence ('kän-sə-kwens) result
con sid er a tion (kən-si-dər-'ā-shən) reason
con stant ('kän-stənt) regular
con stel la tion (kän-stə-'lā-shən) a group of stars
con sti tut ing ('kän-stə-tü-tiŋ) making up
con sul ('kän-səl) one who lives in a foreign country to look after the business interests of his own country there
con tempt i ble (kən-'temp-tə-bəl) mean
con tracts ('kän-trakts) makes
con triv ance (kən-'trØ-vəns) device
con trived (kən-'trØvd) made
con trive to bur y (kən-'trØv; 'ber-ē) manage to bury
con veyed (kən-'vād) given over
cop pers ('kä-pərz) pennies
cord string of the bow
cor nice ('kȯr-nəs) high molding around the walls
cor po re al sen sa tions (kȯr-'pōr-e-əl; sen-'sā-shənz) coarse pleasures
corpse ('kȯrps) dead body
corse let ('kȯr-slət) armor for the body
council of war ('kaùn-səl) meeting to make plans
counsels ('kaùn-səlz) advice
count all your boasts even though you present your many charms
count like mi sers ('mØ-zərz) count as lovingly as do misers their money
county town town where the business of the county (holding court, paying taxes, etc.), is carried on
cours ers ('kōr-sərz) swift horses; here reindeer
cour te ous ('kər-tē-us) polite
court fa vor ('kōrt; 'fā-vər) good will of the ruler or other high personage

court i ers (ˈkōrt-tē-yərz) those in attendance at the court of a ruler
cov er (ˈkə-vər) underbrush large enough to hide behind
cow er ing (ˈkau̇-ər-iŋ) hovering
cre a tion (krē-ˈā-shən) the world
crest fall en (ˈkrest-fȯ-lən) cast down
crest ing the bil lows (ˈkres-tiŋ; ˈbi-lōz) adorning the top of the waves
crev ice (ˈkre-vəs) crack
crew of gypsies band of ragamuffins
crossbrace the piece of wood between the plow handles
crown of his desire thing he wanted most
cru el mor ti fi ca tion (ˈkrü-əl; mōr-tə-fə-ˈkā-shən) very great annoyance
cruise (ˈkrüz) trip in a boat
cun ning (ˈkə-niŋ) tricky
cunningly made skillfully made
cup board (ˈkə-bərd) a closet for dishes
cur mudg eon (kər-ˈmə-jən) miser
curt sy (ˈkərt-sē) bow
cym bals (ˈsim-bəlz) pair of brass half globes clashed together to produce a ringing sound

D

Da co tahs (də-ˈkō-təz), Sioux (ˈsū)
Daed a lus of yore (ˈded-ə-ləs) Daedalus of olden time. The story is that he escaped from prison by flying with wings he had made.
dames married women
Da ri us (ˈda-ri-əs)
daunt ed (ˈdȯn-ted) frightened
dawn daybreak
day beds resting places in daytime
death less fame (ˈdeth-ləs) lasting glory
deck her bo som (ˈbu-zəm) trim the front of the canoe
deems (ˈdēmz) thinks
deer-skin dressed and whitened skins of deer, which had been cleaned, smoothed, and bleached
de file (di-ˈfØl) narrow pass
de funct ten ant (di-ˈfənkt; ˈte-nənt) man who formerly lived there but is dead
de ject ed (di-ˈjek-təd) downhearted
del i cate crafts employ (ˈde-li-kət) use your skill in cooking
dell small valley

de pos it ed (di-ˈpä-zə-ted) put away
de ri sion (di-ˈri-zhən) mockery
des ert (ˈde-zərt) uninhabited by man
de sign (di-ˈzØn) plan
des o la tion (de-sō-ˈlā-shən) ruin
de spair (di-ˈspār) hopelessness
des per ate (ˈdes-pə-rət) hopeless
des sert (di-ˈzərt) fruit pastry, etc., usually served at the close of a meal
des tined to be let loose (ˈdes-tənd) fated to be freed
di a mond (ˈdØ-ə-mənd) precious stone
di min ished (də-ˈmi-nəsht) made less
di min u tive (də-ˈmi-nyü-tiv) tiny
di rect ly (də-ˈrekt-lē) at once
dis as ter (di-ˈzas-tər) great trouble
dis clos es (dis-ˈklōz-ez) lets be seen
dis cov er (dis-ˈkə-vər) find out
dis mount ed (dis-ˈmaủn-təd) threw down off its mountings
dis put ed (di-ˈspyü-təd) argued; talked each against the others
dis qui e tude (dis-ˈkwØ-ə-tüd) uneasiness
dis suad ing (di-ˈswād-iŋ) advising away from
distant days that shall be time to come but still far off
di ver si fied (də-ˈvər-sə-fØd) made to have a look of variety
doc ile (ˈdä-səl) gentle
down of a this tle (ˈthi-səl) lightest thing you can think of
down tim ber (ˈtim-bər) fallen trees
dow ry (ˈdaủ-rē) gift of a man to his bride
draft (ˈdraft) one drink
dread si lence re pos es (ˈdred-ˈsØ-lens; re-ˈpō-zəz) sleeps quietly, so we fear it
dreamy rec ol lec tion (re-kə-ˈlek-shən) faint memory
drink your health wish you good health when beginning to drink, usually at a meal
driv en (ˈdri-vən) blown before the wind
droll (ˈdrōl) laughable
droop ing (ˈdrüp-iŋ) with hanging heads
droop o'er the sod hang over a grave
drought (ˈdraủt) lack of rain
drowned (ˈdraủnd)
dry and dumb (ˈdəm) dried up and still because there is no water to ripple
du cat (ˈdə-kət) old gold coin ($2.28 [1920])
dun geon (ˈdən-jən) underground prison

Du quesne (dü-ˈkān)
dusk y pods (ˈdəs-kē) dark-colored seed vessels
du ty holds him fast (ˈdü-tē) he knows he ought to stay

E

each in its turn the sway one after the other ruled
eager hand (ˈē-gər) hand that could hardly wait
earth-bound ties roots which hold it in the ground
earth en (ˈər-thən) earthenware
earth was young world had not long existed
Eastern lands Asia and Africa
eaves (ˈēvz) edges of the roof which overhang the walls slightly
ech o (ˈe-kō) say over again
ech o ing cor ri dor (ˈe-kō-iŋ; ˈkȯr-ə-dər) long, empty hall in which they could hear their own footsteps
ei ther (ˈē-thər)
elf a made-up creature
ell (ˈel) forty-five inches
en chant ment (in-ˈchant-mənt) magic
en cir cled (in-ˈsər-kəld) wound around
en coun ter (in-ˈkau̇n-tər) meeting
en gines (ˈen-jənz) implements
en ter prise (ˈen-tər-prØz) undertaking; willingness to try different things
ep i dem ic (e-pə-ˈde-mik) a disease which one person takes from another
Ep i me the us (ep-ə-ˈmē-thē-əs)
eq ui page (ˈe-kwə-pāj) horses and carriage
ere (ˈer) before
es teem (is-ˈtēm) good opinion
e vap o rat ed (ə-ˈva-pə-rā-təd) passed away from me
ever of fi cious Ton ish (ə-ˈfi-shəs; ˈtō-nish) Tonish, who was always doing too much
ev er y part has a voice (ˈev-rē) each stripe and star means something
ev i dent in ten tion (ˈe-və-dent; in-ˈten-shən) plain purpose
E wa yea (ə-wȯ-ˈyā) a lullaby
ex ag ger a tions (ig-za-jər-ˈā-shənz) overstatements
ex cess (ek-ˈses) too much
ex ile (ˈeg-zØl) one away from home
ex plore (ik-ˈsplōr) examine thoroughly,
ex pound (ek-ˈspau̇nd) explain
ex press con sent (ik-ˈspres; kən-ˈsent) especial permission being given

ex tend ing themselves (ik-'sten-diŋ) spreading out so as to be at a distance from each other
ex tin guish (ik-'stiŋ-gwish) put out
ex traor di na ry (ik-'strȯr-di-nə-rē) surprising unusual
ex ult ed (ig-'səl-təd) was glad
ex ult ing, glean (ig-'zəl-tiŋ; 'glēn) rejoicing, harvest
eye glass of dew ('ɵ-glas; 'dū) a dewdrop

F

fading losing the original color
fail of the fruits have not the fruits
faint shadow of a trouble only a hint of unhappiness
fair voy age ('vȯi-ij) trip without severe storms or accidents
fal low ('fa-lō) pale yellow
Falls of Min ne ha ha (min-ē-'hä-hä) a waterfall near Minneapolis
false es ti mates ('fȯls; 'es-tə-məts) wrong judgment
fal ter ing ('fȯl-tə-riŋ) stopping
fame being known everywhere
fame so be com ing to you (bi-'kə-miŋ) glory that suits you so well
famous roe buck ('rō-bək) fine, big deer
fan tas tic forms (fan-'tas-tik) strange shapes
fash ioned ('fa-shənd) shaped; made
fashioned flutes made pipes from which he blew music
fast in my for tress ('fȯr-tres) held firmly by my love
fa tal ('fā-təl) destructive
fa tigue (fə-'tēg) weariness
fa vor a ble gale ('fā-və-rə-bəl; 'gāl) wind blowing in the direction he wished to sail
feasting his eyes enjoying looking at
fea tures and to kens ('fē-chərz; 'tō-kənz) parts of the face, and expression
feeling but one heart-beat all having the same feelings and wishes
feet unwilling moving slowly without interest
fen lands ('fen-landz) swamps
fer vent ly ('fər-vənt-lē) warmly
feuds ('fyüdz) quarrels
fev ered mart ('fē-verd; 'märt) market place full of excitement
fib rous ('fɵ-brəs) made of fibers; strong
filled the night made it all light
fis sure ('fi-zhər) narrow crack
fit ful ly blows ('fit-fə-lē) blows and then stops

fit to be made a tool of suitable to be deceived by flattery to do the work of others
flags long, narrow leaves of a plant
flanking parties riders who were going to stand at the sides
flaunt ('flȯnt) make a great showing of
flaunt ing ('flȯnt-iŋ) waving
flaunting nigh ('nØ) making a great show near them
flecked with leafy light ('flekt) spotted with sunlight shining through the trees
fleck its lonely spread ('flek) show as a dark spot against the great stretch of grass
flesh creeps shudder with horror
flex i bil i ty (flek-sə-'bil-ə-tē) ability to be bent
flight of song where a song goes
flit ting ('fli-tiŋ) flying about
flow in music glide along so as to make pleasant sounds
flow'ry dells little valleys with flowers in them
flut ter ('flə-tər) are in motion
fo li age ('fō-lē-ij) leafy plants
fol ly laughs to scorn ('fälē; 'lafs; 'skȯrn) one who is foolish makes fun of
fond loving
for bear (fȯr-'ber) keep from thy stroke; do not chop it down
for bid ding fur ther pas sage (fər-'bid-iŋ; 'fər-ther; 'pas-ij) keeping them from going on
for bore (fōr-'bōr) held back
ford a shallow place where the soldiers could cross without a bridge
fore fath er ('fōr-fä-th̲ər) ancestor
fore head ('fōr-hed) upper part of the face
for est fight ers ('fȯr-əst; 'fØ-tərz) men used to fighting among trees
forest's life was in it it was made from the trees and seemed alive like them
forever and a day for all time
for lorn (fȯr-'lȯrn) poor and lonely
former state condition it had been in
for mi da ble ('fȯr-mə-də-bəl) dreadful
fort night ('fōrt-nØt) two weeks
foul footsteps' pol lu tion (pə-'lü-shən) dishonor of the country, caused by an enemy being in it
fowling piece gun for shooting birds
frag ments ('frag-mənts) scraps
fra grant ('frā-grənt) sweet-smelling
frame of mind feeling this way

fran chise of this good people ('fran-chØz) vote of the men of this colony
freight ing ('frā-tiŋ) burden
freight it with ('frāt) load the boat with
fren zy ('fren-zē) joyous madness
fre quent ed ('frē-kwən-təd) visited
fretted tired; teased
frig ate ('fri-gət) light, sailing warship
fringed with trees with a thin line of trees along it
frol ic ('fräl-ik) play
frolic chase game of running after each other
frost ed ('frȯ-stəd) frostbitten, and, as a result, loosened
froth y ('frȯ-thē) having bubbles
frown ing pine for est ('fraůn-iŋ; 'pØn; 'for-əst) dark evergreen forest
fu gi tives ('fyü-jə-tivz) horses which were trying to escape
full glory re flect ed (ri-'flek-təd) with all its colors showing
full of in ven tion (in-'ven-shən) good at thinking up plans
fur rows ('fər-ōz) shallow trenches made by the plow
furze ('fərz) an evergreen shrub with yellow flowers

G

gain said ('gān-sed) changed
gal lant ly ('ga-lənt-lē) bravely
gal lant ly stream ing ('ga-lənt-lē; strē-miŋ) bravely flying
gaunt ('gȯnt) thin from hunger
gauze ('gȯz) thin, transparent stuff
gave me a good char ac ter ('kar-ik-tər) said I was a reliable man
gave myself up for lost stopped having any hope of being saved
genial favorable to growth
ge nial hour ('jē-nyəl) pleasant spring time
gen ius ('jēn-yəs) a person who can do more or better than ordinary people
gen ius a powerful spirit
gen tian ('jen-shən) a beautiful flowering plant, usually blue
ges ture ('jes-chər) motion
ghast ly spec ta cle ('gast-lē; 'spek-ti-kəl) horrible sight
gi gan tic (jØ-'gan-tik) very large
gilt gold-plated metal
gim let ('gim-lət) tool which bores small holes as it is turned
Gitch e Gum ee ('gi-chē-'gü-mē) Lake Superior
Gitch e Ma ni to ('gi-chē-'man-i-tō) Great Spirit
give back the cry answer

give me thought for thought tell me his ideas and listen to mine
glade ('glād) an open, grassy space in a wood
gladness breathes joy seems to come
gleam ing ('glēm-iŋ) light
glean gather
glens little valleys
glim mer ('gli-mər) gleam
glim mer ing o'er ('gli-mə-riŋ) shining brightly over corn and people
glit ter ing ('gli-tə-riŋ) shining
glo ri fied the hill ('glō-rə-fØd) sent beautiful rays of light upon the hill
glory fell chas tened ('chā-sənd) his light at the height of its brightness cast but a soft light
glos sy ('glä-sē) shining
gold en ears before ('gōl-dən) yellow ears of corn taken from their husks and piled in front of the huskers
good ly root ('gůd-lē; rüt) the much prized potato
go phers ('gō-ferz) ground-squirrels
gor geous ('gȯr-jəs) magnificent; beautiful
gossip of swallows bird notes that sound like chatter
go the entire round make the furrow around the field
Gov er nor ('gə-vᵊn-ər) the chief man of the colony
gra cious ly ('grā-shəs-lē) with kind courtesy
Gra na da (grə-'nä-də)
gran a ried harvest ('grā-nə-rēd) grain and vegetables stored for the winter
gra ti fy ing his utmost wishes ('gra-tə-fØ-iŋ) giving him anything he might wish for
grave ('grāv) serious-looking
gray of the morning faint light before the sun is up
greatest dis qui e tude (dis-'kwØ-ə-tüd) worst trouble
Great Spirit God
griev ous ly ('grē-vəs-lē) painfully
grim stern; unyielding
gri mace ('gri-məs) made-up face
grip ing landlord ('grØ-piŋ) stingy man who rents houses for high rent
grope ('grōp) feel without seeing
grow into tan gles ('taŋ-gəlz) grow wild as in the woods or fields
guard thy re pose ('gärd; re-'pōz) protect you while you sleep
guid ance ('gØ-dəns) showing him the right course to take
guid ed of my coun sel ('gØ-dəd; 'käun-səl) take my advice
guid ing lines ('gØ-diŋ) reins by which horses are driven
guile less ('gØl-əs) pure in heart

guin ea ('gi-nē) English coin ($5.11 [1920])
gul lies ('gə-lēz) small valleys dug out by water
gush ing ('gəsh-iŋ) freely flowing

H

hab it a ble ('ha-bə-tə-bəl) fit to live in
had oc ca sion to go out (ə-'kā-zhən) needed to go somewhere in the town
hailed his coming called out gladly when they saw him
half-faced camp shack with three walls and one open side
half-section of unfenced sod 320 acres of unbroken ground with no fence
hal looed (ha-'lōd) shouted halloo
hal low us there ('ha-lō) give us a feeling at home as of sacred things
ham let without name ('ham-lət) few houses near together, but not called a town
ham pers ('ham-pərz) woven baskets
hand i work ('han-di-wərk) what I make
hand ker chiefs ('haŋ-kər-chifs)
hand of art tasteful plan
happily arranged growing in pretty clumps
har dy gift ('här-dē) fruit of the sturdy plant which is given by the earth
har row ing ad di tions ('har-ō-iŋ; ə-'di-shənz) things added that are painful to hear
hart ('härt) male red deer
Ha run al Ra shid (hä-rün´ äl rə-'shēd) caliph of Bagdad
har vest ('här-vəst) dry seeds
has an ax to grind wants someone to do some hard work without pay
hate is shadow feelings of dislike darken everything
haugh ty ('hȯ-tē) proud
haunch es ('hȯn-chəz) hind legs
haunt ('hȯnt) come back again and again
haunts ('hȯnts) places where one loves to go often
haunts of Na ture ('nā-chər) out-of-doors
hav oc of war ('ha-vək) ruin caused by fighting
hawk-eyed ea ger ness ('hȯ-kØd; 'ē-gər-nəs) watching impatiently and with the sharpness of a hawk
heark en ('här-kən) listen
hearth rug ('härth-rəg) rug in front of the fireplace
heart outran his footsteps wanted to be there before he was
heart's-ease comfort in trouble
heart's right hand of friendship a greeting that shows we feel friendly

heart-strings love
heath ('hēth) land covered with heather, which has a purple blossom
heav 'n res cued land ('he-vən; 'res-kyüd) country saved by God
heavy-rolling flight running with a rocking movement from side to side
heir ('ar) one who takes the property of another after he is through with it
helm ('helm) helmet, a protection for the head; the machinery that steers the ship
he must be cold he lacks feeling
herb age ('hər-bij) grass and other plants eaten by grazing animals
here on earth
he ro ic blood (hi-'rō-ik) descended from brave men
hewed ('hyüd) chopped
Hi a wath a ('hØ-ə-wa-thə)
hid den silk has spun ('hi-dən) threads of down in the pod that resemble those which the silkworm spins
hid e ous ('hi-dē-əs) horrible-looking
hie ('hØ) go; take
high re lief (rē-'lēf) carved so that the features stood up from the box
hire ling ('hØ-ər-liŋ) paid soldier
his prop er sphere (prä-pər; 'sfir) his own place
his rev er ence ('rev-rents) the minister
hith er ('hi-t͟hər) here
hoard ('hōrd) supply of provisions
hoar y ('hō-rē) old and gray
hold ('hōld) lower part of a ship, where cargo is stored
hol lows that rus tle be tween ('hä-lōz; 'rə-səl; bi-'twēn) low, quiet places between large, noisily-rolling waves
home-brew served for wine homemade drinks were used instead of wine
home ly old ad age ('hōm-lē; 'a-dij) common saying
hoodwinked blindfolded
hor ror ('hȯr-ər) great fear
horror of my sit u a tion (si-chə-'wā-shən) great danger of the place I was in
horseplay rude play or jokes
host ('hōst) great number
hot ly pressed ('hät-lē; 'prest) closely followed
hov el ('hə-vəl) small, poor house
hov ered ('həv-ərd) fluttered
hud dled ('hə-dəld) crowded
hue ('hyü) color
hues of summer's rainbow ('hyüz) colors in the rainbow in summer

hu man (ˈhyü-mən) exactly like man
Hum ber (ˈhum-bər) a river in northeastern England
hum ble (ˈhəm-bəl) lowly; not proud
hu mor (ˈhyü-mər) temper
humor better suited to his own mood more like his
hur rah (hə-ˈrä) a word used as a shout of joy
hur ri cane (ˈhər-ə-kān) great storm
hush of woods quiet of the forest

I

I a goo (ē-ˈa-gō)
Ic a rus (ˈik-ə-rus) the son of Daedalus—which *see*
i de as (Ø-ˈdē-əz) thoughts
idle, golden freight ing (ˈfrā-tiŋ) burden of golden-colored autumn leaves
if to windward if the hunter is in the direction from which the wind blows
im ag i na ble (i-ˈmaj-nə-bəl) could think of; possible
im mor tal in their childhood (i-ˈmȯr-təl) so placed that they would never grow any older
im per i al (im-ˈpir-ē-əl) royal
im pe ri ous (im-ˈpir-ē-əs) demanding much
im ple ment (ˈim-plə-mənt) tool
im ply a share of rea son (im-ˈplØ; ˈrē-zən) suggest some power to think
im press ion con tin u ing (im-ˈpre-shən; kən-ˈtin-yü-iŋ) the effect remaining
in a bil i ty (in-ə-ˈbil-ə-tē) that you cannot
in cal cu la ble (in-ˈkal-kyə-lə-bəl) cannot be counted
in ca pa ble (in-ˈkāp-ə-bəl) not able
in cline (in-ˈklØn) slope
in darker for tunes tried (ˈfȯr-chənz) they had when they were poor
in dif fer ence (in-ˈdi-fər-ents) not caring
in di gest i ble (in-dØ-ˈjes-tə-bəl) impossible to digest
in dig na tion (in-dig-ˈnā-shən) anger against what is wrong
in duce (in-ˈdüs) cause
in dulge it to the ut most (in-ˈdəlj; ˈət-mōst) be as cross as he could
in fi nite (ˈin-fə-nət) everlasting
in fi nite ly (ˈin-fə-nət-lē) much more
in gen ious (in-ˈjēn-yəs) clever
in hal ing (in-ˈhāl-iŋ) smelling
in her i tance (in-ˈher-ə-tənts) a gift from our ancestors
in i tial round (i-ˈni-shəl) first furrow around the field
in quir ies (in-ˈkwØr-ēz) questioning

in such wise so fiercely
in tel li gent (in-'te-lə-jent) clever
in tent upon (in-'tent) interested in
in ter mi na ble forests (in-'tərm-ə-nə-bəl) woods that seemed endless
in ter rupt his lay (in-tə-'rəpt) stop his song
in the largest sense in the broadest meaning
in ti mate as so ci a tion ('in-tə-mət; ə-sō-sē-'ā-shən) close companionship
in tol er a ble (in-'täl-ər-bəl) unbearable
in trud er (in-'trüd-ər) an uninvited guest
in ven tion (in-'ven-shən) schemes
Is lands of the Bless ed ('Ø-ləndz; 'blest) in mythology, islands where people lived happily, after death
isles ('Øəlz) islands

J

jas per ('jas-pər) a dark, hard stone
jaun ty ('jȯn-tē) gay and easy
jet black
jib ('jib) swing around
joined to such fol ly ('fä-lē) be partner in such foolishness
joy ance ('jȯi-əns) happiness
judg ment ('jəj-mənt) idea; opinion
Jus ti ci ar (jə-'sti-shē-är) chief judge
justs ('jəsts) mock fights between knights on horseback

K

Kagh ('käg) the hedgehog
keel ('kēl) bottom of a ship
keep support
kept made to go on
khan ('kän) an unfurnished building for the use of traveling traders
king's coun cil ('käun-səl) men who met with the king to advise him
kissed into green ('kist) changed to green when touched by the sun's rays
knight ('nØt) in Great Britain, a man with the title Sir
knights of old men of olden times who went about doing brave deeds
knoll ('nōl) a little round hill
knows full well knows very well
Kwa sind ('kwä-sind)

L

lady the wife of a knight
lam en ta ble (la-'men-tə-bəl) distressed
lamentable tone sad voice
lan guid ly ('laŋ-wəd-lē) carelessly
lank ('lank) thin
lapsed ('lapst) slipped
larch ('lärch) tree which looks like an evergreen but sheds its needles
lar i at ('lār-ē-ət) long rope with a running noose
laud a ble ('lò-də-bəl) praiseworthy
laugh ing ('la-fiŋ)
launch ('lònch) get it afloat
lav ish horn ('la-vish) overflowing horn; from the mythological story of the horn that could become filled with whatever its possessor desired
lea ('lē) ground covered with grass
league ('lēg) about three miles
learn ed ('lər-nəd) highly educated
learn ing ('lər-niŋ) knowledge
leave un moved (ən-'müvd) unharmed
lee of the land shelter of the shore
leg ends ('le-jəndz) old stories only partly true
lei sure ('lē-zhər) time to do what he wished
lev ee ('le-vē) reception given by a ruler or his representative
liege ('lēj) having the right to claim service
light and boon bright and pleasant
light some ('lØt-səm) cheery
like a Turk as people do in Turkey
Lil li put ('li-lē-pət)
Lil li pu tians (li-lə-'pyü-shənz)
limes ('lØmz) fruit like lemons, but smaller and more sour
lin den ('lin-dən) made from basswood
list less ('list-ləs) caring about nothing
live li hood ('lØv-lē-hüd) living
live long ('liv-loŋ) whole
loam ('lōm) earth
lone ('lōn) lonely
lone post of death place where he must die alone
looked west er ly ('wes-tər-lē) turned toward the west, the direction in which the wind was blowing before it stopped
loosed ('lüst) set free

lost their labor got no good from the work they had done
love ly to kens ('ləv-lē; 'tōk-ənz) beautiful signs
low er ('lō-ər) darken
lowly thatched cottage small one story house with roof of straw
loz enge ('lä-zənj) a tablet of medicine
lust strong wish
lus ter of mid day ('ləs-tər; 'mid-dā) light bright as at noon
lus trous ('ləs-trəs) radiant
lust y rogue ('ləs-tē; 'rōg) lively little rascal

M

mag ic arts ('ma-jik) power over spirits
ma gi cian (mə-'ji-shən) one who uses magic arts
magic of his singing charming way he sang
mag nif i cence (mag-'ni-fə-səns) grandeur
Ma ha ra ja (mä-hä-'rä-jä) title of the principal Hindu chief
Mahn go tay see (man-'gō-tā-sē) brave
main tain (mān-'tān) keep
make a mends to the human race (ə-'mendz) make up to people everywhere
make a stand hold out against; fight
man-builded today built by people now
ma neu ver (mə-'nü-vər) planned movement of a large number
man of might strong, important man
man's do min ion (də-'mi-nyən) for the use of people
man sion ('man-shən) large and handsome residence
many a happy return many more
mar i ners ('mar-ə-nərz) sailors
marred ('märd) spoiled
marred the whole scene spoiled the effect planned
mar vel ('mär-vəl) wonderful thing
marveled wondered
Mas sa soit (mas-ə-'sȯit)
match able to win against
matchless having no equal
ma trons ('mā-trənz) married women
mayhap maybe
maze ('māz) confusing number of paths which cross
meads meadows
meas ures ('me-zhərz) melodies
med i tat ed ('med-ə-tā-ted) thought

meeting-house church
mel an chol y ('me-lən-kä-lē) sad
melted them to pity softened their feelings so they were filled with gentle thoughts
mer chan dise ('mər-chən-d∅s) goods
mer chant man ('mər-chənt-mən) a trading vessel
mer est ('mēr-əst) simplest
mer ry ('me-rē) joyous
me tal lic (mə-'ta-lik) of metal
metal true really good iron
me thinks (mi-'thiŋks) it seems to me
Mi das ('m∅-dəs)
mil der ('m∅-əl-dər) glory shone a softer and paler glow cast its light
mil dew ('mil-dü) mold; rust
min gled into one ('miŋ-gəld) so united that one could not be distinguished from the other
min i a ture ('mi-nē-ə-chər) very small
Min ne ha ha (min-ē-'hä-hä)
Min ne wa wa (min-ē-'wä-wä)
mirth ful to ex cess ('mərth-fəl; 'ik-ses) too gay
mis chie vious ('mis-chə-vəs) fun-loving
mis do ings (mis-'dü-iŋz) wrong acts
mis sion ('mi-shən) errand
mists of the deep fog over the water
moc ca sins of magic ('mä-kə-sənz) charmed shoes
mod er a tion (mä-də-'rā-shən) fair way
modest bell bell-shaped flower that hangs over
mol der in dust away ('mōl-dər) lose their form and become earth again
mo lest ed (mə-'lest-ed) troubled
mol ten ('mōl-tən) melted
mon arch ('mä-nərk) ruler
Mo non ga he la (mə-'nōn-gä-hē-lä) river in Pennsylvania
Mon sieur (məs-'yər) French for Mister
moor sandy, wet ground
more en ter prise ('en-tər-pr∅z) willingness to try to do things
Mor gi a na (mȯr-gi-'ä-nä)
mor tal ('mȯr-tᵊl) human
mortal en e my ('e-nə-mē) man who hates you so much he would like to kill you
mortal fear greatest fear
mor tal ly ('mȯr-tᵊl-ē) so as to cause death

mosques ('mäsks) places of worship in Mohammedan countries
moss ('mȯs) a tiny grasslike plant, very soft
moss-green trees trees with trunks covered by green moss
mount to the sky fly out of sight
mow ('maů) ('mō; here for rhyme) A pile of hay or straw
much a miss (ə-'mis) very wrong
much con triv ing (kən-'trØv-iŋ) making great plans
much fre quent ed ('frē-kwənt-ed) often visited
much in clined (in-'klØnd) having a great liking for
Mud way aush ka (məd-wȯ-'üsh-kä)
multiply his heaps make his piles many times greater
mum mies ('mə-mēz) dead bodies which have been preserved in a dried state; here, persons whose minds are dry and not open to new ideas
Mun chaus en (mən-'chȯ-zen) a teller of extravagant tales
Musk et a quid (məs-'kət-ə-kwid)
Musk o day ('məsk-ō-dā)
mute ('mūt) voiceless; quiet
mut te ring ('mət-ə-riŋ) saying in a low tone
muz zle ('mə-zəl) nose and mouth
my design my plan
mys te ri ous (mis-'tir-ē-əs) puzzling
mys tic splen dors ('mis-tik; 'splen-dərz) magic brightness

N

naked sword ('sōrd) sword without a sheath
narrow bound thin wall keeping them out
na tion al con stel la tion ('nash-nəl; kän-stə-'lā-shən) group of stars belonging to the nation
na tive lan guage ('nā-tiv; 'laŋ-gwij) way that is natural to them
nat u ral death ('na-chə-rəl) died without being killed
naught ('nȯt) nothing
nav i gate the az ure ('na-və-gāt; 'a-zhər) sail through the sky
Na wa da ha (nä-wä-'dä-hȧ)
near his cot not far from his cottage
nei ther ('nē-t͟hər)
neither willing nor re luc tant (ri-'lək-tənt) not showing whether she wanted to go or stay
neph ew ('ne-fyü) the son of a brother or sister
nicest goldsmith most skillful worker in gold
niche ('nich) small opening

nim ble ('nim-bəl) quick to do things
no ble ('nō-bəl) coin worth about $1.60 [1920]; man of high rank
No ko mis (no-'kō-məs)
nos trils ('näs-trəlz) the openings in the nose for breathing
note if harm were near to see if there were any danger round about

O

ob lit er at ed (ə-'bli-tər-ā-təd) taken away
ob scure (äb-'skyür) dark
ob scured their pas sage (äb-'skyurd; 'pa-sij) hid their line of movement
ob ser va tion (äb-sər-'vā-shən) careful notice
ob sta cle ('äb-sti-kəl) something in the way
ob tained a foothold (əb-'tānd) got a start
oc cu pied with her grief ('ä-kyə-pØd) full of sorrow
o cean's breast ('ō-shənz; 'brest) calm surface of the sea
O drug useless thing
o'er shad owed Thanksgiving Day (ōr; 'sha-dōd) brought up sad thoughts on the holiday
o'er the comb ers (ōr; 'kō-mərz) over the long rolling waves
of all degrees of all kinds, large and small
of a se ri ous na ture ('sir-ē-əs; 'nā-chər) of a dangerous kind
of fi cial ly rec og nized (ə-'fi-shə-lē; 're-kəg-nØzd) known and stated
oint ment ('ȯint-mənt) precious salve
O jib ways (ō-'jib-wāz) a tribe that lived just south of Lake Superior
ooze and tangle ('üz) mud and roots
ooz ing outward ('ü-ziŋ) flowing from the tree
O pe chee (ō-'pē-chē)
op en hand ed ness (ō-pən; 'hand-əd-nəs) generosity
op er a tions of the en e my (ä-pə-'rā-shənz; 'e-nə-mē) doings of those fighting against us
op pres sion lifts its head (ə-'pre-shən) people are treated unjustly
o rig i nal (ə-'rij-ə-nəl) first
outlaw one who breaks the laws and flees to escape punishment
overcame this hand i cap ('han-di-kap) got over this disadvantage
Owaissa (ō-'wās-ä)

P

pack et ('pa-kət) bundle
pack train a number of animals carrying the supplies of the party

pa gans (ˈpā-gənz) not Christians
painted pul pit (ˈpu̇l-pit) green and purple over-arching leaf of the jack-in-the-pulpit
painted tribes of light gay, bright flowers of spring
painted white white-skinned, like an Indian's face covered with paint
pale skies gray skies of early spring
pal freys (ˈpȯl-frēz) saddle-horses
pal i sades of pine-trees (ˈpa-lə-sādz) tall pines, standing like a wall on each bank
pal pi tat ed (ˈpal-pə-tā-təd) shook
Pan do ra (pan-ˈdōr-ə)
parched (ˈpärcht) dry
par ent (ˈpar-ənt) the giver of life
par take (pär-ˈtāk) share
par tic u lar ly (pər-ˈti-kyü-lər-lē) very
part ners (ˈpärt-nərz) companions
past will no longer be the past (ˈpast) things that happened long ago will seem as real as though going on now
pa thos (ˈpā-thäs) sad sweetness
pa tient weath er cocks (ˈpā-shənt; ˈwe-thər-käks) patient, waiting for the wind to blow
Pau wat ing (pȯ-ˈwā-tiŋ) St. Mary's river, joining Lakes Superior and Huron
pay my court (ˈkōrt) show my respect by visiting you
peace of mind calm thoughts with nothing to disturb them
peas ants (ˈpe-zənts) lowest class of people
peer (ˈpir) peep cautiously
pen non (ˈpe-nən) flag
per form ing these good offices (pər-ˈfȯr-miŋ) doing these kind acts
per il ous (ˈper-ə-ləs) dangerous
per i od i cal (pir-ē-ˈäd-i-kəl) printed matter in the form of a magazine, published regularly (not daily)
per plex i ty (pər-ˈplek-sə-tē) difficulty
per se vered (pər-sə-ˈvird) persisted
per se ver ing ly (pər-sə-ˈvir-iŋ-lē) continually
per son age (ˈpərs-nij) creature
pest disease which kills
pes tered (ˈpəs-tərd) annoyed
pet tish ly (ˈpe-tish-lē) crossly
pheas ants (ˈfe-səntz) wild birds of delicious flavor
phoe be (ˈfē-bē) a kind of bird
phrase (ˈfrāz) expression

phys i cal and mor al cour age (ˈfi-zi-kəl; ˈmör-əl; ˈkər-ij) bravery of body and mind
phy sique (fi-ˈzēk) build and health
piece of cov er (ˈkə-ver) bit of underbrush large enough to hide behind
pierce like a shaft (ˈpirs; ˈshaft) fly through like an arrow
pine-clad hills hills covered with pine trees
pin ion (ˈpin-yən) wing
pit i a ble (ˈpi-tē-ə-bəl) sad
place of de po sit (di-ˈpä-zət) keeping place
plagued the realm (ˈplāgd; ˈrelm) made trouble in the country
plague the Abbot (ˈplāg) annoy the Abbot
plait ing (ˈplāt-iŋ) braiding
Plan tag e nets (plan-ˈtaj-ə-nets) the English kings from 1154 to 1485
plenty enough of everything
pli ant as a wand (ˈplØ-ənt; ˈwänd) as easily moved as a willow twig is bent
plow had vi o lat ed (ˈvØ-ə-lā-ted) had been turned up by the plow, and thus spoiled for the small owners
plow share (ˈplaü-shār) blade of the plow; part which turns up the earth
plun dered store (ˈplən-dərd) goods he had taken by force
Poet Lau re ate (ˈlȯr-ē-ət) poet chosen by the king to write on great events of the nation
point to wind ward (ˈwin-dwərd) turn in the direction from which the wind came
poised it in the air (ˈpȯizd) held it high
po lit i cal bus tles (ˈpə-li-ti-kəl; ˈbə-sᵊlz) activities of politics
pol lu tion (pə-ˈlü-shən) soiling and making impure
pomp (ˈpämp) show
pon der (ˈpän-dər) think
pondering much thinking things over
pon der ous (ˈpän-də-rəs) heavy
Po ne mah (pō-ˈnē-mä)
pon iard (ˈpän-yərd) dagger
por ce lain (ˈpōr-sə-lən) fine white earthenware
pos sessed au thor i ty (pə-ˈzest; ə-ˈthȯr-ə-tē) knew how to control
power of proph e cy (ˈprä-fə-sē) ability to foretell events
prac tice de cen cy (ˈprak-tis; ˈdē-sən-sē) do the right thing every time
prat tle (ˈpra-təl) child's talk
pres ence (ˈpre-zəns) being there
pres ent ly (ˈpre-zənt-lē) soon
pre vent (pri-ˈvent) keep from
Pri deaux (prē-ˈdō)

pried into ('prØd) tried to pull apart
prig one who thinks himself good
prime ('prØm) best
prince ly ('prins-lē) like a prince
pro claim (prō-'klām) show
pro fu sion of flowers (prə-'fyū-zhən) great many flowers
pro ject ed (prə-'jek-təd) extended
proudly we hailed looked at with pride and joy
prov ince ('prə-vənts) one of the divisions of certain countries
pru dence ('prü-dənts) wisdom; sense
Psalm ('säm) sacred song
pub li can ('pə-bli-kən) tax gatherer
pull fod der ('fä-dər) pull up cornstalks by the roots
pulp wet mixture of which paper is made
pump kin ('pəm-kən)
pur pose ('pər-pəs) object; work
pursuit (pər-'süt) chase
put me in mind suggested to me

Q

quail ('kwāəl) the bobwhite
quirk ('kwərk) turn
quoit ('kyȯit) ring
quoth ('kwōth) said

R

ra di ance ('rā-dē-əns) brilliance
ra di ant ('rā-dē-ənt) beaming
raid ('rād) attack made to get something
ram parts ('ram-pärts) protecting walls for defense
rang ers ('rān-jərz) men who live on the range, or prairie
rap tur ous ('rap-chə-rəs) very happy
rar i ties ('rār-ə-tēz) rare and precious things
rav en ous ('ra-və-nəs) very great
rayless disk of red flat, burning circle, not seeming to throw off any rays of light
re ap peared (rē-ə-'pird) came in sight again
rear ('rir) raise
rear ing ('rir-iŋ) standing on her hind legs

re call ing (ri-'kȯ-liŋ) remembering
re ceived in trust (ri-'sēvd) taken, to protect honorably
reck less ('re-kləs) careless
rec og nized ('re-kig-nØzd) saw
re coil (rē-'kȯil) rebound
re cov er ing himself (ri-'kə-vər-iŋ) coming back to his natural state of mind
red-coats British soldiers, so called because of their red uniforms
re deem (ri-'dēm) them buy them back
re dou bled (rē-'də-bəld) repeated
reeds large, tall swamp grasses
re en forc ing (rē-ən-'fōr-siŋ) covering again
re flect ed (ri-'flek-təd) thought
re gions of the morning ('rē-jənz) place where the sun rises; the East
reg u lar or der ('re-gyə-lər; 'ȯr-dər) in straight lines, one behind the other
re lat ed (ri-'lā-təd) told
re laxed (ri-'lakst) loosened; let go
Rel dre sal ('rel-drē-sal)
rem nant ('rem-nənt) few that are left
re mot est corner of Africa (ri-'mō-təst) part of Africa the farthest away
ren der ('ren-dər) give back
re nown (ri-'naůn) fame
re paired to her house (ri-'pārd) went to her house
re pair the mis chief (ri- 'par; 'mis-chəf) make up for the harm
re past (ri-'past) feast
re pel ling (ri-'pel-iŋ) driving back
re pent ance (ri-'pen-tənts) regret
re sem bles (ri-'zem-bəlz) is like
res in ('re-zin) dried sap
res o lute ly (re-sə-'lüt-lē) determinedly
re solved (ri-'zälvd) with his mind firmly made up
re splend ent (ri-'splen-dənt) shining brightly
re store (ri-'stōr) put back
re tired cham ber (ri-'tØrd; 'chām-bər) room away from the main part of the house
re treat (ri-'trēt) hiding place
rev els ('re-vəlz) wild enjoyment
re ver ber a tions (ri-vər-bə-'rā-shənz) echoes
rev er ence ('rev-rens) great respect
richly decked ('dekt) wearing beautiful and costly blankets and other decorations
rich stuffs costly cloth of different kinds

ridges raised lines of ground
ri dic u lous (rə-'di-kyü-ləs) deserving to be laughed at
rills little streams
ring of the same sound of it
rip ened charge ('r∅-pend; 'chärj) precious object in its keeping, now ready for husking
rip pling ('rip-liŋ) blowing in curves
ri val for one hour ('r∅-vəl) equal at the time of greatest beauty
riv et ed ('ri-və-təd) fastened by bending down the end
riveted his attention (ə-'ten-shən) put all his thought
roam ('rōm) wander
robes of darkness blue-black foliage clothing it
roc ('räk) imaginary bird of great size
ro guish ly de fied ('rō-gish-lē; dē-'f∅d) resisted in a joking way
Roha ('rō-hä)
root ('rüt) the potato
ro sy morn ('rō-zē; 'mórn) reddish tint of the sky at sunrise
round-tower of my heart safest place for a prisoner
route ('rüt) way
rue ful ly ('rü-fəl-lē) sadly
rue the day ('rü) regret what I had done that day
rug ged ('rə-gəd) uneven
rug ged vales be stow ('rə-gəd; 'vāᵊlz; bi-'stō) rough valleys furnish
ru ined ('rü-ənd) destroyed
ru mi nat ing ('rü-mə-nā-tiŋ) chewing their cuds
run over with joy be wildly happy
rushes coarse grasses
rus set ('rə-sət) reddish brown or reddish gray

S

Sa chem ('sā-chem) Indian chief
sac ri fic ing ('sa-krə-f∅-siŋ) giving up
sad sea wave ocean seeming sad because you are sad
sage speeches ('sāj) wise remarks
sa lut ed the com pa ny (sə-'lü-təd; 'kəmp-nē) greeted those assembled
san dal wood ('san-dəl-wúd) a highly prized, fragrant Asiatic wood from a tree of the same name
sank deep into my mind made a lasting impression on me
sate ('sāt) old spelling of sat
sat in burs ('sa-tin) prickly husks of chestnuts with their smooth, soft lining

sat is fy his mind ('sa-təs-fØ) find out what he wanted to know
save except
sa vor y ('sā-vrē) pleasing to the smell
scaled the wall ('skāld) got over the wall, as soldiers climbed by ladders over the walls of an old-time city
scars of all wars marks left from injuries got in fighting
scope ('skōp) reach
scorched ('skȯrcht) heated until burned
scoured the seas ('skaủrd) hunted over the seas
scour for spoils ('skaủr) hunt for dainty foods
scour ing down the mead ow ('skaủ-riŋ; 'me-dō) sweeping over the grassland
sear ('sir) withered
sea ward glide ('sē-wərd; 'glØd) flow toward the ocean
Se bo wish a (seb-ō-'wish-a)
se cure him a gainst e vil (si-'kyür; ə-'genst; 'ē-vəl) protect him from harm
sedg es ('sej-əz) grasslike plants with tall heads of seeds
se ñor (sān-'yȯr) Spanish for sir
sense of e la tion (i-'lā-shən) feeling of joy
se quin ('sē-kwən) a coin, no longer in use, worth about $2.25 [1920]
se rene of look and heart (sə-'rēn) with a calm face and mind
service liketh us we like to serve
ses a me ('se-sə-mē) a kind of grain grown in the East and used for food
sev ered ('se-vərd) cut off
Sev ern ('sev-ərn) a river in southwestern England
shadow of an in fi nite bliss ('in-fə-nət) hint of happiness that cannot be measured
shanty small, unfinished house
shaped them to a framework bent and fastened them to form the skeleton of the canoe
share *see* plowshare
sheath ('shēth) put into its case
sheaves ('shēvz) bundles of grain
sheer into the river straight down into the water
shift less ('shift-ləs) poorly kept
shil ling ('shi-liŋ) coin worth $0.24 [1920]
shining land of Wa bun ('wä-bən) bright East (Wabun is the East Wind)
shining shoulders bare, wet shoulders glistening in the sun
shipping passage on shipboard
shirk ('shərk) one who tries to get out of work
shivering shock force that breaks its timbers
shoal ('shōl) sandbar

shoot a main have a match
shot his shining quills cast off some of his smooth spines
shoulder your matchlocks take your guns
shroud rope of a ship
shut tle ('shə-təl) tool used in weaving
sieve ('siv) a utensil for separating the coarse particles from the fine
sig ni fy un ion ('sig-nə-fØ; 'yün-yən) mean joining
sin cer i ty (sin-'sir-ə-tē) honesty
sin ews ('sin-yüz) tough strips
singing pine trees pines through which the wind blew with a pleasant sound
sing led out ('siŋ-gəld) chose
sire ('sØr) father
sit u a tion (si-chə-'wā-shən) state in which things were
skil let ('ski-lət) frying pan
skim ming ('ski-miŋ) flying so close as to brush the surface
skirt ed ('skər-təd) walked along the edge of; grew along the edge of
sky ward ('skØ-wərd) cast hung high
slab ('slab) thick slice
slaugh tered ('slȯ-tərd) killed for food
sledge ('slej) a heavy hammer
sleep shall be broken you will be awakened
sleight-of-mouth tricks ('slØt) mysterious disappearances
slow slop ing to the night ('slōp-iŋ) sinking slowly in the west
slui ces ('slü-səz) gates to hold back the water
smiling fields patches of grain growing well
smirk ('smərk) put-on smile
smite the ore ('smØt) hammer the iron into shape
smol dered ('smōl-dərd) slowly burned
Soan ge ta ha (sōn-gē-'tä-hä)
soar ing ('sōr-iŋ) floating in the air
so bered by his ad ven ture ('sō-bərd; əd-'ven-chər) made wise by his experience
soft ly pic tured wood ('sȯft-lē; 'pik-chərd) beautifully colored foliage showing up in soft tints
sol ace ('sä-ləs) comfort
som ber ('säm-bər) gloomy
soothe comfort
sore of heart weary and discouraged
sorry pass sad state
sound of their shock noise when they struck
sov er eign ('sä-vər-ən) ruler

spa cious ('spā-shəs) large
spake with naked hearts hid no secrets from each other
spare yards extra poles used to support the sails
spars ('spärz) masts
speaks sub lime ly (sə-'blØm-lē) has a noble meaning
spec ter like figure ('spek-tər-lØk) person looking like a ghost
spelled down beat in spelling
sphere of gold ('sfir) golden globe
spikes large nails
spire a slender rod, or tower, extending upward from the top of a building; here, for the weathercock
spir it u al izes ('spir-i-chə-wa-lØz-əz) purifies
spir it was grad u al ly sub dued ('spir-ət; 'gra-jə-wə-lē; səb-'düd) she was tamed
splendor dazzles in vain ('splen-dər) bright show of glory does not tempt
splendor wild light rising and falling
spoils of forest free things that come from trees
sported played
spray ('sprā) twig
sprites ('sprØts) fairies
square heaven of blue blue part of the flag
stal wart ('stȯl-wərt) brave
stanch ('stȯnch) faithful
stanched ('stȯncht) checked the bleeding from
standing in for the shore coming toward the land
stand you in yeo man's stead ('yō-mənz; 'sted) be of help to you in your adventures
star-spangled sprinkled with stars
state and person country and the man himself
state ly ('stāt-lē) standing proudly
stature height
stayed my walk stopped me
stay surety be security
stern the back part of a boat
steward man in charge of the food
stick to your sphere do the things you can do; don't try to do those you can't
stiff not to be bent or changed
sti fled mur mur ('sti-fəld 'mər-mər) a low sound not easily heard
stirred their souls to pas sion ('pa-shən) moved their deepest feelings
store large amount

storm still brave stand firm in a hard wind
stoutest bravest
stout fellow gay young man
Straits of Gi bral tar ('strāts; jē-'bròl-tər) narrow waterway between Spain and Africa
strength al lied to goodness ('a-lØd) bodily power added to virtues
strewn ('strün) covered
strick en ('stri-kən) frightened
strife comes with manhood men have to fight
stroked in rip ples ('strōkt; 'ri-pəlz) gently made into little folds
stub ble ('stə-bəl) short stalks left in the ground after grain has been cut
stud ied the sit u a tion ('stə-dēd; si-chü-'wa-shən) thought over the state in which things were
stur dy ('stər-dē) strong; firm
sub lime ly (sə-'blØm-lē) with great nobility and purity
suc ceed ed to the gloom (sək-'sē-dəd; 'glüm) followed the cloudiness
such an old mus tache ('məs-tash) so fierce a soldier
suit a ble to that char ac ter ('sü-tə-bəl; 'kar-ik-tər) such as dancers wore
sul tan ('səl-tən) title of the ruler in some Asiatic countries
sum mit of the Cedar ('sə-mət) top of the tree
sum moned ('sə-mənd) called
sun be nig nant (bi-'nig-nənt) kindly sun
sun is under the sea sun has set
sunshine of sweet looks brightness of expression
sup ple ('sə-pəl) easily bent
sup port ed the dog's chanc es (sə-'pōr təd; 'chans-əz) said that the dog would succeed
sup pressed (sə-'prest) kept down
sure ty ('shür-ə-tē) security
surge's swell ('sərj-ez) waves of the rising sea
sur passed (sər-'past) did better than
swam ('swam)
sweeping westward moving swiftly toward the west
sweetmeats candied fruits
swell the mer ri ment ('mer-i-mənt) make louder the sound of happy voices
swept down into a valley sloped gradually to low land
swerve ('swərv) go crooked
swoon ('swün) faint
sym bol ('sim-bəl) sign
sym bol iz es ('sim-bəl-Ø-zəz) means

T

tam a rack ('ta-mə-rak) tree that looks like an evergreen but sheds its needles in winter
tang to the spirit ('taŋ; 'spir-ət) fancied taste
Ta qua me naw ('tä-quä-mē-nȯ) river in Michigan
tar nished ('tär-nisht) stained
taught wisdom from the past having learned better things from what had happened before
Ta wa sen tha (tä-wä-'sen-thä) name of a valley in New York
taw ny ('tȯ-nē) yellowish-brown
tax a part of one's wealth given up by law to benefit the public
te di ous ('tē-dē-əs) tiresome
ter race ('ter-əs) a raised level platform of earth
text the subject of a talk
the a ter ('thē-tər) building in which plays are acted
their green re sume (rə-'züm) are again covered with grass
the night is behind us night-time is almost here
there fore ('thar-fōr) for that reason
thick zig zags ('zig-zagz) many paths running this way and that
thinned to a thread grew so narrow she could barely be seen
thongs ('thȯŋz) narrow strips of leather
thresh old (thresh-hōld) piece of timber under the door
thrilled ('thrild) filled with joy
thun der halls ('thən-dər; 'hȯlz) far up, where the thunder dwells
thun der ing down the val ley ('thən-dər-iŋ; 'val-ē) running along level ground with a noise like thunder
thus ac cou tered (ə-'kü-tərd) dressed in this way
thus dis posed (di-'spōzd) so arranged
thwart ed the wi ly savage ('thwȯr-təd; 'w∅-lē) fought against the tricks of the Indians
tinge ('tinj) color; tint
tink ered ('tin-kərd) worked without knowing just how
ti ny ('t∅-nē) very small
tipped with flint having points of flint the hardest kind of stone
'tis meet it is right
tit tered ('ti-tərd) laughed mockingly
titter of winds merry sound of the breeze
toil is the real play work is more fun than playing
toil some ('tȯil-səm) hard
tol er a ble ('täl-ər-ə-bəl) bearable

toll ('tōl) tax; money
took no toll did not rob them
took shipping engaged passage on shipboard
took to his rev els ('re-vəlz) went on with his wild play
tor men tors (tȯr-'men-tərz) flies which bit them
tor tured by their lances ('tȯr-chərd) in great pain from the sharp bites
touch hole ('təch; 'hōl) the place where the powder was lighted
tour ('tu̇r) trip
tour neys ('tu̇r-nēz) meetings where knights fought
to ward ('tō-ərd) in the direction of
tow er ing steep ('tau̇-ər-iŋ) high slope
tow ers ('tau̇-ərz) high parts of the castle
track er ('tra-kər) one who traces the path an animal has taken
trade winds winds which always blow in the same direction
tra di tion (trə-'di-shən) story handed down
traf fic ('tra-fik) business
train those in a company
tran quil ('tran-kwəl) motionless because there was no wind
trans par ent (trans-'par-ənt) able to be seen through
trans port ('trans-pōrt) great excitement
trans port (trans 'pōrt) to remove
trav el ing schoolmaster ('tra-və-liŋ) teacher who went from one place to another
trea son ('trē-zən) attempt to injure the government
tribes of men might prosper all nations might live in better ways
trick ling ('tri-kə-liŋ) of water running in a small stream
trims smooths neatly
tri umph ('trØ-əmpf) victory
tri um phant (trØ-'əmp-fənt) glad of success
tro phy ('trō-fē) prize
troub led spir it ('trə-bəld; 'spir-ət) soul of the dead man which cannot rest
tryst ('trist) meeting place
tur ban ('tər-bən) headdress worn in Mohammedan countries, a cap with a sash or scarf wound about it
tur quoise ('tər-kȯiz) a precious blue stone
tur ret ('tər-ət) a small tower
tusks ('təsks) large, projecting teeth
twin ing ('twØ-niŋ) creeping up and winding about
twinkle of its candle little glow like that from a candle
twinkling moment

ty rant would be lord ('tØ-rənt) cruel master would rule everything

U

un ac cus tomed to vex a tions (ən-ə-'kəs-təmd; vek-'sā-shənz) not used to any sort of bothers
un an i mous ly elected (yü-'na-nə-məs-lē) given every vote
un apt (ən-'apt) unlikely
un bound ed freedom (ən-'baủn-dəd) state where they did as they liked
un com fort a ble state of af fairs (ən-'kəm-fər-tə-bəl; ə-'fārz) hard way of living
un con scious (ən-'kän-shəs) feeling and knowing nothing
un eas i ness (ən-'ēz-ē-nəs) worry
unequal fight ill-matched struggle
unfolded to your gaze spread out before you
un housed (ən-'haủzd) turned out of their homes
unknown crowded nations great masses of people of different races
unwittingly by accident
upon their kind against other men
use less ('yüs-ləs) without having been made good use of
ut most ('ət-mōst) greatest
ut ter itself in words ('ət-ər) speak its meaning

V

va grant ('vā-grənt) idle wanderer
vague ('vāg) not clear
vague lisps talk that could not be understood
vales ('vāᵊlz) little valleys
val or ('va-lər) bravery
var ied riches ('vār-ēd) good foods of different kinds
vault ('vōlt) walled-up space underground
vaunt ing ly ('vȯnt-iŋ-lē) boastingly
veered ('vird) turned
ven om ous ('ve-nə-məs) poisonous
ver dant ('ver-dənt) green
vest that is bright red breast
vex a tion (vek-'sā-shən) anger
vex a tions (vek-'sā-shənz) troubles
vict uals ('vi-təlz) food
vil lain ('vi-lən) wicked man

vir gin air ('vər-jən) clear, fresh air of spring
vir tue of vested power ('vər-chü) because of the office to which he had been elected
vi sion ('vi-zhən) dream
vi sions of sugarplums ('vi-zhənz) dreams of candy
vi zier ('v∅-zēr) a high state officer in Mohammedan countries
vol un ta ri ly (vä-lən-'tār-ə-lē) willingly

W

Wa bas so (wa-'bas-ō)
Wa bun ('wȯ-bən) East wind
Wah wah tay see (wȯ-wȯ-'tā-sē)
wain ('wān) wagon
waist coat ('wāst-kōt) vest
walks of life things they try to do
wand ('wänd) slender stick
wanders piping through the village walks around the town, playing sweet music
wanted nothing had everything he wanted
war ring ('wȯ-riŋ) fighting
war rior ('wȯr-yər) fighting man
wa ry ('wa-rē) easily frightened
was mind ed to try ('m∅n-dəd) felt he would like to test wastes wide stretches of land unfit for cultivation
way side blos som ('wā-s∅d; 'blä-səm) flower growing by the roadside
way side things flowers that grow along the roadside
Wa wa ('wä-wä)
Wa won ais sa (wä-wȯn-'ā-sə)
Way was si mo (wā-'wäs-i-mō)
wea sel ('wē-zəl) a small animal noted for its quickness
wedge ('wej) a tool, thinner at one edge, used for splitting
ween know
well mounted riding on good horses
wend ('wend) go
wheel ing ('hwē-liŋ) circling
whence from where
where the last was bred in the place in which the last sprang
where up on ('hwər-ə-pȯn) after which
wher ev er it list eth ('hywər-'e-vər; 'list-əth) wherever it wishes
white-skin wrapper covering of white bark

Whit sun day ('hwit-sən-dā) the seventh Sunday after Easter
whole round of my isle trip all the way around the island
whose joy is to slay who like to kill
wield ('wēld) use
wig wams ('wig-wȯmz) huts of bark
wil der ness ('wil-dər-nəs) wild country
wildfire jack-o'-lantern gay little man dancing about
willing lands ground ready for plowing
will not eat salt in olden times eating salt with a man (that is, being his guest) bound the guest to do his host no harm, then or afterward
wi ly ('wØ-lē) tricky
winged having wings
winged with feathers ('wiŋd) having feathers at one end, to help them fly
win try hoard ('win-trē; 'hōrd) store of food for the winter
wisdom of the book words which made up the sense
witch er y ('wi-chə-rē) fascination
with in his scope (with-'in; 'skōp) where he could reach it
with one ac cord (ə-'kōrd) with the same idea
with one con sent (kən-'sent) agreeing
without more a do (ə-'dü) not making any objection
wonder ('wən-dər) surprising thing
won drous ('wən-drəs) strange
wondrous birth and be ing ('bē-iŋ) story of the wonderful way he came into the world and lived in it
words cannot paint anything one might say could not describe
work the book out do enough work to pay for the book
wor ship ('wər-shəp) devotion to God
wound ed ('wün-dəd) hurt
wounds ('wündz) old griefs
wo ven tex ture ('wō-vən; 'teks-chər) cloth
wrack ('rak) ruin
wreath ('rēth) garland
wreathed ('rēthd) joyous
wreath ing fires ('rē-thiŋ) flames twisting around
wrought ('rȯt) worked
wrought together in such har mo ny ('här-mə-nē) so combined in the carving

X

Xe nil ('zē-nil)

Y

year ling ('yir-liŋ) an animal one year old
yellow hair the silky threads growing out from the end of the ear
Yen a diz ze (yen-ə-'diz-ē) an idler
yeo man ('yō-mən) free-born man
yes ter ('yes-tər) of the day before
yet unforgotten still remembered
yore ('yōr) olden time
young sun early morning sun

Books Available from
Lost Classics Book Company
American History

Stories of Great Americans for Little Americans .... Edward Eggleston
A First Book in American History .... Edward Eggleston
A History of the United States and Its People .... Edward Eggleston

Biography

The Life of Kit Carson .... Edward Ellis

English Grammar

Primary Language Lessons .... Emma Serl
Intermediate Language Lessons .... Emma Serl
(*Teacher's Guides available for each of these texts*)

Elson Readers Series

Complete Set .... William Elson, Lura Runkel, Christine Keck
The Elson Readers: Primer .... William Elson, Lura Runkel
The Elson Readers: Book One .... William Elson, Lura Runkel
The Elson Readers: Book Two .... William Elson, Lura Runkel
The Elson Readers: Book Three .... William Elson
The Elson Readers: Book Four .... William Elson
The Elson Readers: Book Five .... William Elson, Christine Keck
The Elson Readers: Book Six .... William Elson, Christine Keck
The Elson Readers: Book Seven .... William Elson, Christine Keck
The Elson Readers: Book Eight .... William Elson, Christine Keck
(*Teacher's Guides available for each reader in this series*)

Historical Fiction

With Lee in Virginia .... G. A. Henty
A Tale of the Western Plains .... G. A. Henty
The Young Carthaginian .... G. A. Henty
In the Heart of the Rockies .... G. A. Henty
For the Temple .... G. A. Henty
A Knight of the White Cross .... G. A. Henty
The Minute Boys of Lexington .... Edward Stratemeyer
The Minute Boys of Bunker Hill .... Edward Stratemeyer
Hope and Have .... Oliver Optic
Taken by the Enemy, First in *The Blue and the Gray Series* .... Oliver Optic
Within the Enemy's Lines, Second in *The Blue and the Gray Series* .... Oliver Optic
On the Blockade, Third in *The Blue and the Gray Series* .... Oliver Optic
Stand by the Union, Fourth in *The Blue and the Gray Series* .... Oliver Optic
Fighting for the Right, Fifth in *The Blue and the Gray Series* .... Oliver Optic
A Victorious Union, Sixth and Final in *The Blue and the Gray Series* .... Oliver Optic
Mary of Plymouth .... James Otis